PR

"Well-paced, guided by three-dimensional characters, full of details and blessed with depth beyond its mysteries … a welcome entry to the murder-mystery family."
—*The Globe and Mail*

"A witty and delectably crafted whodunit."
—*The National Post*

"Zingy, high-octane, and brimming with humour."
—*Literary Review of Canada*

"Delightfully entertaining throughout."
—*Winnipeg Free Press*

"A smart, devious whodunit filled with theatrical shadows and veils, *Bury the Lead* is both twisty and hilarious."
—Robyn Harding, bestselling author of *The Drowning Woman*

"A classic, but also topical, whodunit staged with humour and wit."
—Linwood Barclay, author of *The Lie Maker*

"This very witty, sharp, fun, and suspenseful cozy mystery is the best escape."
—Samantha M. Bailey, *usa Today* and #1 national bestselling author of *Woman on the Edge* and *Watch Out for Her*

"Reading *Bury the Lead* is like having cocktails with your most fabulous friends … The minute it's over, you can't wait to get together again."

—Johanna Schneller, Bigger Picture columnist, *The Globe and Mail*

"A word-perfect romp through the world of small-town theatre … I give it a standing ovation!"

—Roz Nay, bestselling author of *The Hunted*

"*Bury the Lead* was made for mystery lovers."

—Andrew Pyper, author of *The Demonologist* and *Oracle*

"The perfect cozy mystery novel … fun, dark, and impossible to put down."

—Amy Stuart, bestselling author of *A Death at the Party*

"A propulsive, juicy little ride … I loved every page."

—Lisa Gabriele, author of *The Winters*

WIDOWS AND ORPHANS

QUILL & PACKET MYSTERIES

Bury the Lead
Widows and Orphans

WIDOWS AND ORPHANS

A QUILL & PACKET MYSTERY

KATE HILTON AND
ELIZABETH RENZETTI

SPIDERLINE

Published in Canada in 2025 and the USA in 2025 by House of Anansi Press Inc.
houseofanansi.com

House of Anansi Press is committed to protecting our natural environment.
This book is made of material from well-managed FSC®-certified forests, recycled
materials, and other controlled sources.

House of Anansi Press is a Global Certified Accessible™ (GCA by Benetech)
publisher. The ebook version of this book meets stringent accessibility standards
and is available to readers with print disabilities.

29 28 27 26 25   1 2 3 4 5

Library and Archives Canada Cataloguing in Publication
Title: Widows and orphans / Kate Hilton and Elizabeth Renzetti.
Names: Hilton, Kate, 1972- author | Renzetti, Elizabeth, author.
Description: Series statement: A Quill & Packet mystery
Identifiers: Canadiana (print) 20250130351 | Canadiana (ebook) 2025013036X |
ISBN 9781487012809 (softcover) | ISBN 9781487012816 (EPUB)
Subjects: LCGFT: Detective and mystery fiction. | LCGFT: Novels.
Classification: LCC PS8615.I48 W54 2025 | DDC C813/.6—dc23

Cover design and typesetting: Lucia Kim
Cover image: Marta Lebek/Stocksy Images
Series design: Greg Tabor

*House of Anansi Press is grateful for the privilege to work on and create from the
Traditional Territory of many Nations, including the Anishinabeg, the Wendat, and the
Haudenosaunee, as well as the Treaty Lands of the Mississaugas of the Credit.*

 Canada Council
for the Arts

Conseil des Arts
du Canada

 ONTARIO ARTS COUNCIL
CONSEIL DES ARTS DE L'ONTARIO
an Ontario government agency
un organisme du gouvernement de l'Ontario

With the participation of the Government of Canada
Avec la participation du gouvernement du Canada | Canadä

*We acknowledge for their financial support of our publishing program the Canada Council
for the Arts, the Ontario Arts Council, and the Government of Canada.*

Printed and bound in Canada

 MIX
Paper | Supporting
responsible forestry
FSC® C103567

To self-acceptance and critical thinking,
both of which are free, and freeing.

Isolated lines created when paragraphs *begin* on the *last* line of a page are known as *orphans*. They have no past, but they do have a future, and they need not trouble the typographer. The stub-ends left when paragraphs *end* on the *first* line of a page are called *widows*. They have a past but not a future, and they look foreshortened and forlorn.

—Robert Bringhurst, *The Elements of Typographic Style*

CHAPTER 1

BLISS BONDAR WAS everything I wasn't—young, wealthy, internet-famous, and possessed of a figure that my father, after a few rum and cokes, would have called "lush." Like me, however, she seemed more than a little bored by the opening press conference of the Welcome, Goddess retreat at the Pinerock Resort. This was surprising, because she was sitting onstage as one of the two stars of the show, staring out at a room packed full of admirers, whereas I was covering the conference for my newspaper, the *Quill & Packet*.

It wasn't exactly hard news. Port Ellis's ritziest hotel and convention centre was hosting a weeklong wellness conference, a change from the usual annual gatherings of horny dentists and outboard-motor salesmen.

The Pinerock had been transformed into a perfumed feminine oasis, with sheer ivory curtains catching the October sunshine and potted orchids replacing the ancient ferns, a setting befitting a pair of modern-day goddesses and their personal-growth-seeking acolytes. Empty for once of ruddy hedge-fund managers and the tennis-forged women who tolerated them, the Pinerock's present clientele skewed younger, more mindful, and definitely less alcoholic.

The press conference was being managed by a slightly built and jumpy young man who introduced himself as Danilo Reyes. He wore a neatly cut dark suit accented with orange sneakers and a chartreuse tie, and he seemed uncomfortable as he outlined the housekeeping details for the session, brushing a sheen of sweat from his forehead with the back of his hand.

"… and with that, we can move on to the main attraction," he said. "Welcome, everyone, to our first annual Welcome, Goddess conference!"

I gritted my teeth against "first annual," a personal bugbear. I was older than almost everyone at the press conference, by a good margin, but at least I had standards. There was one stiff-postured gentleman near the front who looked like he remembered how to use a rotary-dial phone, but otherwise I was lost in a sea of the young and blithe. Around me, they clapped enthusiastically, some snapping their fingers above their heads.

This was definitely not the sort of presser I was used to. Those resembled passive-aggressive boxing matches, minus the actual punching. This was more of a love-in. Then again, it seemed that the journalists in the room were outnumbered by wellness bloggers, podcasters, and alternative healers. I wondered how many of them wrote "influencer" on their passport applications.

Danilo dabbed at his forehead again. Maybe he was afraid of public speaking? If so, he was in the wrong business. He took a deep breath and continued. "You all know and love the visionaries behind our gathering, Bliss Bondar and Bree Guthrie. Today, as members of the press, you have an exclusive opportunity to ask them about the extraordinary community of wellness they've created! I'll be facilitating our discussion, so let's get started with a big round of applause for Bliss and Bree!" He clapped frantically, then hopped across the stage and took the middle armchair of the three, hemmed in by a coffee table and several boom mics.

I'd done my research, of course. I'd listened to the goddesses' podcasts on the power of manifestation, watched their YouTube videos on embodied intention, and scrolled through the endless cosmetics and serums on their website. I'd even bought a concealer, which was manufactured without cruelty or animal products, but did little actual concealing once it was on my face.

But I'd never observed them unscripted, or unedited.

Tossing a long, dark, carefully constructed ringlet of hair over her shoulder, Bliss leaned forward and poured herself a glass of water, neglecting to fill the empty one sitting in front of her business partner. An oversight, or a slight? She lounged in her chair, sipping her drink, her Western ankle boots peeking out from beneath a peach maxi dress with a lace-up bodice. She looked peevish behind her lash extensions, as if she'd been forced into a timeout after a tantrum.

Bree, on the other hand, sat erect and alert. She had wide hazel eyes under straight dark brows that contrasted with the blond highlights in her chin-length hair. If she was wearing any Welcome, Goddess cruelty-free makeup it was invisible to my eyes. She wore a cream silk jumpsuit, chic and understated. The stage lights glinted off a small gold pendant at her throat, and a rather larger diamond on her ring finger: Bree and Bliss were both, famously, young widows. But they had moved beyond mourning, and widow's weeds.

Bliss tapped her white shellacked fingernails idly on the arm of her chair as Bree began to speak.

"Thank you all so much for joining us," she said, in a clear voice that had been trained to project. "We're so glad you could be here for the inaugural Welcome, Goddess gathering. We have a terrific program planned. We know everyone is extremely excited about Clarity K's SkyWords workshop, which is unfortunately sold out. But there are a few places left for Bliss's famous light-channelling meditation."

Did I imagine it, or did Bree sound the tiniest bit sneery?

Bliss took out her phone and began scrolling.

It was an act as hostile as it was impossible to miss, but Bree didn't acknowledge it. She finished outlining the many enlightening activities that would unfold over the week, and then called for questions. I listened for a while as ridiculous softballs were lobbed through the air. What did Bliss and Bree hope to channel over the next few days? What did they think of the energy of their surroundings? Bree answered all the questions in her calm, low voice. Bliss stared off into the middle distance when she wasn't looking at her screen.

In interviews, Bliss and Bree often referred to each other as "spiritual sisters," but today they seemed more like the kind of sisters who roll around pulling each other's hair out. I wondered if they both believed the same anti-science garbage that I'd read about on the conference's website. I'd soon find out.

I made sure my phone was recording and put my hand up in the air. Bree nodded in my direction. "Hello," I said. "I'm Cat Conway from the Port Ellis *Quill & Packet*." Suddenly, Bliss's head jerked up. She stared at me through narrowed eyes. *Odd*, I thought, but I plowed ahead. "I'm just wondering about something I read on the conference's website. One of your seminars focuses on using herbal supplements to counterattack transmissible illnesses. Not in addition to medical treatment, but as a replacement. There are people in your audience who will understand that to mean they should trade vaccines for quack remedies. Do you think that's responsible advice?"

I probably should have used a more neutral word in place of *quack*. Way back when I was in journalism school, we were taught never to use loaded language, because it seldom leads to useful answers. But I was irritated by the sycophantic questions being offered to the goddesses, most of which revolved around how they managed to be so fabulous.

Bree's shoulders squared as she prepared to respond. Before she could say anything, though, Bliss had reached across Danilo to snatch the microphone from her partner's hand. Bree recoiled, but quickly regained her calm smile.

Bliss, however, wore an expression that belied her name. She glared at me, aiming one dagger-tipped fingernail my way. "Did you say the local paper? The Shill and Racket?"

Someone in the audience let out a barking laugh. Danilo studied his shoes and looked like he wanted to find a place to hide. Bree slumped into the posture of a very tired lion tamer.

I made my own voice as calm as possible. "The *Quill & Packet*," I said.

"Right, the newspaper"—here Bliss made air quotes with her free hand—"that wrote that ridiculous series telling lies about holistic health?"

"It was actually a series about the detrimental effects of vaccine avoidance—"

"And you wonder why no one reads the corporate media anymore," Bliss interrupted. "Do you know how many listeners we have on our podcast? Because that's where people hear the truth that no one else will tell them." Around me, people were frantically nodding their heads in agreement.

Bliss's expression grew sorrowful, as if she were a schoolteacher and I was a child in the corner with a dunce cap on her head. "I know your job is to parrot the official line about what's right and what's wrong. But have you ever thought about listening for a change? You might learn something."

Bree's mouth had flattened into a murderous line. She reached over and switched off Bliss's mic, before thanking all of us for our attendance. Bliss didn't even wait for her partner to finish but stood up and stalked off. I watched her go and thought that she was half correct. I wouldn't have said I often knew when things were right, but I could usually tell when they were wrong. And there was definitely something rotten in this paradise.

I WANDERED OUT of the auditorium with Bliss's words echoing in my ears. She clearly didn't know much about my employer if she thought the *Quill & Packet* was corporate media. A microscopic corporation on its way to bankruptcy court, maybe. And that was my fault.

For a few weeks during the summer, I'd been the star of the Port Ellis journalistic heavens—truly a triumph in a teacup—when I'd investigated the murder of the famous actor Eliot Fraser, and managed to find the culprit before the police did.

But my amateur sleuthing had come at a personal cost, and when the media circus rolled out of town, I'd needed a local story to sink my teeth into. It had landed in my lap in the form of a report from the provincial ministry of health noting that vaccination rates were alarmingly low in the county and had been dropping for a couple of years. I decided to investigate, alongside Bruce Collinghurst, the *Quill*'s veteran reporter-photographer. We spent weeks working on a series about vaccine resistance and the online conspiracy theories that fuelled it. We talked to parents, researchers, even a chatty ten-year-old who'd survived a nasty bout of measles. The first installment was published online and in print to coincide with Labour Day and kids' return to school.

Bliss had been right about one thing: a lot of people hated my reporting on the growing anti-vaccine

movement in the tri-lake area. And they'd been demon-
strating their anger for weeks now, gathering to protest
at the *Quill*'s offices. Sometimes they drove honking
around our block in a miniature convoy, disrupting our
access to the newsroom and irritating our neighbours.

The critics who were too chicken to protest in
person expressed their anger via email and dropped
subscriptions and calls to Mayor Gerry Halloran's
popular talk-radio show. Worse, they had pressured
our long-term advertisers to abandon us. The *Quill &
Packet* had already been on life support; now we were
picking out the tie it would wear in its casket.

Sighing, I began to browse through the marketplace that had been set up on the main floor of the hotel
to peddle the wares of the conference participants and
speakers. I stopped at a table displaying books beside a
sign that said Wellness. Judging by the books' titles, it
might more accurately have said Falling Apart-ness. I
picked up a slim hardcover called *Free Your Chi (and the
Rest Will Follow)*, which cost forty dollars. *My rent will
follow*, I thought. I smiled at the young woman running
the booth, who had the skin of a baby and the posture
of Karen Kain. She smiled serenely back. My finger
trailed over *The Big Book of Cellular Decay* and *Radical
Wonder: 14 Ways to Find Diamonds on the Sidewalk of Life*.

One book stood upright, its title in lurid pink. *The
Madwoman in the Colon: Cleanse Your Way to Mental
Clarity*. I leafed through its pages, trying to avoid the

illustrations. "So," I said to the young woman, "is this suggesting that the burger I ate yesterday is standing in the way of my happiness?"

She regarded me with a placid expression, refusing to be drawn into a fight. "You know what they say. Garbage in …"

"Garbage out. So I've been told." She bowed in acknowledgement, the graceful movement of a neck too young to feel random nerve pinches. I looked at the book's cover again, noticing the promise of clarity in its subtitle. "Do you happen to have any of Clarity K's books for sale?"

For the first time, her expression flickered. Clarity K had risen to astonishing popularity after she began posting her spare, cryptic poems on Instagram. Her first published collection, *Um*, had made her the millennial Anne Sexton—though Anne's poems had never been optioned by Apple TV. "I'm afraid not," the bookseller said. "You'll find all of Clarity's merchandise gathered in one place, in the centre of the display aisle." A brief pause, then: "It won't be hard to find."

Was that a dig? I admired subtlety in insults. It was an appreciation my mother had instilled in me early on. Speaking of which … I scanned the book table again, but I couldn't see my mother's opus, *Kicking the Ladder*, which had become a bible for the sort of women who got up at five in the morning to do Pilates and fight injustice. Its sequel, *Grit and Gumption: A*

Warrior Woman's Guide to Finding Inner Strength, was scheduled for release late in the fall, to capitalize on the "people who don't know what to get their mother/sister/wife for the holidays" market.

My mother, Marian Conway, was one of the VIP speakers at the Welcome, Goddess conference. In her Boss Babe workshop, she'd be holding forth on the subject of work-life balance and avoiding burnout—hilarious in the sense that she burned like Edna St. Vincent Millay's candle. Not just at both ends, but in the middle too. She was here somewhere, but I hadn't sought her out yet. My colon wasn't ready for it.

I thanked the bookseller, who inclined her willowy torso slightly in my direction. As I made my way under a banner that welcomed attendees to "activate the feminine divine!" I heard a familiar voice call my name.

I turned and saw my friend and colleague at the *Quill*, Kaydence Johnson, standing behind a table at the foot of a majestic oak staircase (and also, unfortunately, under the head of a majestic stag), her bright red lips curved in a wide and genuine smile. I still wasn't used to people in Port Ellis being happy to see me, and I felt a little glow.

"Look at you, moonlighting in the service of the goddess," I said, giving her a hug. "Don't let Amir know."

She let out a disdainful *pffft*. Of course Amir Mahar, our editor-in-chief at the *Quill & Packet*, knew she was here. He'd given her a couple of days off to sell her handcrafted dresses and scarves. It wasn't like Kaydence had been overworked in the newsroom. Normally, she was our sales and advertising manager, but there hadn't been a lot of sales or advertising to manage recently.

And that was my fault.

I tried to squash my feelings of guilt by picking up one of Kaydence's dresses. The shape was fun and retro, nipped in at the waist and then flaring into a full skirt. If you looked closely, you could see the intricate work Kaydence had done stitching vintage tea towels together. On the bodice was a map of the old roads along the tri-lake area, before Port Ellis became a summer destination for rich urban exiles. The skirt was filled with adorable forest creatures, carefully sewn together to suggest they were hanging out in a woodland paradise. Each dress she'd made was unique and splendid.

"These are stunning," I said. "It must have taken you forever."

Kaydence did a bashful twirl in her dress, the rainbow-tapestry skirt belling around her. "Well, I had my mom to help me with the sewing, but ..." Her voice trailed off. We were both members of the Avoiding the Topic of Mom Club.

I straightened a pile of headbands, which—a sign told me—were infused with healing lavender. The heap of cloth overshadowed a much smaller pile of newspapers next to it. My heart contracted as if clenched in a vise. Kaydence was trying to shift copies of the *Quill & Packet*. It should have sold on its own merits, of course. There was a great story on the front page, an exposé of unpaid commercial property taxes, written by our colleague Bruce. The paper had never been as zaftig as the Sunday *New York Times*, but now it was so thin. Thin like Audrey Hepburn in *Breakfast at Tiffany's*, but not nearly as beguiling.

Kaydence caught my eye. "The advertisers will come back," she said. "It's just a temporary slump."

I wished I could share her confidence. I had thought I was finally making peace with Port Ellis, where I'd spent my childhood summers at my grandparents' cottage. I'd returned less than a year earlier, not exactly with the wind beneath my scorched wings. But against the odds I'd started to fall in love with the town and its people. How quickly fortunes turned. Now I seemed to have written my own one-way ticket out of the place. I pictured Amir, his shoulders slumping in a way that even the most diligently ironed shirt couldn't hide. He'd trusted me. He'd put his faith in my abilities.

"You're spiralling, Cat." Kaydence's voice was loving but firm.

I took a deep breath and was about to thank her when a tiny hand reached up and gave her table a yank. Newspapers and headbands rained down on the grinning face of a child, who had the expression of an angel and the strength of a gorilla on amphetamines.

"Phoenix, for god's sake, what are you doing?" A harassed-looking woman dashed up to the table, holding the hands of two more children. One of them, the goblin's twin, was hooting with joy at the chaos. The woman yanked Phoenix away from the table and bent to gather the goods that had fallen. Kaydence and I knelt to help her. The three children took this opportunity to run screaming away from their mother in the direction of the Pinerock's main doors.

She looked up at us, and I recognized in her eyes that combination of panic, despair, and murderous intent. I'd had only one child, and he was a teenager now, but I understood how close this poor woman must be to the edge. "Just go after them," I said. "Don't worry about this mess."

"It's fine," Kaydence echoed. "We've got it." The woman nodded her thanks, got heavily to her feet, and took off after her brood. We watched her while we piled everything back on the table. "Remind me to talk to my doctor about having my tubes tied," Kaydence said. I snickered.

I craned my neck to see if the woman had managed to catch them, but suddenly there was a stir in the main hallway. A flock of people, some with video cameras and others with headsets and clipboards, swirled around a person who moved calmly through the crowd. Well, as calmly as a person could who was wearing an extraordinary getup—a flowing ivory cloak with an enormous hood that covered and shadowed her head. Within the darkness, I caught a glimpse of a creature out of a fairy tale: glowing silver hair surrounded a smooth, youthful face. The woman's dark eyes were focused on the middle distance, beyond her fans, as if she expected to find divine inspiration between the potted plants.

"Clarity K," Kaydence breathed, in the same reverent tone I might have used if Christiane Amanpour had entered the building. Which seemed unlikely, since she was off covering wars, and not wellness conferences.

Immediately, I grabbed a copy of the *Quill* and ran toward the Clarity cluster. I'd been pestering her PR team for an interview for weeks and had not heard a word in reply. Here was my chance. If I could get an exclusive interview with the world's bestselling poet, it would make a huge splash in the *Quill*. I'd already done my research. I'd read *Um*, which had soared up the bestseller lists. Bookshops had stayed open all night to accommodate the demand for her second book, *It's Giving but I'm Not Sure What*, published in the spring.

I caught up to the group. Two young women protectively flanked Clarity, her own personal messy-bunned praetorian guard. I waved at the one nearest to me. "Hi, Cat Conway from the *Quill & Packet*." I quickly doubled up the paper so it would look thicker and thrust it at her. She stared down her nose at me, as if I'd fouled the air with a gust of garlic breath.

"I'm sorry, what?" she said, and kept walking. Clarity K sailed on with the train of her cloak trailing, a majestic cruise ship surrounded by little tugboats.

"I've been trying to get an interview with Clarity," I said, trotting alongside. "I'd love to talk to her. For the paper here in town." I waved the *Quill* again.

The minion's brows drew together. "That's comms," she said. "We're production." And with that cryptic pronouncement, she turned her shoulder to shut me out. It wasn't going to be that easy to get rid of me, though. I fished around in my back pocket and found a business card. Reaching over her arm, I stuck it under the clip of her clipboard. "If you could pass my request to the PR team, I'd be hugely grateful." She humphed at me, but that was okay. Humph wasn't no. I could live with humph.

Dozens of phones were held high to record Clarity's procession. I wondered what it would be like to be so celebrated for your writing. I loved that she'd made poetry hot again, but on the other hand I couldn't help calculating just how much money she got paid per word. And how much I was not getting paid to write a lot more words.

I shook my head to banish the thought.

My mother had a real skill—honed over decades—for getting inside my head and making me wonder what I was doing with my life. But I didn't have to let my own bitterness give her an assist. It was the first day of the conference, after all. We had time.

CHAPTER 2

I SHOOK MY shoulders to release some tension before I knocked on the door of my mother's hotel room. It wasn't quite enough to shake off decades of irritation, but it would have to do.

"Who is it?' Her voice sounded sharp, even for Marian.

"It's me," I said. Then, when there was no response, I sighed. "It's Cat, Mom."

The door whipped open, my mother regally framed within. She presented her cheek for a kiss, and I dutifully leaned in for a peck. She whirled away before I could make contact, stalking back into her room. All of my mother's movements were sharp and definitive, even the ones pushing me away. She moved like a sixteen-year-old Olympic gymnast trapped in the body of a seventy-two-year-old motivational speaker.

I had to admit, she looked good, if annoyed. Marian wore a sharp-shouldered russet pantsuit—my mother insisted she had been the one to whisper "pantsuit" into Hillary Clinton's ear when the senator was still wearing off-the-rack from Talbots—and a pale grey blouse. The pantsuit matched the colour of the autumn leaves outside the Pinerock, and also two bright spots of colour on my mother's cheeks. Not the best omen.

"I've been trying to reach you," I lied. I followed her into the hotel room, knowing better than to wait for an invitation. Everything was neatly in its place, no dirty socks on the floor, no magazine splayed open on the bed. An enormous vase of flowers sat on the desk, and I didn't have to look at the card to know they were from my father. Stewart Conway's devotion followed my mother on her excursions around the world. And yet, the angrily flushed cheeks. Why?

"The interviewer never showed up," she said, hands in fists on her hips. "She said that Clarity K was giving an impromptu lesson in free verse in the Canoe Salon, and that she'd reschedule. And this is why I don't trust millennials. No sense of responsibility."

That explained why Marian was furious, and also where Clarity K and her entourage had been headed. "I'm sure she'll call you," I said. *"Grit and Gumption* is going to be huge." I hadn't yet read my mother's new manifesto on midlife empowerment, but if it did half as well as *Kicking the Ladder*, it would keep her in designer pantsuits for decades. The fact that she hadn't sent me an advance copy to read rankled slightly. Not that I would let her know.

"Hmmm," my mother said, unswayed by my judgment in literary matters. I dropped my backpack by the door and headed over to the desk. A basket of croissants, scones, and apple fritters sat next to the flowers, the delicious scent telling me that these were a gift from my friend Glenda Gillis, Port Ellis's finest baker. Glenda was also the leader of an underground feminist cabal and a former murder suspect, but those were secondary to her skill with fried dough. I picked a fritter off the top of the pile.

I offered a piece to my mother, but she recoiled as if I were handing out nuclear waste. "I only eat carbs on the first day of each month," she said. "And on your father's birthday."

"Days ending in *y* are my carb days," I said through a mouthful of fritter. She shot me a look that said *I can see that* and picked up my backpack from the floor, thumping it onto a table. She perched on the edge of the bed, jaw tight.

"I'm just not sure what I'm doing here, Catherine. I mean, a wellness conference? I've written a serious book about the struggles of women in an ageist society. I'm on the program between some idiot talking about astral projections and a quack who says you can cure cancer with honey. I mean, really. And now my first interview's cancelled." Her voice trembled. Was my mother about to cry? I couldn't remember the last time I'd seen her weep. She hadn't cried when my dad went in for heart surgery, and she certainly hadn't cried when I told her—in hysterical tears myself—that my marriage had ended.

"I'm sorry about that, Mom." I knew better than to try to hug her. When it came to physical affection, she was pricklier than my fifteen-year-old son, Jake, if that were possible. I'd made my peace with that. But I could try to calm her with words. "I'm sure once—"

A gentle rap on the door cut off my words. I heard a soft voice outside. "Marian? It's me."

My mother rose from the bed and practically bounded to the door. I didn't know what shocked me more: the sight of the woman who entered the room or the pleasure with which my mother greeted her. The woman wore a fitted tweed blazer, jeans that looked as if they had been hand-stitched from the softest organic denim, and elegant low-heeled boots designed for European cobblestones. Her smile, composed of straight and radiant white enamel, was warm and genuine. "I brought you a smoothie," she said, handing my mother a plastic glass full of something that looked suspiciously like pond slime.

"Debbie, you're an angel," said my mother. "I can't thank you enough for all of your help."

An angel? I'd heard Debbie Halloran described many ways, but heaven didn't figure in any of them. Mayor's wife, yes. Society figure, sure, if you believed that there was a Park Avenue in Port Ellis. She was a fixture around town, usually standing slightly behind her obnoxious husband, Gerry, who loathed the *Quill & Packet* the way many small-town politicians hate the journalists who occasionally jerk their leash. Since he owned several radio stations, including the one broadcasting from Port Ellis itself, I suspected that his anger toward the *Quill* was tinged with something even darker: covetousness. Like a tin-pot dictator of the tri-lake area, he wanted all local media in his control.

At least Debbie wasn't vocal in her criticism. She mainly confined herself to organizing the annual tour of Port Ellis's most ostentatious gardens and chairing the hospital board. I'd seen her entering the food bank at St. Stephen's church with an apron on, so she also performed her good works outside of the camera's flattering light. Unlike her husband.

"Debbie Halloran," she said, holding out a French-manicured hand. "I think we met at the NICU fundraiser for the Three Sisters Hospital, didn't we?"

"Good memory," I said.

She smiled, and her eyes crinkled at the edges. It was one of the few signs that she was in her fifties; the sharp claw of money worries had never been dragged across her skin. "That's the job," she said, tucking a loose strand of rich mahogany hair behind her ear and exposing a substantial pearl stud. Debbie, according to rumour, imported a stylist from Toronto, paying for his round-trip Uber every six weeks.

"Debbie's my local guide this week," my mother said. She took a sip of her sludge, careful not to leave lipstick on the straw. "The conference organizers paired us up."

"Please don't tell anyone, but I requested the assignment," said Debbie. "I don't like to abuse my position as First Lady—and I'm sure there were many local women who would have loved to spend time with you—but I felt some responsibility to ensure that you received the homecoming you deserve." I couldn't detect a note of sarcasm. Either Debbie was even better at political subterfuge than I thought possible, or she was a true Marian Conway fan.

"Catherine is going to take me for a tour of the local newspaper office," said my mother. "Would you like to join?"

Debbie's smile faltered ever so slightly. She and I both knew that she couldn't come to the *Quill & Packet* office on a goodwill tour. "That sounds like great fun," Debbie said, "but I have a few things to do before the banquet tonight. I'll see you both there?"

"BEFORE I FORGET," Marian said. "I want you to have the extra key to my hotel room. In case you need a quiet place to work." I was about to thank her for this unusual display of thoughtfulness when she added, "Or I need you to grab something for me while I'm signing books or presenting. I usually have a staffer at these things. Debbie's very helpful, obviously, but there are limits to what I can ask of her. She has other responsibilities."

I took the card without comment and slipped it into my wallet. "Are you sure you want to see my office?" I asked. "It isn't much to look at, trust me."

"Meeting the local press is never a waste of time, especially when one is promoting a book," said my mother, wiping crumbs from the passenger seat and shifting the teetering stack of files—a small part of the research that Bruce and I had compiled for the vaccine avoidance series—from the passenger seat floor to the back seat. She brushed off her hands before climbing into my old Honda CR-V.

"The local press is honoured," I said as we drove through the Pinerock's parking lot, past gaggles of women dressed to welcome the goddess. My fantasy mother would have insisted that she wanted to see where I spent my days for the pure pride of it. The truth was, Marian thought I could do better. I was at peace with that, except when I wasn't. "I'm going to need a half-hour in the newsroom to finish up my story about Bree and Bliss," I said. "You can wander the main street if you like. I know how much you hate it here."

"Mmm," said my mother. "You know, I was thinking last night about that time when your reporting brought down that corrupt developer's empire. Impressive." A less skillful critic might have said, "remember when you had a real job at a real newspaper," but my mother excelled at the subtle jab. I chose silence as my weapon, and we passed through the outskirts of Port Ellis with no words between us.

On one side, the forest pressed up against the road—poplar and beech, maple and pine. On the other side, behind a screen of trees, cottages hugged the shore of Lake Jane. My mother barely looked up from her phone. The town she'd grown up in had transformed since she'd left, gentrifying more each year, shiny veneers on an ancient smile. As soon as she'd graduated high school with a ninety-two percent average, she'd fled this "hick town" as fast as the bus could carry her.

Suddenly she made a little yelping noise, and I jerked around to look at her. She was clenching her phone as if she'd like to crush it. Her top lip was snagged between her teeth. Her breath came in small, angry puffs.

"Mom? Is everything okay?"

She stabbed at the phone and then flipped it over,

tucking it in her pocket. She turned to look out the window, at the community she'd forgotten as soon as it vanished in the rear-view mirror of that bus.

"It's all good," she said. "Everything is fine."

I had to admire my mother's ability to twist reality to her will. To shape it through sheer determination, like Uri Geller bending spoons. Though, in my experience, reality had a way of catching up with you whether you liked it or not.

AS WE APPROACHED the *Quill & Packet* newsroom, my heart began to thud. On the street outside, which was normally quite empty, a half-dozen pickup trucks were parked. One had its front wheels on the sidewalk. The baseball-capped drivers milled around outside, occasionally reaching inside their trucks' windows to blare their horns. One of them was holding a sign that said "SHILL & RACKET 100 YEARS OF LIES."

"Happy readers," my mother said dryly.

"I'm not sure they can actually read," I said, turning into a laneway halfway down the block. I tried to maintain a light tone, but the protesters weren't funny. They were organized, they were angry, and they were trying to shut down the newspaper I'd come to love. They had targeted our advertisers, too, many of whom had sheepishly cancelled their ad buys. It was a stupid and destructive campaign.

We parked behind the *Quill*, and I took my mother through the back entrance. The hallway leading to the newsroom was lined with framed copies of the paper from its glory days, before it had shrunk to pamphlet size. My mother stopped to read the headlines as we passed: "Inferno Ravages Packet Ship, All Hands Perish" and "Port Ellis Man Finds Glory, German Guns on Beaches of Normandy."

Marian let out a small *hmph*, but before she could complain that the *Quill* had failed to document her own rise to glory, I heard a commotion coming from the newsroom at the end of the corridor. I ran toward the noise, my mother forgotten behind me.

In the newsroom I skidded to a stop, shocked beyond speech. Hannah Shim, our brilliant intern, stood just inside the front door, arms out at her sides, while globs of something yellow and slimy dripped down her face. Bruce raced past me to the tiny kitchen and came back with a wad of paper towels. Amir reached for the door, emanating rage from every pore.

"Amir, please don't," Hannah said, taking the paper towels from Bruce. "It will only encourage them."

"Egg them on, you mean." Bruce was our most reliable supplier of snacks and bad puns. He picked a piece of eggshell from Hannah's hair.

I could see Amir freeze in the doorway, his crisp white shirt practically vibrating with tension. Slowly, he turned around and shut the door. He went to the kitchen and came back with a tea towel, crouching to wipe yolk from the floor around Hannah's feet. He seemed calm, but I knew his internal boiler was ready to blow.

I took the paper towels from Hannah's hand and began to wipe the egg from her face, but the wad of paper was too big and clumsy, and I only made the mess worse. She was not a crier, our Hannah, and she was trembling with the effort of keeping tears in. I felt my own eyes prickle. Those assholes. How could they be so cruel to a nineteen-year-old girl?

"A woman's first egging is a rite of passage." *Oh my god, Marian*. I'd forgotten my mother was there. She came into the newsroom and put her Coach bag on a chair. She fished around inside and pulled out a packet of wet wipes. "I was egged for the first time at the G20 protests in Brisbane. Somebody thought I was Christine Lagarde. An honour, really." She leaned closer to Hannah. "Eggs are actually quite good for the hair."

Hannah looked at her, wide-eyed. "My mother says the same thing."

Before I knew it, Marian had taken over, cleaning the egg from Hannah's face with a tenderness I did not recognize. My colleagues appeared star-struck. Bruce wanted to know if Marian had ever met Bill Gates, and if so, did she think he was good at Scrabble. Amir brought her a cup of coffee and apologized for the lack of fresh milk. Hannah accepted my mother's offer of a spritz of Chanel No. 5 to disguise any lingering eggy odours.

"Sorry to interrupt the love-in," I said, "but what are we going to do about those jackasses outside?"

They turned to look at me. "I'm okay, really," Hannah said. She wiped the last residue from her forehead and sat at her desk. "I'm going to write up my story from last night's council budget meeting."

Bruce took a plastic tub of Craisins from his desk, peeled back the lid, and dropped some beside Hannah's keyboard. "Did Mayor Halloran take this opportunity to talk about how much money he's saved by cutting the fat at city hall?"

Hannah stared at him in fake astonishment. "Were you there? How did you know?"

Outside, we could hear the horns blaring. "Did the mayor mention anything about helping us get rid of these idiots?" I asked. My voice was perhaps a tiny bit angrier than necessary. I waited for my mother to make some cutting remark about my role in all this, but she was focused on her phone again.

Amir tilted his head at me. "Cat, you know whose side Halloran is on. He's Team Idiot." He beckoned to me, and I followed him into his office. He closed the door behind us and landed heavily in his chair. Amir was not a person who was given to slumping. The boy who'd been so cool and competent when we

KATE HILTON & ELIZABETH RENZETTI

were camp counsellors together had become a cool and competent newspaper editor. Once, he'd excelled at building fires, and now he excelled at putting them out.

Or at least he had, until the protests started. Now the groove between his eyebrows was a canyon. He moved heavily and sighed more. It was like he was carrying an invisible sign on his shoulders that said "Weight of the world here." Whatever feelings of guilt I had about hurting the paper were nothing compared with my pain at hurting Amir.

I sat in the chair across from him. "I'm so—"

"If you're about to say sorry, don't." He shook his head abruptly. "This is not your fault. You and Bruce did exactly what you were supposed to. You conducted your research and wrote a good series on an important topic." He leaned forward, his dark eyes alive with a flame that I'd worried was extinguished. "That's what we're supposed to do, Cat. Otherwise why are we here?" He closed his eyes and fell back in his chair. "Your anti-vax series had an impact. It just wasn't the impact we were expecting."

For a minute we said nothing. The trucks' horns blared into the silence. "You know," I said, "the wellness influencers were pretty pissed about the series too."

Amir's eyes snapped open. "Why do you say that?"

"Bliss Bondar, one of the influencers, came down

pretty hard on us at the opening presser. Also, she refused to denounce some of the loonier anti-medicine material on the conference program."

A smile slowly spread across Amir's face. "Well, well. Look at you, stirring the pot. I'd call that a story, wouldn't you?"

I smiled back at him. "Give me half an hour and I'll give you that story."

He jumped out of his chair, making a shooing motion at me. "All right then, Conway. What are you waiting for?"

CHAPTER 3

BY THE TIME I headed out to the Pinerock for the Welcome, Goddess welcome banquet, my spirits were much improved.

Bruce had taken responsibility for returning Marian to the hotel so I could hunker down over a draft for Amir. Within an hour, I'd given him a short piece on Bliss's unscripted rant at the press conference, and then, feeling my groove coming back, I'd spent the balance of the afternoon delving into the history of Bliss and Bree's wellness empire. I wouldn't say I was looking for payback after the public smacking Bliss had served up, but neither was I awash with a great generosity of spirit. Fair's fair.

I already knew that Bree and Bliss had gotten

their start as hosts of a podcast called *Black Suits You* after both of their husbands—friends from a college hockey team—had been killed in a car crash. Initially, it was a call-in show for other young widows whose happily-ever-afters had been similarly derailed. But over time, the show evolved into a platform for wellness strategies, with physicians and psychologists giving way to aromatherapists, hypnotherapists, and energy healers. In due course, Bree and Bliss traded the five stages of grief for the endless stages of self-care.

As far as the internet knew, they were the best of friends, but onstage earlier, they'd seemed about as cozy as a polar bear and a seal trapped on an ice floe. Looking at their backgrounds, it was hard to see what they had in common aside from tragedy. Bree had a master's degree in chemistry and had worked in product safety before founding Welcome, Goddess. Bliss, on the other hand, had been a cosmetics tester with her own YouTube channel. She didn't have a post-secondary degree, unless you counted her online influencer certification from some virtual school that no longer existed, if it ever had.

Still, they'd made a good team as podcasters. I'd listened to several of their *Welcome, Goddess* episodes, and the division of labour was pretty clear. Bree did the research, interviewed the experts, and made sure the trains ran on time. And Bliss? She talked to the callers.

Even I—bitter, vengeful, collagen-depleted—had to admit that she had a magical quality on air. She was a presence. She understood how to listen, how to draw out a story with only the smallest nudge. Her callers confided in her as if she were their oldest friend, the person they trusted most in the world. She had them eating out of her glitter-manicured hands. But, toward the end of the pandemic, something changed. She began travelling deep into the weeds of health conspiracies, and her conversations with listeners were peppered with warnings about Big Pharma and surveillance by microchip. The government was herding its hapless citizens with lies about hastily developed and dangerous vaccines. She wasn't the only person to have been sucked down a hole during that time, but she was definitely one of the most influential.

When had Bliss and Bree's partnership gone sour? Because based on what I'd seen in the conference room today, it was well past its best-before date.

I was mulling over the question as I climbed into my car for another trip to the Pinerock. I turned the key, relieved to hear the engine spring to life. My geriatric CR-V owed me nothing. I patted the dash in gratitude, glancing as I did at the kitchen window of the recently shuttered Second Act. It was dinner time on a Friday night and the building was dark. I knew that the owners were trying to sell, but they weren't having much success. As depressing as it was living over an empty restaurant, it was better than receiving an eviction notice. My precarious housing was one more problem I was content to kick down the road for as long as possible.

"HERE COMES TROUBLE," said Doug Jaglowski. His smile was genuinely friendly but there was a hint of *mind your manners* and *don't fuck with my cushy gig.* He was working security at the Pinerock for the Welcome, Goddess conference, an off-season side hustle. During the summer, Doug held down the fort at the Playhouse, the local theatre. He'd had a murder investigation on his patch a few short months ago, and I'd been hip-deep in it. I could see why I might make a fellow jumpy.

"Good to see you, too," I said. "How's the wellness business treating you?"

He shrugged. "No complaints. Bunch of kooks, but harmless enough. Hope you brought your moonbeams and unicorns."

I laughed. "I never go anywhere without them."

He beckoned me closer. "I hear they're going to make a movie about the Eliot Fraser murder," he said, conspiratorially. "You know anything about that?"

I did indeed. I'd agreed to be a consultant on the project for a small upfront fee, with more to follow if the producers got a studio on board. The payment was helping to stretch my budget over the deficit created when I'd lost my bartending shifts at the Second Act.

I told Doug that the producers were hoping to film on site at the Playhouse.

His eyes lit up. "Will they need extras?" he asked.

"If they do, I'll tell them to make sure you're one of them." I extracted a promise to let me know if he happened upon any newsworthy gossip in the course of his duties, and left him happily contemplating his big-screen debut.

I found my mother in the ballroom, halfway through a breadbasket and a bottle of wine. I noted with approval her surprising embrace of carbs, but any warmth I felt disappeared with her next words. "You're late," she snapped. "And you shouldn't wear linen after Labour Day."

I suppressed a sigh. I'd thought I was rocking the jaunty red jumpsuit that I'd had Kaydence sew for me, but all at once I felt scruffy and unsophisticated.

"I think you look fabulous," said Kaydence, who seemed blessedly unoffended by Marian's comment. She was resplendent in a linen maxi dress herself, made from an embroidered fabric that I suspected had graced a dining table at some point in its past. I took a seat next to her, a safe distance from my mother. Kaydence turned to me and whispered, "Your mom got hangry and made them bring her bread from the other restaurant. And wine. It's a dry event."

I glanced at the menu. I'd missed the roasted locally grown purple sprouting broccoli with whipped tofu dip, but still had the chestnut, squash, and sweet potato loaf to look forward to. I reached over and snagged a slice of focaccia out of my mother's basket.

"Why the empty seats?" I asked Kaydence. The table was set for eight, but we were an awkward four with several orphaned chairs.

"We were abandoned for Clarity K after the appetizer course," said the fourth occupant of the table. As I reached out to shake his hand I realized that it was the upright gentleman from that morning's press conference.

"Lewis Kinross," he said.

"What brings you to the altar of the goddesses, Lewis?" I asked.

"Well, I'm an academic by day—I teach in the Faculty of Health Sciences at the University of Southern Alberta." He ran a hand over his balding head. "But I'm afraid I'm treading on your toes this week."

I cocked an eyebrow. "Are you now?"

"Yes, I'm here on assignment from *The Loft*." If his chest puffed a tad, I couldn't blame him. *The Loft* was Canada's premier magazine for intellectuals, the kind that serious people kept on their coffee table while they hid *Us Weekly* in the bathroom. A prime minister had given a disastrous interview to *The Loft* a few years before, and his party had flamed out in the election that followed.

"Has *The Loft* started to care about probiotic supplements and manifesting your money dreams?"

He chuckled. "No, but it does care about disinformation and the impact it has on public health policy. *The Loft* has commissioned me to write an analysis of the intersection of the wellness movement and conspiratorial thinking. That's my academic bailiwick. And thus, here I am."

I realized that I'd seen him on TV and in the newspapers during the pandemic, railing against the people who spread falsehoods about COVID-19. I told him I admired his work, and he nodded, not entirely bashfully. "I return the compliment," he said. "I read your series on vaccine hesitancy. It was excellent."

"Not a widely shared opinion around here," I said.

"You keep fighting the good fight," he said. "So much depends on it. To be honest, I thought there might be a few more serious journalists here."

My mother made an abrupt movement, standing so suddenly she rocked the table.

I followed her gaze to two men clad in black suits and wearing headsets clearing a path through the room. I was not entirely surprised to see Clarity K floating behind them, her ivory cape billowing in her wake.

My mother appeared ready for battle. "I'm going to introduce myself."

"She seems pretty busy, Mom," I said.

"Not too busy to meet a fellow presenter, surely," she said and stalked off. She had never liked sharing the spotlight.

I looked at Kaydence and Lewis. "That's unlikely to go well." I poured myself a generous serving of wine from my mother's bottle and offered it around. Kaydence declined, but Lewis held out his glass.

"To your health," he said, and we toasted.

There was more to say, but our wayward dinner companions were drifting back to the table. Marnie, Gina, and Becca, we learned, were friends from a book club that had read Clarity K's first collection and loved it. They'd registered for the retreat as soon as they'd heard about it, but even then, only Gina had snagged a spot in Clarity's SkyWords workshop.

"It sold out in fifteen minutes!" said Marnie. "But we're still having fun. We got into the mala necklace workshop." She looped a string of bright pink and turquoise beads over her fingers and held them out for me to admire.

"Nice," I said. I guessed that Marnie wouldn't be using them as a meditation aid, but who was I to judge? I didn't meditate *or* accessorize.

"I wanted to see Elizabeth Gilbert," said Becca, "but they say she had a scheduling conflict. They booked Marian instead." She regarded my mother's empty chair with a disappointed air. "It's too bad.

Marian's not vibing with the mood of the conference, you know? She's cranky."

"She can be," I said. I hesitated for a moment, and then added: "I should know. She's my mother."

Becca blushed the colour of her beetroot soda. "I'm so sorry," she said. "I only meant that she's kind of, um, driven, I guess?"

Marnie put a hand on Becca's arm. "We all felt that way, babe. You shouldn't be embarrassed to speak your truth. That's what Clarity K says." She turned to me. "We were chatting about how your mother really represents that boomer model of success. Her energy is so … masculine."

"Do any of you work?" I asked, before I could help myself. I heard a small intake of breath from Kaydence.

Happily, Marnie was prevented from answering by the arrival of their fourth, introduced as Abby. "Oh my god, you guys, you will not believe what happened." She pointed at my mother's chair. "What was that woman's name? Miriam?"

"Marian," I said.

"She tried to follow Clarity into the bathroom. Clarity's security team stopped her and she had a full meltdown. She said that she was a VIP and she'd go where she damn well pleased. I filmed it, look."

Becca reached for Abby's phone and covered the screen. "You haven't met Marian's daughter," she said, nodding in my direction.

"Cat Conway," I said.

Abby froze for a moment, and then Marnie said, "Hey ladies, there's a necklace I'm thinking about buying in the marketplace. Will you come and give me your opinion?"

With identical expressions of relief, they rose as one and practically ran for the door.

Kaydence snorted. "You sure know how to clear a table," she said.

"It's a skill I learned from my mother," I told her.

"Young people don't appreciate the contributions of your mother's and my generation," said Lewis. "C'est la vie. I don't blame her for being cranky, if that's true. She's a hero to many. I certainly admire her."

"She's had a remarkable career," I agreed. Marian had left a senior role at McKinsey to head up WEENA— Women's Economic Empowerment North America—a position that had turned her into a regular cable news pundit on issues of gender and work. She'd been approached by a major publisher to write a book on midlife empowerment, and they'd pulled all the levers they had to make it a hit. She'd had a charmed career, in other words, at least over the past decade or so.

I wasn't accustomed to seeing her ridiculed by anyone except me, and it left me feeling strangely protective of her. At the same time, though I would never admit it, I shared Becca's confusion at Marian's inclusion at this gauzy conference. She was a Ferrari engine surrounded by fireflies. I searched for something supportive to say about her. "She hasn't always been the easiest parent, but she's great with my son."

"How's Jake doing, by the way?" asked Kaydence. I appreciated her efforts to steer the conversation away from my mother.

How was Jake doing? I wasn't sure I knew. He preferred to interact with me from the other side of a closed door whenever we were in the same house. He was slightly more communicative by text, which is how I knew that his grades were decent and he had a reasonable social life.

"No red flags at present," I said.

"Grandparenting is infinitely more fun than parenting," Lewis said.

"How old are your grandchildren?" asked Kaydence.

"Just the one. Olivia is eight," he said, pulling out his phone and showing us a picture of a curly-haired toddler hugging a teddy bear.

Kaydence gushed, and told Lewis that he should come by her booth and check out the kids' clothes. "I have a dress that would be perfect for her."

Now that the tension at our table had dissipated, it suddenly occurred to me that Marian had been gone a long time. I excused myself and went to find her.

There was no sign of her in the corridors around the ballroom, in the lobby, or in the bar. I wondered if she'd retreated to her room for a reset, so I took the elevator up to the second floor and tapped on her door. "Mom? Are you in there?"

There was no response. I was preparing to enter with my key when the door to the room next to Marian's flew open and a woman with greying blond hair and a tear-streaked face launched herself into the corridor, followed by a stocky man in slim-fitting pants and a T-shirt sized to show off his pecs and delts. He seemed like the sort of man who would call his muscles by nicknames. "You are a bastard, Bodhi," the woman shrieked. "A complete bastard."

"Jenny," he said, in a podcast-perfect voice. "It's not what you think. You're putting two and two together to make five."

How many times had my ex-husband told me that I was imagining what I could see with my own eyes? How many times had it been exactly what I thought? Every damn time. But not before I'd made myself half-crazy trying to explain away the signs of yet another betrayal.

The man put a hand on the woman's arm. Where had I seen her before? My mind flashed to Kaydence's booth in the marketplace, where little Phoenix had wreaked havoc among the headbands while her mother, hopelessly outnumbered, tried to contain the damage.

Phoenix's mom shoved the man away, hard, and stormed off toward the elevators.

"I'd let her go," I called. "Just some friendly advice."

I saw a flash of anger on his artfully stubbled face as he turned, and then a practised smile slipped into place. He walked toward me, reaching out to shake my hand. His palm was a lot warmer than his eyes. "Bodhi Rubin," he said. "My wife was having trouble expressing her feelings constructively. Please excuse her."

Bodhi Rubin. That was a name I recognized. "You're one of the speakers at the conference, aren't you?" I asked.

"That's right," he said. "I'm Wonderstruck."

"I'm flattered," I said.

He looked puzzled. "My business," he said. "It's called Wonderstruck. I teach people how to connect to the wonder all around them so that they can sink more deeply into life's mysteries."

"Uh-huh," I said. "Sounds cool." I had five bucks that said Mrs. Bodhi was sinking into the mystery of how she'd ended up with such a navel-gazing, gaslighting fuckwad.

BY THE TIME I made it back to my table, Bliss and Bree were onstage and my mother was in her seat. The book club women had pulled up stakes and were nowhere to be seen.

"Where were you?" I whispered. Marian ignored me and reached for the last roll in the basket.

"You'll have lots of time to hear from us this week," said Bree. "So tonight we have very short remarks of welcome." Was I imagining the pointed emphasis in her words, or the sideways flicker of her eyes toward Bliss? "It is truly meaningful to us to see so many of you gathered together. You are making a powerful commitment to your wellness today and we are here to support you."

Bliss took the microphone. "Everywhere around us, forces of darkness conspire to undermine our bodily integrity. Our autonomy, which is our birthright as humans, is under threat like never before in history. That's why what we're doing here is so urgent. We need you to be leaders in the fight, like our friend Mayor Halloran, who is here with us tonight. Stand up, Mayor Halloran. You are a champion of free speech and free thought and we salute you."

Gerry Halloran, with the meaty frame and crooked nose of a former minor league hockey enforcer, rose from his seat and waved to the crowd. His tight blue blazer rose up around his shoulders. Debbie sat beside him, but instead of gazing at him in admiration, she was reading the program with an air of complete boredom.

"Okay," said Bree, who had regained control of the mic, "that's all from us. Please linger over dessert and get to know your new friends on this journey. We all have so much to learn from each other. We'll see everyone early tomorrow morning for a full day of programming."

On cue, the server placed a pot of brown sludge in front of each of us.

My mother pursed her lips. "What is this?"

"Avocado chocolate mousse," said the server.

"Take it away," said Marian, "and bring me a martini."

CHAPTER 4

I AWOKE THE morning after the banquet to three new messages: two complimentary emails and one less pleasant dog turd wrapped inside a copy of the *Quill & Packet*, left on my front stairs. Fortunately for my ego, the emails arrived first.

I immediately knew who had sent the first message, thanks to its lack of punctuation and capital letters. It read as if it had been typed with one hand by someone who was lighting a cigarette with the other: *ya still got it kiddo*. What I still had was left to the imagination, but I figured that Nick Dhalla, my old newspaper colleague—and one-time fling—was referring to the ever-so-slightly critical story I'd written about Bliss Bondar and Bree Guthrie.

The other message, from Amir, was—like its sender—cooler, calmer, and more formal. And left me feeling much warmer: *Dear Cat, once again I have to thank you for a stellar contribution to our pages. If the* Quill *does founder on the rocks, it will be entirely my fault, not yours. But I don't think it will founder, because your hand is on the wheel alongside mine.*

If there was a tiny flush in my cheeks when I brushed my teeth, it was solely due to last night's wine. Or so I told myself. Nothing to do with the image of my hand next to Amir's. *He's your boss,* I told myself sternly in the mirror. Yes, I'd had a crush on him when we were teenagers, but that was decades ago. Now we were merely shipmates, and our ship was taking on water.

Unfortunately, the good vibes were lost in a fetid stink the moment I stepped outside the front door of the Second Act and my foot sank into a suspiciously soft edition of the *Quill.* Shit oozed from inside and left a rancid stain on Bruce's front-page story about tractor thefts. I wiped my shoe on the pavement and used the tips of my fingernails to carry the newspaper to the garbage can outside Mugs 'n Things.

I thought of the protesters gathered outside the newsroom, honking furiously. I pictured egg dripping from Hannah's hair, her shocked and bewildered face. What I felt wasn't fear, but my old friend rage. Anger was something I had in common with those anti-science idiots. The thought did not comfort me.

For a moment I stood staring at the novelty clocks and umbrella hats in the window display. Mugs 'n Things brought me such comfort. It was one of the few shops in Port Ellis that had not been gentrified, and it sold the same tacky tat I had coveted back when I'd visited with my grandparents: placemats showing a map of the three lakes; signs that said, "What happens at the cottage stays at the cottage."

My anger cooled. The October sun helped, with its last-gasp warmth. The elm trees lining the street filtered pure gold below. Normally I would have honoured the day by riding my bike, but the Pinerock was a good way out of town. I needed to make a call from the car, too. *A car gives you more protection than a bike*, a tiny voice in my brain whispered. *And you can get away faster.*

If I had enough time, I decided, I'd take a stroll up the hill behind the Pinerock when I got there. While technically on the Pinerock's land, the steep hike and famous view over Lake Jane were treated more like public parkland by the local population. Even after huffing and puffing up the forest trail for thirty minutes, swatting at bugs and branches, the magnificent view was worth it: postcard-perfect in any weather, the broad expanse of water broken by small islands of salt-and-pepper-striped rock, the green shoreline sculpted by craggy pines.

In the car, I typed out a quick thank-you to Amir,

and ignored the message from Nick. I put the phone on the passenger seat, hit the speaker button, and then the contact I'd named Dadapalooza. He picked up on the second ring. "Caterina!" My father called me by a bunch of different names: Cathy, Kitty Cat, Billie (after his favourite journalist on *Lou Grant*). He thought of me as a gem, with many sides and facets. Unlike some parents I could name.

"Funny you should call," he said, as I pulled out onto Lakeshore. "Jake's coming over later today."

"Huh," I said, wondering when I had last heard from my teenaged son. "Does he need money?"

My dad laughed, deep and rolling. "We're at the end of our *Lord of the Rings* view-a-thon. Only one more movie to go, although I fear it's six hours long. And the absurd genealogy!" I could practically hear his head shaking. "It's all Shmegulin, son of Begulin."

"I thought you loved that genealogy stuff. You were thrilled when Jake got you and Mom that 23andMe kit for your anniversary."

"And the results came back one hundred percent orc-free." My dad laughed.

"Anyway, thank you for taking an elf arrow for the team," I said, and meant it. My son learned invaluable things from my dad, a history teacher and book lover, about the vastness of the imagination. Jake learned other lessons from his father, my ex-husband, Mark. Like how to suppress all feelings, except those for material goods. This sudden pang of bitterness reminded me why I was calling.

"Dad, I wanted to talk to you about Mom. She's being weird. I mean, extra weird. She's super distracted, for one thing. She disappeared for half an hour last night and I couldn't find her. And normally she'd catch at least ten percent of the mean comments before they leave her mouth, but her filter's clearly not working."

"Well, you know, it's a tricky time—"

"She ate half a breadbasket. And asked for a martini afterwards."

That shocked him into silence. As I waited for him to speak, I turned onto the road that led to the Pinerock. I passed Pepley's Apple Adventure Land and Pumpkin Patch, its parking lot full of city families out for a day of hayrides and apple picking. The road was clear and the sun warm on my hands. I waited for my father to gather his thoughts about the complicated woman we both loved and lived slightly in fear of.

"She's having a particularly hard time right now. The book's coming out soon, and she doesn't know how it will be received. You know how she is when she can't control a situation. Uncertainty makes her nauseous. There was some talk that the book would be eligible for one of the big book clubs if it did well—"

"Oprah?" I whispered.

My father diplomatically chose not to hear me.

"And she's banking on getting a new contract with her publisher, but that's also going to depend on sales, apparently. And then there's ..." His voice was gone, and I wondered for a second if my phone had lost signal.

"Dad?'

"I'm here, Kitty Cat. Just be gentle with your mother, that's all I'm saying."

I was about to tell him that might be easier if he sent me a case of bourbon when a sudden wailing interrupted our conversation. A police car appeared in my rear-view mirror, lights flashing. It raced up on my tail, swerved around me, and disappeared up the road. A fire truck passed me a couple of seconds later, sirens blaring.

I stomped on the gas pedal. "Dad? I've got to go. Something's up."

My hike through the woods would have to wait.

THREE POLICE CARS and the fire truck were parked in a haphazard row by the Pinerock's front door. I found a spot out back, grabbed my bag, and raced toward the entrance. I dodged a group of young women huddled with their heads together, shoulders shaking. I had a sudden vision of my mother falling down the stairs, hitting her head on the bathtub, suffering a heart attack alone in bed. I ran faster.

When I flung open the Pinerock's doors, I was

confronted with chaos. Two police officers were speaking to the front-desk staff, who looked shell-shocked. I didn't recognize either of the cops from my run-ins with the law earlier that summer, so they must have been from a different detachment.

Inside the huge front lobby, the stalls that had been bustling yesterday were empty and unstaffed. Bodhi Rubin, guru of soul connections, sat on a wicker sofa with his arm around his wife, but I noticed his eyes scanning over her shoulder. They caught mine, and flicked away.

No sign of Marian. I fished the phone out of my backpack and typed a text to her: *Where R U?* The answer came back immediately, and she didn't even bother to comment on my disgraceful grammar. Something definitely was wrong. *In the coffee shop*, she wrote.

I ran down the lobby toward the café at the back of the main floor, passing groups of dazed-looking women. Out the window I could see the firefighters heading toward the wooded hill behind the resort. I skidded to a halt. Danilo Reyes, Bliss and Bree's publicist, had tucked himself into the alcove where the payphones used to be. Even in the gloom I could see that he was unshaven, his cardigan misbuttoned. His cheeks were wet with tears. He had his phone clamped to his ear, and when I approached him, he shooed me away with an angry hand.

The coffee shop was sparsely filled, the staff clustered in a whispering huddle by the kitchen doors. In a window I caught a reflection of Marian's silver bob (immaculate, no surprise), and I ran over to her booth.

"Mom," I panted. "Jesus, I'm glad to see you. I thought—" Then my mouth clamped shut, because there was already someone else at the table. Someone with dark hair and an air of calm competence, her bejewelled hand resting on my mother's. It rankled to see Marian tolerating prolonged physical contact from an almost-stranger.

"Debbie," I ground out. "How nice to see you again."

Debbie Halloran patted the seat next to her, indicating I should sit down. "I arrived this morning to help Marian prepare for her Boss Babe workshop, and we heard the ghastly news. So distressing, wasn't it?" She patted my mother's hand, as if seeking confirmation.

Marian snapped a packet of Sweet'N Low the way a nun might flick a ruler at a naughty child. She did not appear distressed.

"Mom? Do you want to tell me what the hell is going on?"

"So much drama," she said. "If anyone should be in hysterics, it should be me. I'm the one who found the body." She took a sip of her coffee. "And you wonder why I left this town? It's cursed."

I sank back in my seat, my thoughts as chaotic as

the clatter and din in the coffee shop. "I'm sorry … you found what?"

"A body, Catherine. A corpse. At the bottom of the lookout. It was quite upsetting, as I'm sure you can imagine." She said this in a tone that suggested she had found other bodies in her time, or perhaps buried them.

I was, for once, speechless. It was Debbie who filled the silence with a gentle, sad observation: "That poor girl. She certainly didn't fulfill the promise of her name."

CHAPTER 5

"WELLNESS DOESN'T SEEM to have done much for her," said Doug. "I'll stick with my bacon sandwiches and beer, thank you very much."

It was harsh, but I could see where he was coming from. It hadn't been me, in the end, who'd exploded his low-key work routine, but Bliss Bondar. The early word was that Bliss had fallen from the scenic lookout at some point during the night. Her twisted, crumpled body had been spotted in the bushes below, first by a couple enjoying the sunrise and again, shortly thereafter, by Marian Conway, out for her morning walk, ankle-weighted and Fitbitted.

My mother and I needed to talk, but I was waiting for reinforcements. I'd left her to the tender ministrations of Debbie Halloran, not that she needed them. Despite yesterday's wobble, there was no fragility on display today, only grit and gumption.

Doug swivelled on his chair, so that he had his back to the monitors showing various corners of the Pinerock: hallways, staircases, the pool, the gardens, the dining room. "I told Martha Mercer that the lookout was a deathtrap. She wasn't interested. 'Put up a fence,' I said. But no. We wouldn't want to spoil the view. You know what spoils a view? A dead body, that's what." Doug shook his head. "A little stone wall that people could sit on, like a bench. That's what they installed instead. Idiots. I'd have put chain link across the whole thing." In the war between form and function, Doug had picked his side.

I was waiting for Bruce to arrive. Amir had agreed that the story was large enough to justify sending both of us. The death of Bliss Bondar would bring journalists from near and far, and we had the home field advantage. Anyway, Bruce was much better than I was with a camera, and I had an inkling that his Marian-management skills might be stronger than mine.

I saw Bruce's antique Subaru pull into the parking lot and went out to meet him. He grinned. "And the death toll keeps rising," he said. There was no malice in his voice. He liked to joke that I was the worst thing to have happened to Port Ellis since the Great Manure Explosion of '75. Bruce was the most laid-back colleague

I'd ever had in the newspaper business. Others (Nick Dhalla, just to pick one at random) appeared easygoing but were ferociously competitive on the trail of a story. It was next to impossible to rile Bruce; I occasionally tried, just to see if I could. He was in his sixties and had seen more than most in his day—a day that still included regular hits of cannabis. His general philosophy seemed to be *you do you*, although he made exceptions for people who stomped on others in their quest for self-fulfillment. All in all, he was one of my favourite people and a major reason why I'd decided—at least so far—to stay in Port Ellis. "What's the plan?"

"My mother was next person on the scene after the couple who found the body," I said. "We need to interview her. She likes you better than she likes me."

"Hardly," he said, smiling at me. He knew all about Marian. "Where is she?"

"In the café. With the mayor's wife, her new best friend."

He looked up from the camera he was fiddling with. "What's that about?" Gerry Halloran didn't have a lot of fans in the newsroom, on account of being a dirty liar and a schoolyard bully; and he never lost an opportunity to slag the *Quill*, his competition in the local media scene. But we tried to rise above the fray. Even with Gerry facing unopposed re-election in the spring, we left Debbie alone. She never waded into the political mud, and she kept her opinions to herself.

I was about to reply when a familiar duo—a short Black woman in loafers and sensible trousers, and a tall white woman in couture—emerged from the hotel entrance. "Hold up," I said, and jogged over to intercept them.

Detective Inspector Cheryl Bell of the Ontario Provincial Police and Martha Mercer, owner of the Pinerock Resort, did not look delighted to see me. Perhaps it was because our last encounters had been soured by my investigation into the murder of Martha's ex-husband, Eliot Fraser. I felt I deserved a little gratitude for my role in solving it—and nearly getting killed in the process. But none seemed to be forthcoming. Was it that I'd dug up some unsavoury information about Martha's family and implied that she'd been involved in his death? Or that I'd temporarily withheld some key information from Inspector Bell? Who could say?

"What are you doing here?" asked Inspector Bell. Martha simply glared.

"I was covering the conference," I said. "Now I'm covering the death of Bliss Bondar. I wonder if you might have a comment for the *Quill & Packet* on the case?"

"Absolutely not," said Inspector Bell, crisply.

"You don't usually attend accidental deaths, do you?" I asked. Inspector Bell didn't answer. My question was intended as a provocation, but it was also food for thought. What was a senior officer from the regional office doing here, mere hours after a tragic fall?

Martha Mercer stepped forward, bristling. "I will not hesitate to have you thrown off my property, Ms. Conway," she said, her blond hair helmet as fixed as her expression of disdain. "There has been a terrible accident. That is all. We do not need you sensationalizing it."

"I understand that you rejected the safety recommendations that your security team made about the lookout," I said. "Would you like to respond to that?"

I felt an arm snake through mine. "I'm sure you're both very busy," said Bruce, tugging me toward the hotel. "We should let you get on with your responsibilities." I allowed it. I knew that I wasn't at my most strategic around Martha Mercer. The woman got under my skin. It was as if she reminded me of someone.

"AS I TOLD Catherine, I was out for my morning walk," my mother explained to Bruce, taking a delicate sip of her smoothie.

For years, my mother had been up with the birds in the morning, which was only annoying because she insisted that anyone who didn't follow suit was missing out on the best part of the day. At various times, she had promoted reading, goal-setting, and clearing email during the first couple of hours of wakefulness. She'd gone through a meditation phase after Arianna Huffington promoted its benefits, but I had the sense it hadn't stuck. Sitting still wasn't Marian's strength.

"Trying new things is essential to cultivating a beginner's mind," she said. "And the benefits of exercise are well-known to everyone." Her eyes slid toward me and she corrected herself: "Almost everyone." She turned her attention back to Bruce. "Efficient growth is one of the main messages of *Grit and Gumption*. Combining priorities in a single activity to catalyze exponential benefits."

"It's so clever," said Debbie. "I love that part of *Grit and Gumption*. If I'm addicted to anything, it's self-improvement." So Debbie had an advance copy of my mother's book. My own must have been lost in the mail.

My mother smiled benevolently. "I wish I could persuade my daughter to adopt that mindset."

"I'm sitting right here," I said.

"So, Marian," Bruce prompted. "You were at the lookout this morning?"

She nodded. "It was close to seven. I took the trail that starts from the parking lot. I'd been up for an hour at least, waiting for the sun to rise, editing the notes for my workshop. It's postponed now, obviously."

"How long had you been on the trail?" I redirected

her. It was a half-hour's steep climb to the top of the ridge, two hundred metres above Lake Jane—more if you ambled along in harmony with the trees; less if you were trying to outrun the natural course of aging or liked to show off.

"I'd been climbing for twenty minutes or so," she said. "I was near the top when the screaming started." As I'd predicted, a power-walking pace at the very least. "I stopped and called out, and a minute or so later, a young couple came tearing down the path toward me. The girl was in a terrible state, crying her eyes out."

"What did they say to you?" asked Bruce.

"They said there was a body and they pointed up to the top of the path." Marian shook her head. "They weren't very coherent. I asked them to clarify where the body was, and the young man said they'd seen it at the bottom of the cliff when the sun came up. I told them to go to the hotel and tell the staff immediately, and I went up to the lookout to see for myself."

Of course you did, I thought. *You never miss an opportunity to be the centre of attention.*

"You're a brave one," said Debbie. "I'm not sure I would have had the stomach for it."

"Any normal person would feel the same way," I said. Debbie and Bruce frowned at me, but my mother favoured me with a smile. We both knew I'd have done the same thing she had. "And?" I asked.

"And it was a distressing sight," said Marian. "Those poor kids. Apparently they were up there for a sunrise proposal. Well, hopefully it will give them a sober second thought. No one should get married that young." Debbie glanced swiftly at my mother and seemed to colour. I wondered how young she'd been when she married Gerry. Many of my own mistakes could be explained by youthful inexperience. Although by no means all of them.

Marian continued, "The body was at the bottom of the cliff, as they'd said. I'm no expert, but I doubt she suffered. Well, not after landing, anyway."

Debbie blanched and took a long sip of water, then excused herself. I swallowed a laugh. My mother's sangfroid was legendary, but it could take some getting used to. "Did you notice anything up at the top?" I asked. "Any reason to suspect it wasn't an accident?"

"Such as?"

"Oh, I don't know," I said. "Signs of a struggle? Drag marks? A suicide note?"

"No," said my mother. "Nothing like that. But I wasn't looking for it either." She paused. "I recognized her, you know. Even from so far away. She was face-up, her hair full of blood." She exhaled slowly, as if taking it in for the first time. "It was shocking. Shocking."

I reached out and gripped her hand. She returned the squeeze briefly and then pulled away. I thought, then, of how she'd permitted Debbie to coddle her earlier and it gave me an uneasy feeling. Over the years, I'd allocated ninety-nine percent of the responsibility for our fraught bond to my mother's personality, but maybe I'd miscalculated. If my mother (and my son, for that matter) turned into a spiky hedgehog ball in my presence alone, what did that say?

I banished the thought. "Did you see anyone else out there?"

"No," Marian said. "Not a soul."

Had I detected an infinitesimal pause before she replied? Perhaps I'd imagined it. But my Spidey sense tingled. My mother's presentation of reality was often Photoshopped to show her best side. Was she withholding something?

"Bruce, would you excuse us?" asked my mother. "I want a private word with Catherine."

"Certainly," said Bruce. "I'll go interview some of the weepers in the lobby, shall I?"

"I like that fellow; he's a sensible sort," said Marian, after he'd left. "Before Debbie gets back, I wanted a word about my book."

"The one you haven't sent me?"

"Honestly," said Marian. "That publicist is hopeless. No work ethic. All of twenty-two, I'm sure."

"She managed to get a copy to Debbie," I said.

"I gave her one of my personal copies," said my mother. "You're getting a press copy. Which is what I wanted to chat about. I'm wondering if you can get some of your contacts to help promote the book. You must have some favours you can call in?"

I had a few, but I wasn't planning on spending them on puff pieces for my mother. I was still rebuilding a career that had collapsed like a rotten bridge in the too-recent past. The Eliot Fraser story had restored my reputation with my old journalism colleagues in the city, but I still shuddered at how close I'd come to professional death. I told her I'd do what I could but that I'd mostly lost contact with my old circle.

"All the more reason to move back to the city," she said. She held up a hand. "I've heard you. You like it up here, god only knows why."

She was good, I had to give her that. "I'm on the clock, Mom. I'll see you later, okay?"

Her eyes flickered. "If you're determined to stay in Port Ellis, wouldn't it make sense to invest in some property? I could help, you know. Think about it."

One favour for another. Efficient, you might say. And I had some thoughts already, including a great title for my mother's next book: *Strings Attached*.

CHAPTER 6

AS I HEADED out through the lobby, I saw Bruce interviewing a group of weepers in one corner. Always as
good as his word, Bruce. If my mother was a twisty
mountain path, Bruce was a straight, smooth road.
You knew where you were going with him.

I headed back through the parking lot, to the edge
of the woods. The cops were still busy wrapping caution tape around the trunks of trees, crushing thickets
of brush underfoot. Inspector Bell was inside the cor-
don, arms folded, talking to someone I assumed was
another detective—his city-mouse dress shoes gave
him away. I counted the cops in uniform tramping
around: there were five, including Dick Friesen, who
ran the tiny local police department. A few more in

plain clothes. So many cops. Too many cops to be investigating a mere accident.

There was no sign of Bliss's body. The medical examiner must have taken her away. Taken *it* away: a broken corpse where yesterday there had been a lively, pretty, mouthy young woman. She'd been bitchy to me the day before, but I felt the pain of a death that had come too soon, too violently. At least she'd not had a chance to read the story I'd written about her, with its acid undertones.

If I'd been cruel to her in life, maybe I could help her in death. Two cops stood guarding the bottom of the path, but I didn't recognize them. They weren't locals like me. They'd never explored these woods. They hadn't ducked out of the Pinerock one night when they were fifteen, leaving the music of the solstice gala behind, holding the sweaty hand of Darryl Danby.

Darryl and I had ended up at the top of the cliff, at the fateful lookout. We'd been making out like two crazed rabbits until his fingers groped inside the top of my Reitmans dress and squeezed so hard that I screamed with shock. He'd stomped away, leaving me sobbing and alone. *I always did have bad taste in men*, I thought, as I circled around the edge of the parking lot, looking for the second, secret trail that led to the lookout.

I skittered down one side of a drainage ditch and scrambled up the other, swatting away cattails and burst milkweed pods. Pacing the edge of the treeline, I saw a crushed water bottle and crept closer. The underbrush here looked recently trampled. I'd know this was the right path if I found a clearing with a rotting picnic table in a few hundred steps. Darryl had tried to carve our initials in it with a corkscrew he'd stolen from the Pinerock's kitchen.

Pine needles and dried leaves crunched under my feet. The sunlight made the forest blaze, crimson and gold and orange. Too pretty a day for death. Suddenly, a strange noise broke the silence. The wailing of an animal caught in a barbed-wire fence.

I froze. Forgot to breathe. What if someone had pushed Bliss from that lookout, and that someone was still here? The wailing subsided into wet, burbling sobs. Not nearly so alarming. My heart slowed to a normal pace. I followed the sound until the trees gave way to a small clearing, with a dilapidated picnic table at its heart.

Sitting on the table, his head drooping between his knees, was Danilo Reyes. I came into the clearing, and his head jerked upright in fright. "Jesus," he said, clutching his chest. "You scared me to death." His face crumpled. "I can't believe I just said that. I'm a monster."

"No," I said. "You're just upset. You lost a friend today."

He stared at me. He wore glasses with chunky red

frames, and they sat crookedly on his nose. "What do you know about it?"

"Not much. How about you?"

"We should never have come to this sad-ass town. 'Hold the conference in Toronto,' I said. 'You can get a decent coffee and a banh mi.' But did they listen?" He flung up his hands, and I noticed he held one of Glenda's famous mondochunk chocolate muffins. "But no," he continued. "It had to be here. In the middle of nowhere. With bugs. And bad Wi-Fi. And ... and"—he shook his head in disgust—"nature."

"Nature is Satan's church," I said solemnly, quoting a movie I'd seen once at an arthouse theatre.

He shot me a surprised look. "You've seen that film? So there is some culture around here."

"I'm actually from Toronto," I said. "But I spent my summers here when I was growing up."

"Bliss insisted the conference had to be here. She had some strange connection to this town." As he said her name, he started to sob again. He snuffled, and stuffed the muffin in his mouth. As a fellow stress eater, I sympathized.

Danilo made a strange noise, a cross between a gargle and a moan. His shoulders convulsed. I bounded across the clearing as his eyes bulged behind his chic glasses. "Danilo? Are you okay?" He shook his head furiously, his hands at his throat. I knew that gesture: choking. For an awful second, I was thrown into the past, Eliot Fraser writhing at my feet with the same desperate struggle on his face.

Danilo heaved again, one hand clawing at me. My first-aid training kicked in. I pulled him off the table, braced him, and hit him sharply between the shoulder blades with the heel of my hand. He continued to convulse. I made a fist, pulling my arm back like I was trying to strike out Barry Bonds, and whomped him again. A mondochunk shot from his mouth, arced through the air, and landed wetly next to a clump of mushrooms.

He sucked in air like a drowning man, then hurled the rest of the muffin toward the trees. After a second, he said, "I told you this place is cursed." I sat down on the rickety bench at his feet, and patted his knee. I couldn't disagree.

"And that crappy dinner was Bliss's last meal," he said glumly. "It seems so cruel."

We sat there and pondered the terrible unfairness of life. I stirred. "How's Bree doing, by the way? She must be so upset."

Danilo snorted. "You'd think so, wouldn't you? She's holed up in her room. She won't talk to me."

Onstage yesterday, there'd been tension between Bree and Bliss. Anyone could have seen it. But Bliss hadn't appeared despondent, or frightened. Quite the opposite. "Do you think," I began, and stopped. "Do you think Bliss might have chosen this ending?"

He whipped around, his face full of shock. "Are you kidding? Bliss? She would never. She believed in herself. Even in her bullshit. She saw herself as a saviour, not a victim."

"Maybe an accident, then." I was trying to probe gently, but Danilo was onto me.

"Are you planning on writing a story?"

"I'm trying to get at the truth. You don't have to talk to me, obviously. But if you do want Bliss's truth to be told, I can help with that. You can give me information that's not for attribution, for example, so that your name never appears in the story." It felt gross to wheedle the grieving this way, but I'd long since made peace with the gruesome bargains of my profession.

"I don't have much to tell you," he said. "Apart from the fact that she definitely didn't hurl herself off that cliff. But—"

I waited. He gazed off into the distance, perhaps weighing the debt he owed to someone who'd saved him from death by muffin. He made a decision.

"That inspector did say that she wanted to speak to me. That we shouldn't leave the area." He turned to look at me, the sunlight bouncing off his glasses. "Because it could be a murder investigation."

I MADE MY way back through the woods, mulling over Danilo's words. He'd fortified my hunch that a murder investigation might be underway, but I'd have to get further confirmation before I could write anything. I'd need to go back to the newsroom and find out what Bruce's reporting had uncovered.

My pace slowed as I neared my car. "Oh, for god's sake," I muttered to myself, and then, forcing brightness into my voice: "Hi, Debbie. What's up?"

Debbie Halloran looked upset, which could have been the work of her awful husband or my awful mother. She solved the mystery without small talk, which I appreciated. "I'm worried about Marian," she said.

"Marian once told the British prime minister that he didn't know the difference between 'who' and 'whom,'" I said. "She's made out of some mineral they find in the earth's core."

"Yes, I get that aspect of her," Debbie said. She fiddled with the amber beads at her throat. "But she's also hiding something. Something she's very anxious about."

I met Debbie's eyes. There was a crease between her eyebrows that was familiar, because I had the same one between mine. The gulch of concern. It only got deeper with time. I remembered Marian's strange disappearance from the dinner table the night before. "Do you have any clues?"

"I think it might have to do with her book," Debbie said.

"But it's not even out yet."

"Exactly. That's the thing. It's not out yet, but some-one's already trying to sabotage it." Her head whipped one way and then the other, as if a phantom book saboteur might be lurking in the Pinerock parking lot. "Check this out." She showed me her phone with a screenshot on it. Someone had written: *I took a bullet for the team, y'all. I read the new Marian Conway. And let me tell you, it's even more full of bullshit corporate jargon than the first (which she didn't even write). If you want to learn about empowerment, save your dough and buy a Dolly Parton record instead.* I flinched when I read that. Brutal.

"That's from Goodreads, where there are dozens of one-star reviews," Debbie whispered. "And that's not all." She flicked through a few screens, and suddenly I was watching a video of a young woman fanning herself with a copy of *Grit and Gumption*. "This book ain't got no grit or gumption," she said. "But you could use it as a fan when your AC goes out."

"Ouch," I said, and Debbie nodded.

"BookTok's gone feral. Goodreads, Amazon—all of it. Terrible reviews everywhere. Marian thinks there's a targeted campaign against her." Debbie leaned closer. "Who would want to destroy your mother?"

WHY WAS I learning about my mother's emotional upheaval from Debbie, of all people? I fumed as I drove back to the newsroom. But I also knew, deep down, that this was at least partly my fault. I'd allowed the distance between me and Marian to expand to canyon-like proportions, so that now we shouted to each other across a void, spending vast effort for minimal connection. For years, I'd blamed her—she was the parent, after all—but at forty-five, I could take some responsibility too.

My mood always got worse when I was hangry. If I went more than a couple of hours without eating, I suffered—and the people around me suffered even more. At least I could count on Bruce for a tub of celery sticks and some disgusting dip he'd whipped up at home; I wouldn't starve. But dollar-store licorice laces and jujubes were my real soul foods.

It was a relief to find parking spaces in front of the *Quill*. The protesters were taking the day off, or maybe they were plotting in a dank basement somewhere. I was determined to enjoy the brief reprieve from chaos. As I locked my car I noticed that I'd parked next to a Mercedes suv, freshly washed and smelling of money.

The reprieve from chaos lasted precisely as long as it took to walk into the newsroom. I could hear raised voices coming from behind the closed door to Amir's office. My colleagues stood in a knot between the jumble of ancient desks: Hannah in overalls and a faded Pink Floyd T-shirt; Bruce—who had been to six

Pink Floyd concerts and remembered two of them—
swaying in agitation from foot to foot. I'd never seen
Bruce agitated, and I didn't like it. "Is that—"

Bruce nodded. "The Talbott wolf pups. And they're
eating Amir alive." Before he could say anything else,
the door to Amir's office whipped open. A middle-aged
man strode out, dressed in what I thought of as upscale
golf—expensive chinos and a zippered blue cardigan.
His eyes passed over us without seeing anything useful. Behind him was a woman who had the grace to
at least look a tiny bit sheepish.

Neither of them bothered to stop and say hello,
and we all knew what that meant. There had been
rumours that Dorothy Talbott's kids wanted her to sell
the paper, and the current downturn didn't help. We
could start writing the paper's obituary now.

Amir stood in the doorway, arms folded. Even
from this distance I could see his left thumbnail was
chewed ragged, as if he'd allowed himself to take out
all his anxiety on just one finger. I started to say something, but he shook his head at me and turned back
into his office, shutting the door behind him.

A funereal silence descended on the newsroom.
Bruce was the first to break it, holding up a sketchy
Tupperware. "Anyone for a cucumber slice?"

"Not everything can be solved with crudités," I
said, and immediately regretted my snappishness.
The *Quill* had been in decline for a while, but it was

my series on vaccine deniers that had turned up the volume on our death rattle.

"You know," said Bruce, taking a seat at his desk, "that was my series too. So don't think you can hog all the guilt, little Miss Misery Guts."

I laughed, and the sour mood popped. Hannah came and perched on my desk. "What did you find out this morning?"

I told them what I'd heard from Danilo and Doug. I added that I'd seen an unnaturally large gathering of police around the area where Bliss had been found. Bruce had managed to find and interview the couple who'd first spotted the body. They hadn't seen anyone else up at the lookout, they said. They'd seen no sign of a struggle.

"We're getting somewhere," I said. The feeling of doom was slowly being replaced with something more familiar and thrilling: a story that only we could unravel. We might be tiny but we had contacts that the national papers didn't—at least half the town was still talking to us. "Hannah, would you mind calling the OPP and asking what they have? It might be nothing but we want them on the record." Hannah nodded, and went to her desk to make the call.

I took a cucumber peace offering from Bruce's tub. We started to thumb through the photos he'd taken that morning: conference guests weeping, cops milling, empty stalls. I had a sudden thought. I picked up my phone and typed out a quick text: *Kaydence, do the exhibitors have a group chat by any chance?*

It took only a moment for her response to flash back: *We do, but I've had it muted for the past couple of days. It was all keto recipes and people bitching that Clarity K was getting special treatment.*

I tapped out another message: *Take a look at it, would you? There might be some useful conversations going on.*

Bruce and I huddled together as I flipped open my laptop and logged on to the paper's content management system. I opened a story file and put our bylines at the top. *The death of celebrity influencer Bliss Bondar outside the Pinerock Resort is being investigated as a possible homicide*, I typed.

"What do you think?" I asked Bruce. He pondered for a minute, and then said, "We have Danilo telling you that. Police are shtum of course. Not enough yet."

My phone rang, and before I could say anything Kaydence was already in mid-flow. "It's all anyone's talking about on the group chat. Mostly people have no clue but"—she paused, as if she had pulled the phone away from her ear—"Athena from Web of Wellness Books says that she was questioned by a cop who told her it was definitely a murder investigation. I'm going to give her a call to see what she'll tell me. I'll let you know. And Cat—"

"Still here."

"I just remembered something else weird."

"Which is?"

"I'll tell you when I see you."

After I'd hung up, I told Bruce what Kaydence had said. His foot jiggled now with excitement rather than agitation. He nodded at my laptop, as if to say, *What are you waiting for?* I'd only written a couple of grafs when the door to Amir's office suddenly sprang open, and he thrust his well-chewed thumb upward into the newsroom. An okay from the boss. He must have been reading my story as I wrote it.

I felt carried forward on a wave of something warm and buoyant. We might not be able to save the paper, but together we would sure as hell try. With my team around me, I continued to write.

CHAPTER 7

BREE HAD DECLARED that the conference would continue. It was what Bliss would have wanted, she announced on TikTok. The conference had been her dream, and Bree would ensure that it came to fruition. It wouldn't hurt Bree's bottom line either, but I couldn't be entirely cynical; a lot of people would lose money if the event fell apart, from the venerable Pinerock to the tiny independent vendors in the marketplace.

I found Kaydence at her market stall the next morning, decked out in a British monarchy–themed dress—a dizzying combination of beefeaters, carriages, castles, and crowned heads. She was helping Phoenix's mom, who had upgraded her battle tactics since I'd last seen her. Jenny had one child strapped to her back like a piece of camping equipment, while Phoenix and her twin were buckled into a double stroller. "Phoenix and Ariadne are allowed to select a hair band one at a time," the woman was explaining to Kaydence in exaggerated tones clearly not meant for her. "Provided that they do not misbehave. They will be allowed out of the stroller to look at the hair bands but not to touch them."

"All good," said Kaydence. "Let me know how I can help."

"Ariadne gets to choose first because she listened to Mommy this morning." Jenny released one twin from bondage and allowed her to examine Kaydence's table. A warning squawk emanated from the stroller. "Mommy is going to lose her mind if you make that noise," their mother said to no one in particular. "And if Mommy loses her mind, she is going to throw the iPad in the lake." A stunned silence greeted this pronouncement. "Is that the one you want, Ariadne? You have three, two, one seconds to make a choice. Good. Your turn, Phoenix. Then we are all going for a long walk."

I glanced at Kaydence, who had never been known for her poker face. She was barely managing to contain her amusement. But Kaydence didn't have children. As I well knew, they were no laughing matter. Neither was Jenny's marriage, based on the fight I'd seen between Jenny and Bodhi Rubin outside my mother's hotel room.

"You're doing a great job," I told her. "It's not easy." She looked at me with swimming eyes that told me she was barely hanging on beneath the drill-sergeant veneer. "Mine's a teenager now but he was a holy terror in his day." Jake was still difficult on a good day, but I wasn't going to tell her that. There had been years where I'd survived my lonely marriage by convincing myself that my hard labour would be rewarded at some point in the future. Like the horizon, that destination seemed to fade and drift with every step forward, until I realized I would never reach it, at least with respect to my ex-husband. I continued to hold out hope on the parenting front.

She extended a hand. "Jenny Baker-Rubin," she said. "You're so kind to say that. It's a lot. My husband was supposed to be helping out this week. I should have known he'd get caught up in his own stuff. It would have been so much easier to stay home with the kids than to try to entertain them here. But he said it would be a free vacation. Turns out that was more of his bullshit." Her words poured out in a rush. I got the sense she hadn't been treated to adult conversation in a while.

"Mommy said a bad word," yelled Phoenix.

"She'll say some more if you don't zip it," said Jenny. She coloured. "I'm sorry. I don't know what's wrong with me. I can't seem to keep it together today. I'm sure some exercise will help."

She packed the twins into the stroller and headed for the exit at a fast clip. I shook my head. Gentle parenting strategies, exercise, mindfulness: none of these was going to contain the Vesuvius of rage bubbling inside Jenny Baker-Rubin.

I turned to Kaydence. "What's the big secret that you couldn't tell me over the phone?"

"Shhh." Kaydence looked around nervously. "Not here. Wait for me outside. I'll get someone to watch my table."

As I waited for Kaydence, I walked around the building to take in the view of the lake. I closed my eyes and inhaled the scent of the lake water, pine, and woodsmoke. "Admit it," said a voice at my shoulder. "You love it here."

I smiled at Kaydence and was about to respond when a shout rang out from the far side of the lawn and a group of women, goose-fleshed in bathing suits, ran toward the lake. "Go, go, go, go," urged an amplified male voice. "Push through your resistance! Awaken your wonder!" Some of the women raced to the beach and began to wade in. A few intrepid souls went all the way to the end of the dock, where they seemed to hesitate. Bodhi Rubin walked out to meet them and bellowed, "Do you want to sleepwalk through your life, or do you want to live?" Obviously Bodhi was not well-versed in the dangers of hypothermia. Or perhaps he was; his hoodie and fleece trousers indicated he had no plans to swim himself.

Several women leapt from the dock into the freezing water, while the beach-wading contingent seemed to find new energy. The air filled with shrill shrieks. "What the hell is this?" I asked Kaydence.

"It's the Ice Plunge Reawakening," she said. "Totally sold out, believe it or not. People paid extra to be bullied into a freezing lake by that asshole. He says you can't perceive wonder without risking exposure."

The screaming grew louder, interspersed with chanting from Bodhi. "Embrace the wonder of awakening your senses."

"Electrocuting them, more like," I said. "How long can you be away from your stall?"

"As long as I need," said Kaydence. "What do you have in mind?"

"Butter tarts," I said.

I RELAXED INTO the relative quiet of the car. "That's better." I pulled out of the driveway and pointed the car in the direction of Glenda's Country Bakehouse on Main Street. "So. Tell me what you know," I prompted.

"It's about Bliss and Bree," Kaydence said. "There's a presenters' lounge on the second floor with a coffee station. The day before Bliss died, I went up there to have a break and I caught them arguing. The door was open and they were going at it. Bree was furious that Bliss had visited the convoy and invited them to come to hear her Claiming Your Truth lecture."

"What?" I whipped around to stare at Kaydence and the car swerved, nearly taking out a stand of silver birches minding their own business by the side of the road.

"Eyes front!" she yelled. I gripped the wheel tighter and turned my attention back to driving. Bliss had been in contact with the anti-vax crowd? Worse, she'd been their ally? These were the same people menacing the *Quill*, the same people who'd thrown eggs at Hannah Shim. Who wanted to shut the paper down. There were only a few dozen of them at most, but when they started honking and shouting they seemed more powerful than they were—a little dog with a loud bark. We'd jokingly started to call them "the convoy" after the legitimately huge anti-government protest that had shut down Ottawa earlier in the year, but the protesters didn't seem like much of a joke anymore. They were serious, and dangerous. And Bliss had been in their midst. But why?

Kaydence had released her death grip on the dashboard. "Bree sounded pissed," she continued. "She said she didn't want the conference overrun with crazies more than it already was, and that Bliss was endangering them by inviting people who refused to get vaccinated. Then Bliss said that vaccines were a vehicle for government control and she'd heard that they were inserting surveillance chips into people."

"What happened then?" I asked.

"Bree said that she couldn't understand why someone who'd dropped out of a third-rate university seemed to think she was an expert in epidemiology. Bliss said that there was a lot to learn outside of the classroom and Bree had some nerve to talk down to her when she was responsible for all the growth in their business lately. And then Bree said Bliss was destroying the business's reputation with her conspiracy theories and if she kept it up, there would be consequences."

"Nice work," I said. Kaydence's eavesdropping made me consider the chessboard from a different perspective: Bree was now suspect number one as far as motive went, but it was hard to imagine the elegant young woman shoving her business partner over a cliff to her death. On the other hand, I'd been wrong before and might have paid dearly for my miscalculation if my luck had broken the other way. Bree would stay on the list.

We passed an unmarked driveway, and I pointed it out to Kaydence. "Bruce and I found out that the convoy is camping up there. The owner of the land is letting them park trailers and set up tents. Even provided some porta-potties. Bet you can't guess who it is?"

"The mayor," said Kaydence, tonelessly.

"Good guess. Gerry Halloran himself." Kaydence didn't seem pleased, nor particularly surprised for that matter. I was disappointed; the news had caused Hannah Shim to pump her fist in the air and Amir to utter a rare "Damn." Once I'd heard that the protesters had found a place to camp near the Pinerock, I'd done a land-title search. It hadn't been easy; the land was registered to a numbered company, and it had taken calls to several real-estate agents until I found one old-timer who told me the mayor's father had bought the land forty years before. Not everyone in town was Team Halloran, thank god.

Now Bruce was quietly sniffing around, trying to discover why the mayor of Port Ellis thought it was a good idea to harness himself to a bunch of people who did not seem invested in the principles of peace, order, and good government. I was planning on helping him with this reporting, once I got out from under the stories about Bliss's murder. Normally Kaydence would have wanted to talk about these hidden connections, helping me look at every possible angle. But she lapsed into silence, her gaze fixed out the window.

A MERRY JINGLE of bells greeted us when we opened the door to the bakery. The tables were packed with women styling Lagenlook and drinking oat milk lattes.

It was a good problem to have, I knew, and I was delighted to see my friend's business doing so well, but it seemed we would have to take our coffee and pastries to go. Since Eliot Fraser's death, it had become public knowledge that he'd had Glenda eliminated from a national baking competition when she wouldn't sleep with him. Her bakery was now a mandatory excursion for every women's retreat in the county.

Glenda slid out from behind the counter to greet us. She walked over to a table in the window, still occupied by the one man in the room, and removed his plate and mug. "Okay, sir, time to go," she said. "You've been here for two hours, and I need the table."

If the man was put out by her peremptory manner or gender discrimination, he didn't say so. Regulars knew better than to get on Glenda's bad side. A few months ago, she'd banned Eliot Fraser from the bakery, posting his headshot in the window with a red line slashed across it and a message in all caps: "WE DON'T SERVE A-HOLES." No one wanted to be next.

Glenda summoned Megan, her long-suffering assistant, to wipe the table down and take our orders. She sat down, perching on the edge of her seat. "I don't have long," she said. "Give me the highlights."

I started to recount what we knew about the murder at the Pinerock, but Glenda shut me down. "I can read about that in the *Quill*," she said. She squeezed

Kaydence's hand. "How's it going with your family, honey?"

I was mystified. I knew almost nothing about Kaydence's family; other than a few mentions of an aunt she sometimes thrifted with, she rarely talked about them. There was a family photo on her desk of late high-school vintage, showing Kaydence and her mother sitting bloused and pussy-bowed in the foreground; her father looming over the proceedings with a proprietary hand gripping his wife's shoulder; and her brother standing slightly to the side as if he meant to make a run for it. Kaydence's expression suggested she wouldn't be far behind.

"Mom's okay," Kaydence said. "I managed to persuade her to come and live with me for a few days to help me get ready for the market." She gave me a half-smile. "My mom is an incredible seamstress. Master level. She taught me everything I know." A short laugh. "Literally everything. She homeschooled me. Sewing was my extracurricular." She turned back to Glenda, the smile gone. "But Dad insisted she move home and play host to some folks from out of town."

Glenda nodded. "Convoy tourists."

My head was spinning from this flood of unexpected information about Kaydence, the person I thought I knew best in Port Ellis. "You were homeschooled?"

Kaydence sighed. "My dad is a lay pastor in an evangelical church in Big Bay. He doesn't like being told what to do by anyone, including the government. I had to emancipate myself so that I could go to a regular high school."

"You mean legally?"

Kaydence nodded. "That's when I started living with my aunt. Her best friend was a social worker and she helped me through the process. It was horrible. It took a long time before my father would speak to me again. And my mother was really conflicted. It was like being orphaned."

"He's crazy," said Glenda. "Seriously. I was looking online, and I think I've figured out what's wrong with him. Oppositional defiant disorder. Textbook case."

Megan put a brownie down in front of me and I took a bite. The premium-quality chocolate hit my bloodstream like redemption. I suppressed a moan of pleasure.

"Last week you thought it was narcissistic personality disorder," Kaydence said. She turned to me. "He's never been an easy person, obviously. But the pandemic made him so much worse." Based on what she'd already said, "much worse" put him in dangerous territory. My heart ached for Kaydence.

She continued, "He has heart problems—which run in his family, by the way—but he's convinced that they were caused by the vaccine. Since I'm the one who persuaded him and my mom to get it, the heart stuff is my fault. He cut off contact again after the *Quill* series came out. He says if I want to peddle fake news for the woke libs, I'm not his daughter. And somehow he's got my little brother Kyle believing his bullshit." She dabbed at her eyes with a napkin, while Glenda put a protective arm around her shoulders. "You'd think I'd be used to it by now, but it's awful. It's so hard on my mom."

"Kyle used to be so normal," Glenda added. "A regular Port Ellis bro. Hockey. Snowmobiles. The type who'd come and plow out your driveway after a snowstorm. But then, during lockdown, he started listening to all these podcasts. Really crazy stuff."

The pieces were all dropping into place. "Kaydence, are you saying that your dad and your brother are in the convoy?"

She looked at me with infinite weariness. "My dad's the leader of the pack."

CHAPTER 8

IN MY DEFENCE, Johnsons were a dime a dozen in the tri-lake area. Like the Mercers and the Talbotts, they'd been early and prolific settlers, and many of their descendants had stuck around. It hadn't occurred to me that Peter Johnson, the creepy loudmouth parked outside my office, could be anything but very distantly related to my bubbly friend.

"I'm so sorry, I didn't know," I told her, as we walked back to my car. "This must be such a difficult time for you. Why didn't you tell me?"

"It's mortifying," said Kaydence. "I mean, look at them." She pointed across the street to Centennial Park, where two dozen protesters were walking in circles around the old bandstand, their faces taut with anger and contempt. Elevated above the crowd, on a stage that had once hosted Oscar Peterson, Duke Ellington, and Louis Armstrong, a woman shouted into a megaphone: "What do we want?"

"Freedom," the group roared back.

"When do we want it?"

"Now!"

"I mean, honestly," Kaydence continued. "Freedom from what? I don't talk about it, because then people want me to explain it, and I can't."

"At least they aren't at the *Quill*'s front door today," I said. "Amir must have made some calls."

"Isn't that your friend from dinner the other night?" Kaydence pointed at an older man making a beeline for the centre of the action. Lewis Kinross.

"Oh, shit," I said. "That's not going to end well."

"Leave it," said Kaydence. "You'll only make it worse."

But I was already running. By the time I caught up with him, the protesters had closed ranks and Lewis was surrounded by a tight, angry ring. One man was screaming in Lewis's face, which was now tense with alarm. He held one hand out, a peace gesture, and I noticed he held his phone, which was recording video. One of the protesters gripped his wrist, shaking it, and the phone smashed to the ground.

I pushed through the crowd, receiving an elbow in the ribs. A sign swung toward my face, and I shoved it out of the way. I felt a familiar anger rising—anger at bullies, at people who only find courage in gangs. The last time I'd given in to that rage there had been disastrous consequences. But I couldn't think about that now.

"Lewis!" I shouted. "Time to go."

"Oh, check it out. We've got someone from the Shill and Racket here." A young man stepped in front of me, blocking my access to Lewis. Dark red hair, a patchy goatee, eyes narrowed in contempt. I knew that face, and not only from pushing past it to enter the *Quill* office. A less scruffy, friendlier version lived in a picture frame on Kaydence's desk.

"Hello, Kyle," I said, edging past him. "Your sister, Kaydence, is a close friend of mine." I knelt quickly and picked up Lewis's phone. I stood to hand it to him, and tugged his arm. "Time to go," I repeated. I'd hoped that the mention of Kaydence's name might soften Kyle. I was mistaken.

"It figures you two would be in league with my sister," said Kyle. He thrust his face into mine and hissed, "Spreading lies."

"You have it all wrong," said Lewis. "I'm an independent journalist, working on my own story. I want to hear you out." He let out a forced chuckle, smiling and nodding at the protesters surrounding him. I wondered if this bonhomie worked on his first-year students. It certainly wasn't going to work on a bunch of conspiracy nuts with violence on their minds.

The crowd pressed closer. Kyle Johnson snatched Lewis's phone. I lunged for it, but he danced out of my reach. He stopped the video, and his finger hovered over the trash icon. "This is what we do to liars," he shouted. "We delete them." The crowd behind him shouted their approval.

A trickle of sweat slid into the small of my back. Someone kicked my calf. A hand grabbed a fistful of my jacket and I was hauled sideways. I swung around, fist clenched—

And met a pair of familiar green eyes. Normally quite jolly, those eyes, but now furious. Kaydence shoved herself in front of me, squaring up to her brother. "Kyle, you fucktard," she gritted out. "What do you think you're doing? Aren't you supposed to be working at city hall today? Mom is really happy that you finally have a job. Are you going to screw this one up too?"

Astonishingly, he wilted in front of her scorn. "I got the day off," he mumbled.

"Really?" she said. "Is a riot day like a snow day?"

Somebody in the crowd snickered. Kyle glowered, and puffed himself up again. "I have permission from Mayor Gerry himself to exercise my right to free speech. Who are you to talk, anyway? At least I'm not hanging out with a bunch of murderers."

Kaydence barked a disbelieving laugh. "You're nuts, Kyle. What murderers?"

Kyle had regained his mojo, bouncing on the toes of his Timberlands. "We heard about Bliss." He spread his arms wide. "We all heard. Dead at the bottom of the lookout. She starts telling the truth, people start to listen. And then *bam*"—he slapped his palms together—"she ends up dead. What a coincidence."

"Ain't no such thing as a coincidence with these fascists," said an old woman in a purple ski jacket. She carried a sign suggesting that the prime minister should perform a sex act on himself. I recognized her: on the days she wasn't trying to undermine local government, she was a volunteer at the library, teaching kids to read.

Lewis stirred beside me. "This is exactly what I wanted to talk to you all about. This kind of disordered thinking—"

I yanked his arm, perhaps harder than necessary. "Lewis, you need to shut up."

He shot me a wounded glance. But I was worried less about harm to his ego than our limbs. The crowd had pressed tighter once again. Kaydence, Lewis, and I were squished into a tiny ball, the filling in a shitshow sandwich.

"Yeah, Lewis," Kyle spat. "Listen to your boss here."

"Your fake-news boss," said the old lady, whose name, I suddenly remembered, was Brenda.

Kaydence laughed again. "Fake news? You people really need to come up with some new lines." If we got out of here alive, I was going to buy her a lifetime supply of Glenda's doughnuts.

Kyle's face twisted in fury. He leaned closer, his red head next to hers. "Shut up, pervert."

Pervert?

I turned to whisper into her ear. I'd planned to say *run*, but when my mouth opened I suddenly felt a shocking pain in my teeth and lips. My head flew back, my eyes watering. Someone had whacked me with the business end of a sign. I felt myself swell with fury, both hands up to reach out and claw—

A siren split the air and a voice, amplified by a loud-speaker, called out, "Okay, friends! Let's take it down a notch! This is no way to resolve our differences."

In a second, the heaving mass had turned toward the sound of Gerry Halloran's commanding voice. He was striding through the grass, a megaphone swinging in his hand. Again, he raised it to his lips. "I get you. I understand your fight for freedom!" The crowd shouted their enthusiastic agreement.

Now Gerry had reached the bandstand and stood at the top of the stairs. He placed the megaphone on the ground and raised his hands in a gesture more suited to an evangelical preacher. "My friends, violence is never the answer. I know you're worried about your families. I know you feel like no one's listening to you. I want you to know I've heard you. I'm on your side. Do you trust me?" The protesters bellowed their support, but now the mood was shifting to something softer and less terrifying, like a giant inflatable slowly leaking air. Brenda from the library had tears running down her cheeks. "Now," Gerry said, "I need you to do something for me. I need you to go home. Be with your families. The fight will go on, but not today."

Gerry came down the stairs and shook hands with his fans, who began drifting away in small clusters. I had no illusions. I knew they were scuttling back to their basements and bedrooms to send out their twisted messages about what had happened. My role in the altercation. The death of Bliss Bondar. The messianic presence of the mayor. It would all be skewed to fit some ridiculous narrative that now included me.

The constables, who had been useless up to this point, offered to escort Gerry to city hall as the last stragglers melted away. On the way past, one of them asked me if I was all right.

"I'm fine," I muttered, resisting the urge to say *No thanks to you.*

"Are you sure? You're bleeding," he said. I wiped the back of my hand across my mouth, feeling the warmth of blood but also, hearteningly, the presence of teeth. Good. I didn't have the money for dental surgery.

"I got broadsided by one of the signs," I said. "I didn't see who did it." I had my suspicions, but I wasn't going to add to the volatile atmosphere.

Lewis unwrapped his cotton scarf and offered it to me to dab away the blood. It would be ruined now, but I figured he owed me that much.

"Oh my god," said Kaydence. "Was that you, Kyle? Did you hurt Cat?" She shoved him hard in the chest, knocking him off balance. He stumbled backwards as a constable stepped between them and held out a warning hand. Kaydence yelled over him: "Get the fuck out of here before I call Mom and tell her what you've been doing today."

He gave her a glare that would have melted vinyl siding, but he went.

WE PARTED WAYS with Lewis outside the *Quill* newsroom. He looked at us, shamefaced. "I feel I owe you both an apology," he said. "It's entirely my fault that you became involved."

He wasn't wrong. "What were you doing out there, Lewis?" My tone was sharper than I'd intended.

"I was hoping to talk to them on their own turf," he said. "For my magazine story. About their reliance on shoddy data—"

"Please tell me you didn't phrase it that way."

He winced in embarrassment. "I'm sorry to say that I did. I wish I had a fraction of your experience. Things might have gone differently." He gave us a little wave and wandered down the street. I hoped he'd have the good judgment to head straight back to the hotel.

As we entered the newsroom, Amir emerged from his office. "What on earth?" he said. "Cat, you're bleeding."

"You should see the other guy," I told him.

"And who was that?"

"My brother," said Kaydence.

Amir's brow formed a knot, the kind you see in very old pine trees and very outraged editors.

"I'm not actually sure it was Kyle," I said. "But somebody in the crowd had an issue with my face." I asked Kaydence to check the kitchen for an ice pack. My lip was starting to swell.

When she returned with a mug full of ice cubes, I remembered what she'd said to her brother in the heat of battle. "Did you say your brother is working at city hall?"

"I don't have the details," she said. "My mom tends to put a positive spin on things. Like, when Kyle was taking extra shifts at the car wash, my mom said that he was a management trainee."

"What does she say about this job?"

Kaydence rolled her eyes. "Personal assistant to the mayor. I mean, if he's assisting the mayor, it's probably by emptying his garbage can. But Mom needs to believe that life is better than it actually is."

Who could blame her? The poor woman was

trapped in a loveless marriage to a zealot, and her underemployed son was cruising into incel territory. I'd be a fantasist too.

Amir asked me to step into his office. I sat across from him, piling ice cubes in the centre of Lewis's bloody scarf and then tying it to make an ice pack. I held it to my lip while I explained how we'd rescued Lewis Kinross from the crowd of protesters.

"Do you want to go home for the rest of the day?" Amir asked.

His laptop was open to a budget spreadsheet, glowing red like an August sunset. "Of course not," I told him. "It's a scratch. I'll run home and change my shirt and I'll be good to go. Give me an assignment, boss."

"If you're sure," he said. I nodded. "Then go back out to the Pinerock and see what you can find for a follow. We need a big story to stay alive past the end of the month. If anyone can find it, it's you. Go work your magic."

As I stood, I could see over his shoulder and out the window that fronted onto Main Street. Centennial Park was empty now, save for a couple of dog walkers. Near the bandstand, a sign—the one that had collided with my face?—lay abandoned on the lawn, flapping in the wind. In giant block letters, it read "DON'T LISTEN TO MEDIA LIES." Even from this distance I could see that the letter *i* in *media* was drawn to look like a knife, dripping blood.

CHAPTER 9

I DROVE KAYDENCE back to the Pinerock. She seemed fragile, so we kept it light, singing along to the Sheepdogs on the radio. When the announcer came on to tell us that Mayor Halloran's call-in show would follow the traffic report, Kaydence and I dived for the off button at the same moment, and blessed silence filled the car. I left her at her table in the marketplace and went searching for Bruce.

Bruce had located Inspector Bell's not-so-secret headquarters and was chatting up the uniformed officer stationed outside. He introduced me to Constable Pamela Jones, of the Hawker Jetty Joneses. Constable Jones looked to be barely out of high school, her curly blond hair subdued into a severe bun. She looked startled when she heard my name. "You're Cat Conway?" she said, in a tone that suggested surprise that I wasn't a three-headed hellhound frothing at the mouth. "I'm not supposed to talk to you."

"I don't bite," I said.

"Inspector Bell does," she said with a cheeky grin. "No hard feelings."

I assured her that there were none taken.

"Say hi to your uncle Len for me," Bruce told her. "And tell him he still owes me a beer."

As much as I felt like Port Ellis was home these days, exchanges like this reminded me of my outsider status in a community where residents of twenty years' standing were still considered newcomers. I wasn't feeling optimistic about my ability to deliver a barn-burning story in the absence of any sources willing to talk to me. I needed a strategy. "Watery overpriced coffee?" I offered. "I'm buying."

Bruce and I parked ourselves in a prime location in the café and I pulled out my notes. "Where's Hannah, by the way?" I asked.

"She's up at the lookout taking some photographs for the story, assuming there is one," said Bruce.

"There's always a story," I told him.

He smiled. "That's the spirit," he said. "First best, we solve the murder. Second best, we have celebrity reflections on the impact of the murder. We've inter-viewed your mom, and I can follow up with her once

I have a feel for where the story is going. Who else do we need to talk to?"

"Clarity K, obviously, but she's got a wall of handlers around her. I have a request in with her PR, but they haven't responded. I'm going to her SkyWords workshop tonight, so I might get an opportunity there?"

He nodded. "What about Bree Guthrie?"

"I have an in. I saved her PR guy's life yesterday." Bruce looked quizzical, so I told him about my first-aid skills. He was duly impressed. "Can you take Bodhi Rubin on your own?" I asked. "That guy gets up my nose." The café had a view of the playground on the west lawn, and I watched Jenny Baker-Rubin struggling to push the twins on the swings with the youngest on her back. That woman needed a real vacation, a therapist, and a good lawyer. But I remembered only too well how impossible it seemed to leave a marriage when you'd been made to feel that your value as a human was bound up in your success as a wife and mother. Staying was a choice, sure, but who would willingly fall into an abyss of failure and self-loathing? It had taken me years to get there.

"Cat? You okay?"

I shook off the dark tendrils of memory. "Yup. Fine. I was thinking about the security footage. Doug Jaglowski has access to it. He'll probably say no to giving it to us, but he might agree to look through it himself and see if there's any action in the parking lot before the murder."

"Maybe he'd let Hannah help him?" Bruce suggested. We'd noticed that people had trouble saying no to Hannah Shim. She was unfailingly polite and reasonable, and although young, she had the extraordinarily competent air of someone who would be useful to know someday. I nodded. It was a solid idea. I said I'd broach it with him.

"What do you make of all of this?" I asked Bruce.

"The murder?"

"The wellness industrial complex."

Bruce took a sip of his coffee and winced. "Truly disgusting," he said. "Worse than the swill at the *Quill*, and that shit is free." He pushed his mug aside. "Generally speaking, I like the idea that people are questioning received wisdom about health. Corporations are way too invested in the system, for starters, and the system itself was designed for dudes who look like me. But this feels like a different kind of corporate takeover. It isn't encouraging people to do their own research and think for themselves. It's encouraging them to give their money to new masters. It's depressing."

I had to agree. Wellness was a multi-trillion-dollar industry these days, and Bliss Bondar and Bree Guthrie had claimed a decent stake. It made me wonder anew if money was our motive. "Let's go find Danilo," I said. "He knows more than he's saying about that business."

Danilo was in the presenters' lounge, consoling himself with baked goods. He was wearing leggings with a long, flowing floral tunic and rhinestone-studded loafers. His entire vibe said *Screw it*. Bruce and I exchanged a smile. Someone who'd stopped trying to keep their messy self in check was a promising interview.

Danilo enfolded me in a hug, his eyes bright with tears. "I can't thank you enough," he said. "If you hadn't been there ..." I patted his back before trying to reverse out of his clutches. He held on for a few awkward seconds before releasing me.

"An experience like that," said Bruce, meaningfully, "can make a person think."

Danilo nodded furiously. He'd been doing a lot of thinking, he agreed. What was he doing with his life? He was pouring all of his energy into other people's success. If he did his best work, it was invisible, and his employers thought they'd done it themselves. He was an artist at heart, he said. Didn't he deserve his share of the spotlight? Did he want to live in the shadows forever?

I did a gentle redirect. "What was it like working with Bliss?" I asked.

"She was a nightmare," he said, before clapping his hands over his mouth. "I can't believe I said that."

"We're on the hunt for information here," Bruce assured him. "Not looking to get you fired."

Danilo let out a sigh of relief. "Between us? She wasn't very bright, but she didn't know it. She thought she had the inside track on how the world worked. She was condescending and wouldn't take my advice. Bree talked to me about it. She wanted to do damage control. She wanted me to keep the mic away from Bliss when she started in on one of her rants—good luck with that! She loved an audience more than anything."

"And Bree?"

"I like her, you know, as a person," he said. "She's respectful, professional. But as a boss, she's been distracted lately and making my job harder. I couldn't push back against Bliss if Bree didn't show up to our meetings, you know? And since Bliss died, Bree's gone AWOL. She's in her room, but she won't answer the door, won't respond to emails or texts … all she's told me is that the conference should go on according to schedule. I'm doing my best, but everyone wants to know what's happening and I have nothing to tell them. It's so stressful!" He popped a brownie into his mouth reflexively. "An event like this needs leadership. I thought maybe your mother would rush to the front of the line."

I must have looked startled, because Danilo shot me a look that said *Come on, girl.* "You have to admit, the alpha energy pours off Marian," he said. "As soon as I met her, I got exploding black-hole vibes. I thought I'd have to protect myself with one of those X-ray aprons they give you at the dentist's. But ... nope. She's just kind of disappeared. I tried to text her to reschedule her Boss Babe seminar, but I didn't hear anything back. Is everything okay?"

I had no idea how to answer that question. Was Marian okay? The review-bombing of her new book had upset her, but her weird behaviour suggested more than a bruised ego. There was some glitch in her normally immaculate mechanism. And it wasn't me that she'd turned to for help—it was Debbie Halloran, ever-present, ever-competent. Marian's fantasy daughter: established but non-threatening, financially secure, socially adept.

I shrugged. "My mother isn't one to share her feelings," I said.

"I know, right?" said Danilo. "I'm honestly not sure why they asked her. Don't get me wrong," he added hastily, "she's impressive as hell. She just isn't ..."

"Pulsing with Mother Earth energy?" I suggested.

"Exactly," he said. "Bree said that one of the sponsors was a huge stan of Marian's, and they kinda twisted Bree's arm to get her on the program. Anyway, thank god for Bodhi Rubin and Clarity K. They've really stepped up. By the way, are you going to SkyWords? I can get you passes if you need them."

Bruce demurred, so I said I'd take Hannah with me. With Danilo softened by conversation and carbs, it seemed like a good time to press a bit. "So, you had an inside seat at the Bliss and Bree circus. How was their business doing?"

I felt Danilo withdraw. "Outside my pay grade," he said.

"But you had a sense of it."

He sighed. "It had dipped after a few years of massive growth. Bree said that Bliss was driving solid, loyal customers away. There had been some online backlash against Bliss's anti-science videos. Bliss said that she was growing their following, but Bree said that the people she brought in weren't buying products, they were only there for the comments. Bliss and Bree were barely speaking to each other when she died."

He clamped his mouth shut like a miser zips his wallet when he's given away too many coins. His expression was unreadable. It wasn't grief over Bliss, obviously. Fear, maybe? But fear of what? A jobless future? Or a murderer who'd left a job unfinished? I squeezed his shoulder and told him I'd see him at SkyWords.

As Bruce and I waited for the elevator, I asked him what he thought of Bree as a suspect.

"I'm not sure," said Bruce. "I don't have much of a picture of her yet. Or of Bliss, for that matter. We need to talk to more people who really knew them."

I agreed, but it didn't seem as though anyone at the Pinerock had. There were fans here, and employees, and a handful of professional colleagues.

"So it seems," said Bruce. "But here's what I'm thinking. Your company is on the rocks, you hate your business partner, you feel judged and wronged, maybe you're planning to blow the whole thing up. What are the chances that you invite a support person to come to the conference with you?"

"High," I said. "You're very good, you know."

He shrugged modestly. "I have my moments," he said. "I'm going to ask around and see if the cleaning staff saw anyone coming in or out of Bliss's or Bree's room at odd hours. I can ask Doug about it too; he's in my bowling league."

AT 5:30 P.M., Hannah and I joined a line of women bundled up in blankets and beanies, wending our way past the playground and into the woods. The walking trail through the forest was narrow, and it gave our short journey the gravitas of a processional. Within a few minutes, we arrived at a large clearing with logs arranged like benches around a fire pit. Women from the conference milled about, whispering excitedly. I recognized one of the hotel cleaners, still in her uniform, looking thrilled. Apparently Clarity felt some sense of obligation to the little people who had created her.

Two men dressed in black were standing at the edge of the clearing with djembe drums slung over their shoulders. As we filed in and took our seats on the logs, the drumming began, quietly at first and then with increasing intensity.

"Are those the bongo guys from Centennial Park?" I whispered to Hannah.

"Good eye," she said. The two men had started a popular tradition the previous summer, inviting anyone who was interested to bring a percussive instrument and gather at the bandstand on Sunday afternoons. It had taken off, the park filling with people of all ages, playing music and hacky sack and mellowing out. That is, until Gerry Halloran got an earful from a wealthy cottager whose son had purchased some MDMA at the event, and directed his bylaw officers to enforce the permit requirement for gatherings of that size.

The drumming built to a crescendo and then stopped abruptly. Two young women emerged from the forest, wearing the blank expressions of professional handmaidens. Clarity's minions: I recognized the one who'd brushed me off the first day of the conference. Behind them, a white-robed figure glided to the edge of the flames. Two elegant hands emerged from the deep pleats of the garment, grasping the edges of the hood and folding it back to reveal the glowing silver hair and sculpted features of Clarity K.

"Impressive," I murmured to Hannah.

"She's wearing a Creativity Cocoon," she whispered

back. "She told one of the vendors in the marketplace that they'd be available for purchase for Christmas."

"Shhh!" A woman in front of me spun around and glared. I recognized her as one of the women from the opening dinner. Marnie? Becca? I waved.

Clarity K began to speak. "Welcome, friends," she intoned. "As humans have done since time immemorial, we gather together around the sacred fire. The fire is light. It is life. It is the place where we celebrate and where we mourn. This evening we do both. We celebrate the gift of being here, of connecting with one another and the natural world. We celebrate our internal fire, our creative spirit. And we mourn the loss of one of our brightest stars." She turned her face up to the sky. "We remember you, Bliss."

Around us, tears glistened on the faces of dozens of rapt women. Clarity continued to speak, but my attention was distracted by a movement in the woods. It was Danilo, stepping into the clearing like a nervous forest creature, and behind him, shrouded in an oversized black hoodie, was Bree Guthrie. I elbowed Hannah in the ribs and pointed. Hannah pulled out her trusty iPhone. Bree might be fragile, I thought, but she was in touch with her inner fire; the look of hatred she was directing at Clarity had the heat of a flame-thrower.

Now, at last, the main attraction was beginning. Clarity's acolytes moved through the audience with baskets, honouring each person with an individual sparkler. Once they had been distributed, the poet called for quiet. The drummers moved to the fire and lit a pair of torches. "Spread out," Clarity told the group. "Create a sacred circle around yourself, and the fire will come to you." I chuckled to myself. It was as pretentious a health and safety warning as I'd ever heard. "When it does, let your secret self guide your hand and send your message out to the universe."

Hannah handed me her sparkler. "It's all yours," she said. "I've got an assignment." She slipped past me and I quickly lost sight of her in the trees.

The drummers moved with care through the clearing, and as they passed, tiny explosions erupted. Streaks of light illuminated the clearing as dozens of hands etched their messages onto the night air. The glade smelled of woodsmoke and sulphur. I watched my sparkler flare, and offered my own heartfelt wish to the sky.

And then it was over. The crowd dispersed. Hannah reappeared, tapping busily on her phone.

"What are you doing?" I asked her.

"You can create still images from the long exposure setting and then use an app to flip them so that you can read them ..." she began, and then, seeing my baffled face, said, "Never mind. You'll see. Give me a minute." She paused, and then turned her phone toward me.

The first image was a photograph of me, with the

words *More* and *Money* floating across my chest in electric letters. I could feel myself blushing. "You can delete that one," I said.

She nodded and hit the trash icon. "Here's Clarity K." *Peace + Love* sparkled in the air above her.

"Oh, that's complete bullshit," I said.

We flipped to the hotel cleaner, who'd written *UNION* in sprawling letters. "Now for a couple of interesting ones. Here's Bodhi Rubin's wife." Jenny Baker-Rubin was standing alone, slightly apart from the crush of participants. Her message was more of a scrawl than the others, but it was still legible: *I Hate You*.

"That's one angry woman," I said.

"And now for my last trick," said Hannah, and swiped across to the next image.

It was Bree, and her SkyWord, in full caps, read *MURDER*.

CHAPTER 10

THERE WERE NO protesters outside the *Quill* or in Centennial Park the next day. Maybe they were all gathered for a workshop on prepping for societal breakdown. Or maybe their brush with the law had taken the fun out of civil disobedience. In any case, it meant I could sit at my desk in peace, staring at the photos Hannah had taken.

Murder. Did Bree have a suspect in mind? Did she think there was a murderer hiding under Clarity's creativity cloak? Or was she trying to deflect attention from her own guilt? If she'd loathed Bliss as much as Danilo had suggested, she would definitely be on the police's radar. My fingers spread outward on the photo, zooming in on Bree's face. It was blurry, thanks to the time-stop effect, but still I could see her jaw hard-set, her knuckles white on the sparkler. I wrote *Bree Guthrie background* on my notepad and underlined it three times.

It was quiet in the newsroom, and I took a moment to look around at the shabby desk chairs, the water-damaged walls, the floor pockmarked with burn scars. The vinyl tiles had not been replaced since the days when reporters had used the floor as their ashtray. It was dingy and kind of gross, but it had lived, that newsroom. For how much longer, though?

There was a sliver of light under the door to Amir's office, and I was just about to get up and ask if he wanted to order a pizza when my phone buzzed. Even before I got it to my ear, Kaydence was speaking, rushed and clipped. I heard her say *Marian* and *police*—not words I was used to hearing together.

"Whoa, slow down. Start from the beginning."

Kaydence took a deep breath. "Cheryl Bell came by my booth. She asked if I'd seen Marian Conway. They were hoping to have a word with her."

I perched on the edge of my chair, trying to think. "But they're interviewing everyone who's at the conference, right? They're not singling her out."

"I'm not sure about that. Cheryl Bell said, 'Let us know the minute you see her.' And she said it in that quiet scary voice she has. I nearly peed myself. One more minute and I would have confessed to murder myself." Kaydence let out a squeaky giggle.

I wrote *Marian WTF* on my notepad, circling it with an unsteady hand. "But you haven't seen her, right? I've been trying to call her for hours."

There was a moment's uneasy pause on the other end of the line. "I did kind of see her a couple of hours ago."

"Kaydence, Jesus. Did you lie to the cops?" I didn't know whether to be worried for her or to buy her a drink.

"I didn't lie. They asked if I knew where Marian was. And I didn't, not at that moment. I just kind of didn't mention that I'd seen her earlier."

"Where was she?"

"Out the back way. Walking toward the clearing where there's a secret trail to the lookout. She was wearing a very chic puffer coat, moving like she was heading to a sale at Saks. Your mom's hard to miss."

I made Kaydence promise to call me the second she saw my mother again. I hung up, and immediately dialed Marian's number. It went straight to voice mail. "If you've got a legitimate reason to be calling, please leave a message. I do not need my air ducts cleaned." I laughed at that, but it ended up a half-sob. I'd forgotten that Marian could be amusing, when she chose.

My next call was a Hail Mary pass. My son, Jake, like most teenagers, regarded unexpected phone calls the way I regarded trips to the accountant. Rarely pleasant and often upsetting. To my surprise, he picked up on the second ring. "Hey, Benoit Blanc," he said. "I heard there's another murder up there."

"So it seems," I said. Even in my distracted state, I noted with pride that he'd pronounced *Benoit* correctly, which meant he might actually pass grade-ten French. "Listen, have you heard from Marian at all?" He'd always called her by her proper name. From the moment I'd given birth, my mother had shunned all titles associated with grandparenthood. "Nans are goats," she liked to say.

"Not for a couple of days," Jake said. "She sent me a picture of some typos on the menu at the Pinerock, and told me to stay in school or I'd end up in Port Ellis serving people Sezar salad. But nothing since then. Is everything okay?"

It was the same question Danilo had asked. I still had no answer, and my blood pressure was climbing into the red zone. I asked Jake to check in with his grandad, to see if Marian had been in touch. I told him I loved him, he grunted *uh-huh* and hung up.

I flung myself backwards in my chair. I must have said *fuck* more loudly than I intended, because the door to Amir's office opened. He came and sat one desk over, not saying anything. It was one of the many things I loved about him, this ability to sit in silence without needing to immediately offer solutions.

Did I say love? I meant like, obviously.

"I can't find my mother," I said glumly. "The police

want to talk to her, and she's disappeared. And do you know what's even worse?"

"What?"

"I haven't eaten in five hours."

Amir burst out laughing, a proper laugh that set his maroon tie shaking. He'd undone the top button of his shirt, which, for Amir, was the equivalent of stripping naked and running across centre court at Wimbledon.

"Well, my friend, I can't tell you where your mother is. But the hunger thing? That I can fix."

THE MOON WAS fractured in the black waters of Lake Marjorie as we sped along the road that took us into our past. Amir drove at a speed that suggested he couldn't wait to reach a home-cooked meal, but not so fast that he couldn't avoid a darting deer if he had to. Classic Amir: efficient, capable, no-nonsense. Qualities I'd only come to appreciate too late in life.

I shook my head to get rid of this thought, and he looked over at me. "Does your lip still hurt?"

"It's fine," I said. "I won't be able to get my monthly injection of fillers, but that's okay."

He snorted. "Seriously, though. Do you want to report it to the cops? We could call Dick Friesen."

Now it was my turn to snort. "The same Dick Friesen who posted a QAnon meme on his Facebook page? I swear he's buying doughnuts for the convoy."

"Good point. That's another story we should do, when things settle down." He drummed his fingers on the steering wheel. "If they settle down."

I cracked the window a tiny bit, and the gorgeous autumn wind rushed in. Pine, woodsmoke, a hint of motor oil. Amir's face was in shadow, but I could read the tension in his shoulders. I thought about the Excel spreadsheet, and the baby Talbotts who'd stormed out of the newsroom as if their money was being burnt in front of their eyes.

I didn't want to ask the question, but I couldn't not ask. It was in my nature to seek out information, even if that information would hurt me. "Are we going to be okay, Amir? The *Quill*, I mean."

His hands tightened on the wheel. "Well, I think it's obvious that Dorothy's spawn are putting the squeeze on. They want her to sell. But we're going to fight like motherfuckers to make sure that we keep going."

"Okay, hearing you say 'motherfuckers' is scaring me more than anything. I have a feeling you've never actually said that word before. Wait—no, you called Terrence Wiley a motherfucker that summer at Ravenhead. The summer it rained all the time. Just before you pushed him off the dock."

"Right, just after he called me a Paki son of a bitch."

I was shocked into silence. What was there to say? That I was sorry I hadn't stood up for him? I didn't remember Terrence spewing slurs, but considering that he'd been a bra-strap-snapping jerk, it didn't surprise me. Still, I felt a sickness in the pit of my stomach.

Amir smiled at me, but in the darkness it looked like a snarl. "You think that convoy garbage is new, but it's not. It's always been here. They just used to be quieter about it."

AMIR'S PARENTS FOLDED him into a bear hug the moment we stepped inside their cottage. His mother tall and broad-shouldered like her son, his father a smaller, elfin presence, practically hopping with joy. Amir finally managed to extricate himself and pulled me forward. "I found this starving waif by the side of the highway," he said.

"Look at you," Mrs. Mahar said, taking both my hands in hers. "How long has it been?" She turned to her husband, marvelling. "She's still so pretty. But Amir's right. She could do with a good meal." When was the last time my own mother had said I looked undernourished? Spoiler alert: never.

"It's so lovely to see you again, Mrs. Mahar." She gathered me in a warm hug, and it was all I could do not to burst into tears. "You must call me Azra, or Auntie if you want to pretend we're back home." She cocked her head, looking closely at my face. "Did you hurt yourself?"

Amir slid a hand onto my back, propelling me into

the tiny living room. "It's nothing, Ammi. Cat tripped in the newsroom and hit herself on the edge of her desk. We have to get new flooring one of these days."

I shot him a look, but he refused to meet my eyes. "That's me!" I said, as heartily as I could. "Butterfeet."

Mr. Mahar chuckled. "Butterfeet! You always were the funny one, Cat. Come in, sit, sit."

Very little had changed in that living room over the decades, a bittersweet stasis. As I sank onto the ancient plaid sofa, I remembered the time Amir and I had brought our campers here for a drink of water on a stifling August afternoon. Mrs. Mahar had brought out a plate of gulab jamun, and one of our snotty eleven-year-old charges said that the sweets looked like raccoon turds, which sent all the other kids howling. I'd wanted to strangle the camper, but when I looked over at Amir he just seemed resigned, which was somehow even worse.

The Mahars' cottage sat on the edge of the former Camp Ravenhead. His parents had cooked for ungrateful children, year after year, and tried to get them to eat the vegetables they grew in a patch beside the dining hall. Amir once told me that his mother had been a pharmacist in Lahore, and his father an accountant, but in Canada their new life had involved stirring giant pots of macaroni and cheese on an industrial-sized stove.

Amir collapsed in an armchair underneath a framed 3D print of mountains. Azra bustled off and returned with a teapot on a silver tray, surrounded by intricately painted glasses and a small dish of nuts. She poured the tea, handing each of us a glass. I gulped mine down perhaps a bit too greedily. The smells from the kitchen were torturing me.

"Whatever you're cooking smells amazing, Mrs. Ma—Azra."

She laughed, and I noticed that her animated dark eyes were shaped exactly like Amir's. "You'll have to thank Mohsin for that," she said. "It's his night to cook. And I think it's just about time to eat."

For the next half-hour, we plowed our way through lamb biryani, fluffy naan, and an addictively crispy dish of fried okra. Amir ate with relish, and bite by bite the tension left his shoulders. We talked about my family, and I lied and said that Jake loved to come visit Port Ellis. I left my mother out of the conversation, not having the energy to explain what I did not understand.

Amir asked if there was any more news about the redevelopment of Camp Ravenhead. The Mercers, who ruled Port Ellis alongside the Talbotts, planned to turn the lakefront property into a retirement village. Once that happened, the Mahars would most likely lose their cottage; the Mercers' Ten Commandments included "thou shalt amass wealth" but not "thou shalt demonstrate loyalty to others." Mohsin's face clouded over at the question, and he shook his head. He quickly switched topics.

"What is this we hear of a death at the Pinerock? And perhaps foul play?"

"So many deaths lately!" Azra chimed in. "It's like we're living in a real-life version of that program we like with the sad detective. The one who wears the lovely pea coat."

"*Shetland*," her husband said.

"We're trying to figure it out ourselves," I said. "What we do know is that there's a wellness confer- ence at the Pinerock—"

Mohsin held up a hand, stopping me. "I'm sorry. What exactly is wellness? And why does it need a conference?"

Amir laughed so hard I thought he was going to choke on his biryani. I thumped him between the shoulder blades, while trying to explain the idea that people felt they were broken inside, and they needed yoga with puppies and cold plunges and sound healing and expensive supplements made from grass to heal themselves. Mohsin stared at me, mouth agape, as if I were speaking Klingon.

"Well," Azra said as she stood to clear plates, "I just hope that poor girl wasn't murdered. This was never a violent town—until recently." I knew she was talking about the murder of Eliot Fraser, which had shaken Port Ellis's smug sense of itself as a lakeside utopia.

"You know how people are," Mohsin said. "Violence fascinates them. The Fraser business was good for the newspaper, no?" He hitched his head to one side, and for a moment I couldn't understand what he was trying to indicate. My eyes travelled around the pine-panelled walls, landing on a bookshelf whose bottom shelves were packed tight, absolutely crammed, with newspapers.

It took me a minute to find my voice. "Is that—"

Amir sighed. "Yes. Every issue of the *Quill* since I came back to run it." He turned to his parents. "You know you can read it online, right?"

"Not the same thing," Mohsin said.

"It is so vastly improved," Azra said. "Much better since you took over. Before it was all stories about people's garbage cans being stolen."

"But ..." Amir's dad spoke slowly, peering up at his son from under bushy white brows. "It is a little thin lately, neh?"

I could feel Amir begin to tense again. Before I could say anything, Azra jumped in, as if she'd been waiting for her husband to broach this difficult topic. "And what's this about a mob? I went to pick up my books at the library and Pierrette told me that a gang was roving the streets. And that they were angry at— I'm not even sure what."

"Angry about politics," Mohsin said, shaking his head. "In this country! They should travel a little bit. Get some perspective."

I stood, and started stacking plates. "It's nothing

important," I said. "Just a few readers upset about some stories we published. Amir's on top of it. He's getting the advertisers back on side, and the publisher is behind us a hundred percent."

I expected my nose to shoot out of my face as I told these terrible falsehoods, but Mohsin and Azra just nodded, satisfied. With their house threatened, they could hardly entertain the thought that their son might lose his job too. As I took Amir's plate he held my eyes, every inch of him telegraphing *Thank you, you big fat liar.*

"You know," Mohsin said, "we used to think this one was heading toward politics." He jutted his chin at his son. "All the time with the Model UN, or volunteering on some losing political campaign."

"They weren't all losing." Amir sighed. "And it's important that we're all engaged in choosing our leaders. Otherwise we end up with—"

"With Gerry Halloran." Azra shook her head, and I could tell she was restraining herself from saying something tart about the mayor. She reached over and patted Amir's shoulder. "One day, if you get bored with the newspaper, maybe you will follow that path. What do the young people call it? Your plan B?"

I expected Amir to laugh off the suggestion, but he simply nodded at his mother. I was biased, obviously, but Amir seemed precisely the kind of person we needed in public life. A dogged, possibly even irritating devotion to fairness was his main character trait, and how many politicians could you say that about? Too bad, though. Politics couldn't have him. The *Quill* needed him too much.

I finished stacking the dishes, and followed Azra to the kitchen down a short hallway lined with photographs. A wedding photo of Mohsin and Azra, serious-faced, trapped in the bleached light of a 1970s portrait studio. Pictures of Amir at his high-school graduation, on assignment for a Vancouver newspaper, surrounded by hoodie-clad bros at the launch of the tech news site that he had started (and lost) in Silicon Valley. And one photo of Amir with his arm around an elegant woman with high cheekbones and a swan's neck.

I peered more closely at it, almost forgetting the dirty plates in my hands.

Azra paused beside me. "Ah, Julia," she said. "She never takes a bad picture."

I did not want to ask the question—every part of me said *Don't ask the question*—but somehow the question popped out of my mouth anyway. "Who's Julia?"

Azra looked at me, her face full of surprise. Or possibly pity? She turned toward the kitchen and said, "Amir's wife."

THE WATER IN the sink was not quite as hot as my fury. I punished the poor dishes with my sponge, practically throwing them at Amir. We'd somehow convinced the Mahars to let us clean up, and now we washed and dried in miserable, tense silence.

"There was never a right time to tell you—"

"That you have a wife?" We were trying to keep our voices down, which was frustrating. It's nearly impossible to convey rage when you're whispering.

"Ex-wife," Amir said, drying a fork. "We're just working out the final details, then we'll be divorced."

I kept my head over the sink, working on a bit of rice stuck to a spoon. I didn't want Amir to see the hurt in my face. I had no right to be hurt; he was my friend and my boss, nothing more.

After a minute I whispered, "I just don't know why you didn't tell me."

He stared out the window above the sink, at the pine trees barely visible in the darkness, and said, "Because I was ashamed." He looked up at the ceiling and expelled a long breath before catching my gaze and holding it. "We met in Palo Alto when I was doing the start-up. Julia's a portfolio manager for an early-stage investment company. We kept running into each other at industry events, hit it off, and for a while, it seemed like we were a great match. We worked all the time, so we decided it made sense to move in together. That way, we could at least see each other at the beginning and end of the day. Then there was some concern about my visa being renewed and we kicked around the idea of getting married, and then suddenly we'd gone to city hall and done it. It's hard to explain the pace of life there. Everything moves so fast. One day, you're being touted as the next big thing in online news, you've got angel investors taking you out for dinner, you have a gorgeous wife who believes in you—and then the attention moves to someone else and you're sleeping beside a person you don't really know who's completely disappointed in you. I was married for a grand total of eighteen months. If it weren't for the photo out there, it would almost feel as if it hadn't happened, which, frankly, I might prefer."

I closed my eyes, feeling his pain and mine.

I handed him the spoon to dry, and our fingers touched. Before I could think about it, I gave his hand a squeeze, and met his eyes in the black mirror of the window. We looked like exhausted ghosts.

CHAPTER 11

I WAS STILL unsettled by Amir's news when I woke up the next morning. No matter how many times I told myself it was none of my business, it smarted that I hadn't known about his wife. *Julia*. It was one thing to pretend not to see the flickers of attraction between us, but another to ponder whether they were a figment of my imagination. His pained explanation had helped me understand, at least a little bit, how shame had kept him from sharing that part of his life with me. He'd driven me home and we'd made small talk like strangers. Or like two people on thin ice, delicately reaching toward each other, terrified that any movement would send them plunging into the depths below.

I really needed to start thinking more pleasant thoughts.

But then the phone rang, and revealed that the universe had different plans for the day. "You need to help me," said my mother, her voice husky with what sounded like fear or tears. Either way, unprecedented, and deeply alarming. "They're coming to take me away."

I sat upright in bed. "Mom? What's going on? Who's coming?" I fingered my lower lip, still puffy from its close encounter with our local band of assholes. Now my brain was conjuring images of a gang of anti-corporate thugs kidnapping my mother. My neural pathways were having a rocky morning.

"The police!" she said. "Who else? You need to get out here, now!"

DEBBIE WAS WAITING for me in the parking lot, sitting in the cab of a red pickup. When she saw me pull in, she flew out of the truck and ran toward me, waving both hands over her head.

I rolled down my window. "Hi, Debbie."

"Hurry up and park!" she said, her customary politeness fraying at the edges. "Inspector Bell has agreed to let us sit with Marian while she does her interview, but she said she wouldn't wait more than half an hour. That was thirty-five minutes ago!"

I pulled into a spot and got out of the car. Debbie grabbed my arm and pulled. "Come on!"

I resisted the urge to yank my arm away. Debbie meant well, I knew; she obviously cared about Marian. If I couldn't understand why, that probably said more about my half-hearted efforts in therapy than it did about Debbie's mental fitness.

Debbie steered me through the front door of the Pinerock and toward Cheryl Bell's command centre. She knocked on the door, which was opened promptly by Constable Pamela Jones of the Hawker Jetty Joneses.

"They're here, Inspector," she announced.

"There, you see?" said Inspector Bell. "No need to call the press, or the prime minister's office, or even your lawyer. Unless of course you'd like to do that, which is your right. But to be clear, you are not under arrest, and you are free to leave at any time."

"Hi, Mom," I said.

"Catherine," said my mother, with great dignity. "Thank you for joining us. I was telling Inspector Bell that I thought your experience with"—she wrinkled her nose as if detecting the milk had gone off— "newsworthy events would be of assistance in the circumstances."

"Just so there's no misunderstanding, you are here as a personal support to your mother, at her request," said Inspector Bell. "Not to report on any 'newsworthy events.'"

"Understood," I said, taking a seat next to Marian. "Shall we?"

Inspector Bell opened the manila folder in front of her. "I'd like to go over your movements on Friday night after the banquet in the hotel."

"Was Bliss's death a homicide?" I asked.

Inspector Bell glared at me. "We are looking at all possibilities," she said. "Which includes understanding where everyone was when the incident occurred." She looked at my mother. "Mrs. Conway. You told us that you attended the dinner, after which you went straight to your room, called your husband to say goodnight, and then went to sleep. You slept right through until your alarm went off at five thirty a.m., at which point you answered some emails and waited for the sun to rise so that you could go for your morning walk. All correct?"

"That's what I told your officer."

"And you stand by that statement?"

My mother's posture hardened. "What are you getting at, Inspector?"

"We have a witness who saw you outside between one and two a.m." In contrast to Marian, Inspector Bell relaxed ever so slightly into her chair. "Could I ask you to take a moment and think again? With all the excitement, it's possible you forgot a detail or two."

The air around my mother crackled with anxiety. Or frustration. She'd made a career of being a step ahead of the crowd, but today she was firmly on the back foot. I heard her take a deliberate breath through her nose and exhale through her mouth, one of the self-regulation techniques she espoused in *Kicking the Ladder*. I didn't make eye contact with her. It was never wise to engage when she was on the edge.

She exhaled again. "Ah," she said. "Well, I'm embarrassed to say you've caught me, Inspector." She extended her wrists across the table as if inviting Cheryl Bell to snap her handcuffs onto them. "The truth is that I stepped out before bed to have a cigarette. I know, it's a terrible habit. Filthy. I'm truly ashamed. But with the stress of the new book, I'm afraid I've fallen into old patterns." She shook her head. "I'd hate to have my fans—or my daughter, for that matter—think that I don't practise what I preach. But even I slip up from time to time."

I'd seen my mother from my bedroom window, back in her McKinsey days, wandering casually through the backyard to the garden shed only to emerge ten minutes later with a furtive expression. I'd found the flowerpot full of butts as well as the package of cigarettes and the lighter stashed in a pair of gardening gloves. But that had been a long time ago, and I was genuinely startled to realize that Marian's stress had escalated to those toxic levels again.

"I see," said Inspector Bell. "So you went outside around what time?"

"I'd say midnight," said my mother. "I called my

husband but then I couldn't sleep. I went down the service stairs and into the woods near the path to the lookout. I thought there was less chance of someone seeing me there than in the parking lot."

"And did you see anyone while you were out there?"

"Absolutely not," said my mother. "I would have told you right away if I had."

"Okay," said the inspector, as if she doubted it very much. "Anything else you remember?"

"Not a thing," said my mother.

Inspector Bell shut her folder, her mouth a thin line. She looked as though she wanted to bang her forehead a few times on the table. *I feel you*, I thought.

"That being the case," she said, "I have nothing further to ask you at this time. You'll be staying here at the Pinerock for the next few days?" It didn't sound like an inquiry, or even a request, but my mother wasn't a person who accepted direction well.

"That's the plan," she said airily. "I'll let you know if it changes. And thank you for all of your hard work on this case, Inspector. I'll be sure to send you a signed copy of *Kicking the Ladder*." She smiled modestly. "It's one of the bestselling books on female leadership of the past decade. I'm sure you'll find some advice in there that you can use."

She sailed out of the room, Debbie trailing in her wake.

I shot the inspector a sympathetic look, and followed.

UP IN HER room, my mother threw herself diagonally across the bed, a forearm over her eyes. Debbie hovered nearby. "Can I do anything to help?" she asked.

"Could you order me an Americano from room service? Decaf?" said Marian.

"Of course! Whatever you need," said Debbie. She busied herself with the order.

My mother peeked out from under her arm to find me leaning against the far wall. She seemed to collect herself, and sat up, reaching for her phone. "Might as well see what we've missed," she said, tapping her finger on the device.

"Marian," said Debbie, "are you sure that's a good idea? You know how upset you've been."

My mother sat up and fixed Debbie with a forbidding stare. "Don't manage me, Debbie," she said. "I hate that." What she hated was having her attention drawn to the fact that she required it.

"My apologies, Marian," said Debbie, with the grace of a professional politician's wife. "You know what? I'm going to run down to the café to get our coffee. Room service takes forever in this hotel. Do you want anything, Cat?"

I thanked her but declined. Debbie was nothing

but generous, and it made me uncomfortable. As soon as she left the room, my mother gasped. "What now, Mom?" I asked, not kindly.

Wordlessly, she held her phone out to me. I took it and turned the screen so that I could read it.

"Isn't this your website?" I asked.

She nodded miserably. "It's been hacked."

In the field reserved for praise, glowing blurbs had been excised and replaced with tiny poison pen letters, although the attributions to Marian's famous admirers remained:

> "One wonders if ChatGPT was employed in the production of this unfortunate attempt to crack the wellness market."—Melinda French Gates

> "Marian Conway's new book is a cynical play with one objective: to part you from your money. Don't waste your time looking for a fresh idea in these pages—you won't find one."—Margaret Atwood

> "A major disappointment."—Anne-Marie Slaughter

The sight of my mother's horrified face quelled my impulse to laugh. "Who would want to humiliate me like this?" she whispered. "The one-star reviews were bad enough, but this? Someone wants to destroy me."

I sat down and put an arm around her. "They won't

succeed," I told her. "You're Marian Conway, remember?" I gave her a squeeze. "I'll help you, I promise. Let's start by putting a call in to your website manager. Do you have any idea who might want to hurt you this way?"

She cleared her throat. "Maybe," she said. She reached for the tissue box and dabbed at her eyes.

There was a long pause. "This isn't the time for subtlety, Mom," I said.

"I think it's Clarity," she said, finally. "I used to know her, before she was famous. Before she was Clarity K, even. Her name was Camilla Khe, then. She was my summer intern at WEENA, ages ago."

"Why would she try to sabotage you?" Marian stared at the Lawren Harris print over the desk as if wishing herself into the picture. "Mom?"

She sighed. "She complained about me to HR. She said I bullied her. It was nonsense, of course. I did nothing of the kind. But these young people are so thin-skinned. They can't take constructive criticism. Camilla was a smart young woman. I was only trying to help her along, improve her skills."

"I see." I'd been on the receiving end of Marian's unique approach to self-improvement, which could be as lacerating as a steel-wool loofah. I could well imagine that a sensitive would-be poet might have balked at being singled out for Marian's special treatment. "And what happened when she complained?"

My mother cleared her throat. "It was determined that she wasn't a good fit for the organization."

"You fired her?"

"Certainly not. The HR manager fired her. On my recommendation. Fully backed by the board, I might add."

That explained why Clarity had instructed her handlers to keep my mother away from her. But I couldn't see why, from her current position in the stratosphere of social media fame, she would stoop to anonymous online harassment. Not when she could dash off a few lines about having had a bad boss, plant a few indirect hints about Marian's identity, call it a poem, and let her fans do the rest.

"Did you tell the inspector that you were being harassed?" I asked.

Marian looked offended. "Of course not. It has nothing to do with what happened to Bliss. It's a personal matter."

"I think Inspector Bell might prefer to make that call herself," I said.

Marian huffed. "She's having enough trouble investigating the facts in front of her without my adding irrelevant information into the mix. I'll bet she doesn't even know that Bliss was sleeping with that odious faux mystic. Bondi? Brody?"

"Bodhi Rubin? Bliss was sleeping with him? How do you know that?"

"For a luxury resort, the walls are unacceptably thin," she sniffed. "They kept me up half the night with their squealing and moaning. As if that weren't enough, I saw him sneaking out of her room the night she died. A grown man. Pathetic."

"You didn't share that tidbit with Inspector Bell either?"

"Not my business," said Marian.

She was a front-row student, Marian was, with her hand perennially extended to the sky, and a tendency to dismiss the quiet kids in the rear as weak-minded. Cheryl Bell wasn't one to hog the spotlight, but she was, I suspected, as relentless as Marian in her own steady way.

We'd find out for sure when she figured out that Marian was screwing with her investigation. Inspector Bell, I knew from experience, didn't care for that sort of thing. Not at all.

CHAPTER 12

THE DOGWOOD CONFERENCE room on the main floor smelled like a fire in a scented candle factory. My olfactory system could barely handle the overload of vanilla and chypre. There were no lit candles on the tables, so they must have been pumping Eau du Spa in through the vents. Nearly every chair was filled, and nearly every body was female.

Onstage, Bodhi Rubin was exhorting his audience to unearth the feminine divine. "Each one of you contains the unquenchable flame that is passed down from mother to child, the most powerful force in the universe." He trotted across the stage, his eyes flitting down to the fitness tracker on his wrist. Measuring his caloric output, most likely.

Or maybe I was just one of those bitter gorgons who had murdered her inner divinity in order to survive.

"When was the last time you were struck by wonder?" Bodhi asked, bouncing on the tips of his vintage Air Max sneakers. "When was the last time you inhaled the mineral scent of your mate, tasted his elemental nature, felt the protective warmth of his flesh?"

I was about to snort, but someone beat me to it. I saw Lewis Kinross sitting at a table to my left, an empty seat next to him. I crept over and tapped him on the shoulder, and he glanced up and smiled. He patted the empty chair and I sat. He had a notebook open in front of him, its pages covered in illegible scrawls. I felt a moment's pity for the poor fact-checker at *The Loft* who'd have to decrypt those squiggles.

"What if you took notice, really noticed, the ordinary magnificence of your mate, at least once a day?" Bodhi jogged to the back of the stage, where a gong hung on a frame. He picked up a mallet, his voice reaching a crescendo: "I invite you to rediscover the transcendent in the mundane! Chime together!"

With that, he whacked the gong. As a bone-rattling clang rang across the conference room, a young woman across the table clapped her hands to her ears. "Oh my god," she moaned. "That is literally violence."

Lewis shot the girl a filthy glare. "It is neither literal nor metaphorical violence," he snapped. "It is the sound of a musical instrument."

The girl jerked back, wrapping her cardigan around herself. "Okay, Boomer," she said. "Let's not have an aneurysm at the table."

Lewis looked as if he were going to snap his pen in two. I wondered if he was this huffy with his students back home. His Rate My Professor page must have all the drama of a *Real Housewives* reunion. I made a mental note to check it out.

Onstage, Bodhi stilled the gong with one hand. "We can be wonderstruck at the most unexpected moments. Glimpsing a crimson leaf on a sidewalk. Hearing the delighted shouts of a child on a playground. Even here, in the midst of tragedy—" His jaw clenched, and he placed his hand over his heart. I noticed that he wore no wedding ring. "The tragedy that robbed us of a bright spirit. Do you know who found bliss in everyday life? Bliss did."

His eyes glinted moistly in the bright stage lights. The girl across the table muffled a sob. Lewis looked like a man who'd found an empty box of Raisin Bran in the cupboard.

"Bliss once stopped me when I was getting into my car," Bodhi continued, "and she pointed out there was a ladybug on the windshield. She didn't want it to blow away." His voice tightened, became strained. "So she took it on her finger and carried it over to the grass." He paused and lifted one arm to wipe his eyes, a movement which also displayed a lovingly tended triceps.

Bodhi tried to speak, faltered, dropped the mallet to the ground. "I'm sorry," he whispered. "I think I have to exist alone with my sorrow for a moment." He placed his palms together to his third eye, bowed, and hurried off the stage.

There was rustling and murmuring around the room. "Do you think he'll reschedule?" the woman across the table asked. "I don't want to sound like a cold bitch, but I shelled out two hundred bucks for this workshop."

"Maybe there's a grief refund," I said. "Like an 'Act of God' clause."

"Maybe there's an idiot clause," Lewis muttered, "for anyone who signed up in the first place."

I patted his shoulder in farewell as I got up from the table. I had no interest in seeing a Zoomer-Boomer cage fight, and I also wanted to catch Bodhi with his guard down. Weaving my way through the tables, I made my way to the curtain at the edge of the stage and pushed it aside. It was dark backstage, but I could see a door ajar at the end of a corridor, light filtering through.

As quietly as I could, I crept over and gently pushed the door open. "No need to knock on an open door" has always been my motto, and it's only gotten me thrown in jail once. Bodhi was inside, phone held up to his face. He was repeating the same anecdote about Bliss's compassion for the insects of the world, and I thought—perhaps unkindly—that it was interesting she hadn't been able to find a similar empathy for people who got their children vaccinated.

After he finished his damp little monologue, Bodhi punched the button to stop recording. He hunched his shoulders to his ears and shook his head like a boxer after a bout. I let out my loudest, fakest *ahem* and he whirled toward me.

"What do you want?" he snarled, and set his feet in a fighting stance. His eyes were now as dry as a sick dog's nose.

"Hiya," I said, holding up my hands to show that I was weapons-free. "That was a powerful performance out there." This was not entirely untrue; my ears were still ringing.

Bodhi's shoulders relaxed ever so slightly, but he still sounded sulky as he said, "It wasn't a performance. It was a gateway to revelation."

"Well, I certainly found it revelatory," I said.

"You did?"

"Absolutely." He hadn't invited me in, but he hadn't told me to get lost either, and I slid one foot gently forward and then another, like a toddler learning to skate. Then I was in the room. I leaned my hip against a table. "You have a commanding presence onstage. Everyone at my table noticed it." I wondered if Lewis Kinross and the woman in the cardigan had come to blows after I left.

Bodhi smirked in approval at my discerning taste.

I thought, not for the first time, how easy it was to use the key of flattery to open the door of ego. It had worked with poor Eliot Fraser too, when he gave me the last interview of his life.

Bodhi sat at a small table, unscrewed the cap of a bottle of coconut water, and poured himself a glass. He did not offer me any.

"I often think how lucky I was to have found a new path through life," he said. "I might have been a guidance counsellor forever if not for one moment of epiphany." He then began to tell a story I had already read, a dozen times, in various interviews and on his website. He was still plain old Larry Rubin then, and he'd been supervising the grade-eight lunchroom, miserably trying to make it through to the final bell. He'd looked down at his bowl (it was alphabet soup day, nobody's favourite). The letters in the tomato broth spelled out *WONDER*.

He continued in the practised cadence of a man who'd told his origin story more times than Peter Parker. "And I thought to myself, when was the last time I felt wonder? I couldn't remember! So you know what I did?"

"What?" I tried to inject as much enthusiasm as possible into my voice.

"I went into the principal's office and quit. On my way home, I bought a notebook at the dollar store and wrote down as many moments of boring joy as I could. Finding lots of chocolate chips in your muffin. Walking alone at night and hearing a train. Pretty soon I had stacks of notebooks all over our house." I pictured Jenny Baker-Rubin trying to tidy the teetering mountains of joy.

"Anyway," Bodhi continued, "I must have struck a chord. So many people had been wandering around with their noses in their phones, blind to the sublime." At that moment, the phone on the table vibrated with an incoming text, but he ignored it. I hoped Jenny wasn't having a toddler crisis. "I'd found my audience. Corporations wanted to hire me to give their people a lift. Couples needed to be reminded about the moments of desire that brought them together." The phone vibrated again, and fell silent.

"And Bliss and Bree brought you on their podcast to talk about Wonderstruck."

"One of their top-rated episodes," Bodhi added.

"I listened to it. You clearly had a bond with them." I paused for a moment, feeling my way forward. "What you said onstage about Bliss was so poignant. I think we could all feel the pain in your voice."

Bodhi wrapped his beefy arms around his chest. "She was a beautiful soul. A light-channeller. And a very good friend."

I let the words settle between us. "And that was all?"

His shoulders drew back. "What's that supposed to mean?"

I drew in a deep breath. "Well, it looks like Bliss may not have fallen from the lookout. She might have been pushed. Which raises the question: Who no longer wanted Bliss around?"

Bodhi shoved back his chair. "What the hell are you insinuating?"

"I'm not insinuating anything. But I've heard from a source that you were perhaps in Bliss's room the night she vanished. Maybe offering a guided meditation for two in the soaker tub, who knows?"

That one punched home. Bodhi's face blanched white. His jaw trembled with suppressed rage. After a moment, he hissed, "I think you'd better get out of here, and take your absurd accusations with you. And if I see one word of this in print—one word—you'll be slapped with a libel suit so fast your hair will catch fire." He lunged toward me and I flinched back, but he was just reaching behind me to yank the door open.

"Not to mention," he said through gritted teeth, "I know where your mother was when Bliss died. You might want to check your glass house before you start throwing stones. Now get the hell out."

So much for the wonder in everyday encounters.

IF I HAD a nickel for every door that had been slammed in my face recently, I'd be able to buy a nickel-plated suit of armour. At least, I thought, I'd solved one mystery: Bodhi was likely the one who'd seen my mom enjoying her illicit cigarette and ratted her out to the cops.

Maybe I was too much for Port Ellis? As I felt my way through the backstage dimness, trying not to trip, the metaphor was a little too on-the-nose. After nearly a year in this town, I was still treading gingerly, still offending people at every turn, still unable to make people trust me. Still unsure who I should trust.

My fingers found a doorknob, and suddenly I was out in a brightly lit corridor. I found a wicker chair next to a drooping ficus that looked like it shared my opinion of the world. I needed allies, and information. The first text, to Bruce, I tapped out rapidly. The second took more thought.

Janet Genovese had been a terrific source when I'd worked as an investigative reporter for the biggest newspaper in Toronto. She was a fund manager at one of the major Bay Street equity firms, but really she was a 1940s gossip columnist trapped in a 2022 power suit. She knew not only where all the bodies were buried, but who had held the knives that stabbed them. And she loved to share that information ... As long as I had something to share in return.

If Bliss and Bree had been planning to expand the Welcome, Goddess empire, Bay Street would be buzzing with news. Maybe there had been an IPO floated, or perhaps they were looking for an angel investor. If so, the money hounds would have sniffed out any bad blood between them. I typed out a text to Janet, giving her just enough information to pique her curiosity, and hit Send.

The corridors of the Pinerock were still crowded as I made my way outside. There was less sniffling, and more lingering around the tables that sold supplements and paraben-free water bottles. Poor Bliss: a lifetime in search of wellness, a terrifying plunge in the dark, and then this. Oblivion in all senses.

I squeezed past a woman in a purple jacket who was examining a Zen on the Go portable diffuser. Then I stopped short, turning back to look at her. It was Brenda, volunteer literacy teacher and weekend convoy warrior. Last time I'd seen her, she was screaming insults in Centennial Park. I scanned the crowd. Was that Kyle Johnson's red mullet I saw over by the French doors to the Canoe Salon? He disappeared in a flash. What were the protesters doing here? Were they looking to avenge Bliss's death?

I grabbed my phone to snap a picture of Brenda, but she'd vanished along with Kyle. Maybe I'd imagined the whole thing.

I made my way out to the rose garden behind the hotel, where gardeners were at work preparing it for its winter rest. In the centre was a gazebo, a place I knew a little too well. I'd given Darryl Danby a second chance on the gazebo's bench, after our failed make-out session at the lookout. Unfortunately we'd been spotted by his girlfriend, Carly, and I'd become embroiled in a tenth-grade version of a toxic love triangle.

Like I say, bad taste in men. Or, to paraphrase Dorothy Parker, I'd put all my eggs in the wrong bastards. I sat on the ill-fated bench and tried not to think about all the wrong bastards, and whether Amir was the latest in that line. At least I'd got one good egg out of all of it. I made a mental note to call Jake and see if he wanted to come up to Port Ellis for Halloween weekend. He certainly wouldn't find any place more haunted.

I looked up to see my reinforcement arriving. My backup squad was one grey-haired man in a Gordon Lightfoot concert T-shirt and an ancient Tilley jacket, but he was all I needed. Bruce flopped down next to me, and without saying a word extracted a cloudy baggie from one of his many pockets and handed it to me. Before I even opened it, I knew what was inside would be (a) good for me, (b) keep my bowels moving, and (c) possibly not be delicious. But I was starving, and Bruce was the human equivalent of the Giving Tree, so I munched on my raw jicama and counted myself lucky.

Bruce worked his way through his own baggie, stopping halfway to ask me what I'd discovered. I said, "Do you mean apart from the fact that my mother is crazy, and half the town wants me gone, and all the people at this so-called wellness conference are motiv-ated by one of the deadly sins?"

"Have you ever thought about how unequal those sins are?" Bruce asked, wiping his fingers on his jeans. "I mean, is sloth such a bad thing? I've never seen a picture of an unhappy sloth."

"Or lust," I said. "Nothing wrong with lust. If it's on both sides, that is." Immediately, my treacherous mind shot to Amir. Did he feel the same way about me? I couldn't tell; Amir dealt with challenges and triumphs with the same calm reserve, which was one of the things I found sexy about him. Or had, until he betrayed me with his silence about his wife. A terrible thought gripped me: Who else in the newsroom knew about Julia? Did Bruce know, and had kept it from me? Or had I just been so selfish, so consumed with my own troubles, that I hadn't bothered to find out the important details about my friends' lives?

Bruce's phone rang with the opening bars of "Smoke on the Water" and he fished it out of another pocket. He listened for a moment, and said, "We'll be right there." He folded his baggie and stood. "We're up," he said. "Kaydence says Bree's about to make an announcement in the ballroom."

BREE GUTHRIE LOOKED like someone who was au-ditioning for the role of Grieving Best Friend. Her back was hunched in a question mark, and she'd forsaken her elegant jumpsuit for a pair of yoga pants and a baggy T-shirt that said "I make chemistry puns periodically." She clutched a soggy rag in her hand. A few strands of hair clung limply to her pale forehead. Danilo had his arm around her, and she leaned into him. She closed her eyes, and spoke into the microphone in front of her.

"I think you all know about my mourning journey," she said, and her voice was barely above a whisper. "When I lost my husband, I thought the sun had gone out. The only one who understood was Bliss, because she'd gone through the same thing. You're not supposed to be a widow when you've barely been a wife, and she knew what that felt like. Talking about our grief with all of you"—she spread her hands wide, taking in the ballroom full of people—"it healed us. You healed us." She let out a little hiccup, a sort of half-cry. "And now we've lost Bliss, too."

Two women beside me hugged each other. I had my phone out, recording, while Bruce took notes. I looked around the ballroom, at the sad eyes and quivering chins. Bree lifted her head from Danilo's shoulder and seemed to find the strength to go on: "This is harder than anything, but I feel like we need to continue for Bliss. To carry on her work. Our work together, which is to heal. To be one."

The women next to me started clapping, and soon

the whole ballroom was applauding. My phone pinged with an incoming text. I slid open the text app. Janet Genovese, as always, had risen to the bait of gossip: *Girl, it's been forever! We need to catch up over a martini. Or at least a call. Do they have cell service where you are lol.*

Onstage, Danilo was comforting Bree with a hug. He spoke into the microphone: "Let's do this for Bliss!" he shouted. Bree looked up with tear-blotched cheeks, and I pictured her writing *MURDER* in the air. Nowhere better to hide than under a cloak of pity, I thought.

Another ping on my phone. The second of Janet's text arrived: *Funny you should mention the Crystal Twins. Sad news about the nutty one. They were doing the rounds earlier this year, looking for investors. We passed.* I stared at the text. Was that it? There had to be more. I jiggled my phone, as if that would help the reception.

Finally, a third ping: *They haaaated each other.*

CHAPTER 13

BACK AT THE microphone, Bree seemed to stand taller, as if squaring her shoulders for a fight. The chorus of voices shouting "For Bliss"—like an attacking army in a gothic fantasy film—died away.

"As I said, healing has been the foundation of our business. Bliss and I agreed wholeheartedly on that point. With her death, the responsibility of charting a path for the future of Welcome, Goddess falls to me and me alone. It's a duty that I take seriously. I know that many of you rely on us for guidance about your health, and I want to be a source that you can trust. Consequently, I'd like to take this opportunity to reaffirm my belief—and my company's commitment—to evidence-based products and services.

Wellness without science isn't healing—it's misleading. And I want no part of it."

Bree stepped away from the microphone. Danilo looked at his feet as if praying for a Taylor Swift–style exit through the stage floor. A low murmur bubbled through the throng of women, like tiny warning jets of hot water from a geyser, growing in intensity.

Until it erupted.

"Who got to you?" yelled one woman, jumping to her feet.

"You're working for Big Government!" shouted another. "Big Government killed Bliss!"

"Murderer!"

The word rang in the air. Bree folded over, arms clutching her stomach, shoulders hunched. She looked terrified, the mad scientist who could no longer control her own monster. Danilo grabbed her by the waist and tugged her toward the wings.

"Bliss knew the truth!" The call came from a chorus of united voices. At the ballroom entrance, a collection of signs sprouted like weeds after a rainstorm. The signs were battered from tours of duty at Centennial Park and the *Quill & Packet*, showing signs of weather and strife, but they were still legible: Freedom. Choice. The protesters formed an unruly line and began lurching down the middle aisle of the ballroom, thrusting their placards into the air and chanting in rhythm. "Bliss knew the truth. Bliss knew the truth. Bliss knew the truth." Brenda pumped her fist in the air. Kyle stomped alongside a tall, bearded man who looked like a bit-part actor cast in the role of demented street prophet.

My breath caught in my throat. I needed to move, but I couldn't go anywhere without drawing attention to myself. Any second now, I thought, the protesters would see me, and then what? Surely one of them would want to finish what they'd started the other day before the police intervened.

Bodhi Rubin was at the microphone, calling for calm. "Let's all breathe together," he insisted. "We are all one. We are all part of the same healing journey."

A megaphone crackled to life with a metallic screech. "This is Inspector Cheryl Bell of the Ontario Provincial Police. Everyone will take a seat immediately."

Ignoring the command, one of the protesters launched an object directly at Bodhi. He dodged the wooden Buddha statue that clattered against the microphone stand as he ran into the wings, the head skittering after him, its peaceful expression undisturbed by the outburst of violence.

There was a collective intake of breath, and the chanting petered out. Inspector Bell's voice blasted through the room with the force of a siren. "I will say this once," she said. "Put the signs on the ground. Now." Half of the protesters dropped their placards.

Several officers advanced down the middle and side aisles. "Last chance. Those signs are weapons and will be treated as such." Lumber crashed to the ground, leaving two spindly signs aloft like rejected trees in a clear-cut zone.

"Peter! Kyle!" a woman cried out. "Don't be foolish." The remaining placards wavered and then slowly fell. I recognized Kaydence's brother as one of the holdouts. He had his camera held high, filming the scene. The older man beside him wore a trucker hat low on his brow and a pastor's collar around his neck. That would be Peter Johnson, family patriarch and shit disturber.

"That poor woman," muttered Bruce.

"Cheryl Bell?"

Bruce snorted. "She can take care of herself. No, Deeandra Johnson, Kaydence's mom. She's a sweet lady. Deserves better than that sanctimonious sack of shit she married."

The police were directing the protesters out. Most looked as though they couldn't wait to breathe the free air, but a few stalwarts waited for their police escorts. It made for a better story on social media, I imagined, to create the impression that you were being manhandled. As Kyle and his companion passed, I met the older man's gaze. Unlike his son's hot, undisciplined fury, Peter Johnson's anger was ice cold, his mouth set in an implacable line. Kaydence's father was not a man you'd want to cross. Unfortunately, it appeared that I had done just that.

"Glad you were here," I said to Bruce. My heart was still racing with fear. There was more I wanted to say, but I couldn't find the words. The last person I'd trusted like this had tried to murder me with a giant paddlewheel, so Bruce's steady friendship was particularly heartwarming. It was a complicated sentiment to express.

It reminded me, also, that you could never know what dark motivations drove a person. Bree might seem like a delicate flower, but she'd taken the earliest opportunity to rebrand the business in her own image. Could she have been the one who pushed Bliss to her death?

Bruce waved me off. "I've been to more than a few concert gigs that went sideways," he said. He shook his head. "I never thought I'd see a crowd go wild for Peter Johnson, though. He's nothing but a Bible-thumper. Hardly the type to excite a bunch of goddess worshippers."

The audience, most of whom had frozen in their seats at Inspector Bell's command, began to reanimate, forming a subdued and orderly line, and filing out of the auditorium. I scanned the crowd, looking for Kaydence. I hoped for her sake that she'd missed the excitement. I'd had moments of being humiliated by my mother, of course, but that was nothing compared to Kaydence's family burden. Her father had a gleam of madness in his eye, whereas Marian's glittered only with ambition. Marian was a pain in the ass, but Peter Johnson was scary.

"Come on," said Bruce. "Let's drop in on Doug. He'll be in the mood to gossip after all that."

We found Doug standing in the hallway outside the security office, his arms folded across his chest and his chin jutting out, surveilling the passing conference-goers. "Bruce," he said curtly.

"Well, that was sure somethin', wasn't it?" said Bruce. Was it me, or had he picked up a folksy twang somewhere between the ballroom and here?

Doug's expression turned eager. "You were in there when it kicked off?"

"Sure was. Saw the whole shootin' match."

Doug reached out and clamped a hand on Bruce's shoulder. "Come on in and tell me all about it." He glanced at me. "You can come too, I guess."

He settled himself behind his desk and we sat across from him. "You'd think the cops would want all the assistance they can get, but nope. I go and offer to help clear the room, and doesn't Pamela Jones tell me to stay here and keep an eye on my security cameras? Pamela Jones, if you can believe it, giving me orders! Barely out of high school."

Bruce huffed in solidarity. "Man of your experience," he said.

"It's like they don't know that you managed the biggest security crisis in Port Ellis history," I offered. Doug had been on duty at the Playhouse when Eliot Fraser dropped dead onstage. I didn't recall any particular heroics, but I was following Bruce's lead.

Doug appeared mollified. "I appreciate that, thank you both." He leaned forward conspiratorially. "I've been looking at the backup security tapes from the night Bliss Bondar died. I was going to tell Inspector Bell what I found, but you know what? They have the originals. Let them figure it out on their own. They don't want my help, so the hell with them."

Doug turned his clunky desktop monitor toward us and we adjusted our chairs to form a semicircle. "I'll tell you what else," he said. "I'm no spring chicken, but I notice things." He tapped an index finger under his right eye. "When this contract ends, I'm going to study for my private investigator's licence. The wife keeps telling me I need a hobby."

He pecked at his keyboard while he talked. "I was trying to find that girl, Bliss, on the tapes. We don't have cameras in the hallways here, just in the elevators and the parking lot. The guests don't like being watched, but they sure worry about their cars. Anyway, here she is getting on the fourth-floor elevator at 1:18 a.m."

In the video, Bliss was wearing jeans tucked into chunky pink Ugg boots, and a heavy sweater. She had something soft bundled against her chest—a pillow maybe? A set of towels? A blanket?

"I thought she was staying on the second floor," I said.

"Nope," said Bruce. "She switched rooms with Bree. I talked to the cleaning staff. Bliss pitched a fit about the smell in her room. She was convinced there was black mould and they were concealing it with bleach. She threatened to leave the conference, so Bree stepped in and offered an exchange. The staff swore that they'd never seen any mould and that they used the same cleaning products in both rooms, but Bree had a larger suite and a nicer view up in 406."

My eyes were aching from squinting at the screen, but I felt the discomfort vanish in a rush of pure adrenaline. My mother had been wrong. It hadn't been Bliss banging the gong with Bodhi and keeping Marian awake that night. It was Bree.

I wondered who else knew, and what it meant. Could Bree and Bodhi be scheming together? Was it a fling, or something more serious? Were they planning on joining their empires as well as their lips?

Doug's voice cut into my thoughts. "And then I checked the parking lot footage," he said. "Bingo!"

A video began playing on the screen. A hooded figure concealed by a cape slipped out of the emergency door at the rear of the hotel at 1:20 a.m. "Clarity!" I said.

"Exactly," said Doug. "I figured I'd solved the case and Clarity was the killer." He put his hands behind his head and leaned back in his chair. "Or so I thought."

He was savouring his big reveal, Hercule Poirot in a security booth. "And?" I asked, impatiently.

"Hold your horses, I'm getting there," he said. "Look at her feet."

Once more, I watched the hooded figure step out of the emergency door. As she did, the cape parted at the bottom for a moment to reveal ... "Uggs! Doug, you genius!"

Doug shrugged modestly. "So if I need a reference for the PI course, I can ask you?"

"Consider it done," I said. "You're a natural."

I turned to Bruce. "Why was Bliss wearing Clarity's cape?"

"That's one question," said Bruce. "But more importantly ..."

I finished his sentence. "Did the killer mistake Bliss for Clarity?"

CHAPTER 14

I'D JUST LEFT Bruce and was heading for my car when Kaydence hand-flapped me into an alcove, like I was James Bond and she was my Moneypenny. Servers shot past us carrying room-service trays, and I could see, through an open doorway, the sweaty chaos of the kitchen. That was Port Ellis for you: many toiled so that some could be idle.

"I'm supposed to give you this," she whispered. She thrust an envelope at me.

"Tickets to see Beyoncé?"

"Kinda better, honestly."

When was the last time anyone had given me an actual piece of paper? I resisted the urge to sniff the envelope. Inside was a single piece of paper, on which a divinely messy hand had scrawled: *A conversation would be illuminating, wouldn't it?* There was no name at the bottom, merely two parallel slashes.

I waved it at Kaydence. "What is this? Slash from Guns N' Roses wants to meet me? Because if so I'm all in."

She leaned closer, shooting a suspicious eye at a waiter running past. "It's Clarity. That's how she signs her name now."

"So I should call her Double Slash?"

My friend had no time for my sarcasm. "She radiates peace, you know? I wasn't expecting it." Kaydence's face had taken on the glow of a medieval saint, lost in rapture.

I stared at her for a moment. Were we talking about the same Clarity? The one who divined meaning from sparklers? Who dispensed the wisdom found on coffee mugs? Who might possibly be having a deadly feud with my mother? That Clarity?

"Her skin is like rose petals, honest to god," Kaydence said, and led me toward Clarity's suite.

IN THE ELEVATOR, my phone pinged again. It was Janet Genovese, hot on the gossip trail. *Just met one of the partners at our monthly DEI seminar. We talked murder (so bad I know). Didn't realize the nutty one was sniffing for investors again and*

The text ended. I gritted my teeth. The elevator's opening doors chimed at the same time as my phone. A new text landed: *she had a silent partner this time, deep pocket$*. I texted back, *Any idea who?* And immediately Janet responded, *Nope sorry! Don't forget you owe me a drink lol.*

By now we were standing in front of a set of double doors. To the left, a small plaque noted that it was the Prime Minister's Suite. So Clarity outranked both Bliss and Bree in the glamorous-accommodation sweep-stakes. Interesting.

"Give me your hands," Kaydence said.

"Are you arresting me?"

"No, sanitizing." She took a small bottle from her pocket, and squirted some on my hands. It did not have the chemical pong I associated with the years of the pandemic, and I lifted my hands to my nose. The smell of a personally curated hothouse.

"Clarity has her sanitizing lotion manufactured in the tea terraces of Sri Lanka," Kaydence said.

"Wow," I said. "Poetry sure pays better than it did when Keats was burning pages to stay warm."

"Poetry is only one of the branches in Clarity's tree," Kaydence said, gently knocking. I was busy look-ing for a scar on her forehead where the chip had been implanted when the door swung open, and we were ushered in for an audience with the queen.

Inside, it was dim, quiet, and smelled like the cloud

that takes you to heaven. In the outer room, where we stood, two of Clarity's minions were focused on their devices. The one who had let us in, wearing wheat-coloured palazzo pants and an oat-coloured tank top, glared at me. I was wondering what I'd done to offend her when the second acolyte shot a scolding glance at her colleague and asked if we wanted a drink. I was tempted to request a tequila just to hear a gasp shatter the calm. Instead I asked for water. Kaydence said she was fine, but her nervous swaying belied her words. A third minion said that Clarity would be out shortly.

I wandered over to the window. The setting sun set the forest ablaze. I craned my neck, but the cliff and the fatal lookout were on the far side of the hotel, out of sight. The suite was huge, and had a spectacular view. I remembered my grandparents telling me, long ago, that Prime Minister Pierre Trudeau had enter-tained his friend Barbra Streisand in this suite. At the time, I had only the faintest idea who either of those people were. And now it was Clarity's lair. It made sense—if it was good enough for two divas, why not a third?

"I am also taken by this sky."

I nearly jumped out of my skin, and whirled away from the window to find Clarity behind me, hands calmly folded in front of her. She really was too young to be talking like Obi-Wan Kenobi. There was an otherworldly stillness to her. Could this angelic-faced

young woman really be the bitter demon who was trying to destroy my mother's book? Could she have had
some deep-seated beef with Bliss, possibly a fatal one?

Clarity glided over to the sofa, and I followed her.
"I was hoping we could have a cleansing discussion.
I heard about what happened downstairs, the disrup-
tion." She shook her head sadly, a wing of silver hair
brushing her cheek. "This conference was supposed
to bring people together, in healing and growth. Now
we have chaos and violence. And, of course, the extin-
guishing of a bright soul. Who should still be with us."

My finger hovered over the record button on my
phone. "Is this an interview?" I asked. "Are we on the
record?"

Clarity wrinkled her exquisite nose, as if I'd passed
gas in her presence. "I would like to contribute to a
healing dialogue," she said, which I translated as *yes*. I
pressed the record button. "Though of course, I have
no knowledge of the tragic events of the past few
days." I glanced over at Kaydence, who still looked
like she was standing on a hotplate. So this was why
I was here: Clarity needed to dry-clean her reputation, to remove any stink of connection to a murder.
It rubbed my fur the wrong way.

"Did you know that Bliss was wearing a cloak very
much like yours on the night she was murdered?"

I wanted a reaction and got one. Clarity jerked
back, and her mouth opened in shock. On the sofa

across from us, the minions stirred. Clarity regarded me for a minute, and the serenity in her eyes was replaced with something altogether more crocodilian. "It wasn't my Creativity Cocoon, if that's what you were asking." She turned to her aides. "Zed, can you please bring my cocoon so that Ms. Conway can examine it."

A moment later, my lap was draped in the plushest cashmere. The goat who'd made this sacrifice must have been as carefully groomed as Kim Kardashian. I'd only once felt something equally soft, when my ex-husband bought me a Max Mara coat for successfully producing an heir, an offering he'd referred to unironically as a "push present." My fingers slid along the silk lining, where the initials *CK* were discreetly embroidered.

"Ethically sourced cashmere, of course," Clarity said. "We work with a Nepalese collective, a small group of women who live in harmony with their animals. They harvest the wool at the waxing of each moon, when the goats are calmest. We're helping them expand their enterprise."

I could only imagine what it would cost to placate a herd of Nepalese goats. Or, for that matter, to import your hand sanitizer from the tea terraces of Sri Lanka. Clarity K's empire truly spanned the globe, I thought as I examined the cloak.

My hand froze in mid-stroke. The suite. The expanding cashmere business. My mind flashed to

Janet's text: *a silent partner with deep pocket$*. Someone who saw Bliss as a useful idiot, perhaps. And a valuable one.

Clarity was going to be Bliss's investor. Was Bree part of the plan? Or were they going to cut her out on their way to girl-boss nirvana? Was I looking at two warring factions, Clarity and Bliss versus Bree and Bodhi? My thoughts chased each other as I struggled to formulate a question that wouldn't get me kicked out of the suite.

What the hell. Sometimes the straightest path to the truth was the shortest one.

I said, "Were you Bliss Bondar's secret business partner?"

The minions gave a collective gasp, and even Kaydence let out a yelped "What?" Clarity's brows lowered, and I could see her small, perfect teeth clenched together. After a second, she addressed the room: "Could you all leave me and Ms. Conway alone for a moment, please?"

The minions shuffled out into the hallway, and Kaydence followed after I mouthed "It's okay" at her. And then I was alone with Clarity K, or rather, I was alone with Camilla Khe, because the pretence evaporated as soon as the door closed.

She reached over and hit the button to stop my phone recording. "Did your crazy-bitch mother put you up to this?"

I reeled at this sudden switch in temperature. We'd gone from frangipani blossoms to a prizefight in Vegas in the blink of an eye. I shot back, "Are you the one trying to sabotage her book?"

She spread her arms wide. "Do I look like I need to sabotage Granny's bullshit femifesto? I mean, come on. I put that poison behind me. The settlement I got paid for a lot of therapy. In fact, Marian did me a favour. I was actually at my therapist's when I found my new path. He had one of those fridge-magnet poetry kits, and I started to play with it during our sessions." Clarity's lips curled upward. "Turns out I had a fucking gift."

"You do," I said, and I meant it. It might not be my thing, but her work reached a lot of people who wouldn't otherwise pick up a book.

Clarity leaned forward, dropping her hands between spread knees. "Can we work out a deal? Dirt for dirt. I'll give you something that will go viral."

"And in return?"

She raised her eyebrows at me, like I was the dullest knife in the drawer. "Murder is kinda off-brand for me, Cat. The further I can distance myself from this nonsense, the better."

"How do I know you *are* distant from it? I have no idea where you were the night Bliss went missing."

"I was right here in this suite, working with my team on a video about SkyWords. After they left, I had to go over social media numbers with my core crew. Then I collapsed in exhaustion. Zed slept on the pull-out couch, and the other two curled up on the love seat. Even though they have their own rooms." She shuddered. "They never leave me alone. They're like burrs on my soul."

It sounded like something the famous poet might say, but the scrapper formerly known as Camilla would as well. There was nothing transparent about Clarity, despite her adopted name. And yet I felt, now that we were alone and isolated from any audience, that I was finally getting a glimpse of something authentic. The real girl under the robes was starting to tell me the truth.

"Were you and Bliss going into partnership?"

She got up, went over to the corner, and rooted around at the base of a potted fern. She came back with a KitKat in her hand, which she unwrapped. She broke off a piece and held it out to me, and I took it.

"This part is off the record," she said. I nodded. She finished the chocolate bar. "Bliss was onto something. I mean, she was batshit. Not in the same way as your mother. Much more cosmic. She called herself a starseed, sent to this planet to enlighten the masses." Clarity wiped her fingers on the sofa. "But somehow she connected with people. She tapped into their paranoia. And because she was a pretty white girl, she got away with it." She shrugged. "I could see the trajectory. I could see the business case for Bliss."

"But not Bree? She wasn't part of your plan?"

"Bree was so over Bliss. I think she was out there hunting for side deals of her own. That's the part you can use in your story. Bree knew that Bliss and I were talking about setting up shop together. That's not for attribution. Maybe say, 'a well-placed source says.'"

I did not need journalistic advice from someone who was a stranger to the rules of punctuation, but I kept that to myself. I touched the Creativity Cocoon with the end of my pen. "Bliss had her own cloak?"

"She loved mine, so I had one made for her. I even had her initials embroidered in the lining, like mine. We'd talked about manufacturing a line of capes. Not from Nepalese cashmere, of course. Maybe a nice poly-cotton blend." She touched the cloak absently. "I guess that dream is dead."

Clarity seemed more grief-stricken over the death of her clothing line than her human partner. Suddenly she stopped, and her head jerked up. Her eyes went wide, and I saw, for the first time, the panicked young woman behind the placid facade. "If Bliss was wearing her cloak the night she was murdered—"

She didn't have to finish the sentence. Bruce and I had already wondered if we were dealing with a case of mistaken identity. If Bliss had been wearing the cloak, she would have been indistinguishable from Clarity. Which meant that whoever had shoved her off the cliff perhaps had intended for Clarity to visit the great coffee house in the sky instead. And who hated the world's bestselling poet with that kind of heat?

I watched the realization dawn on Clarity's face; the same horrible suspicion that had been tormenting me since Doug had shown us the video footage. There was one person at the Pinerock who loathed Clarity. What she didn't know was that this person also happened to have disappeared for a while on the night of the murder. I stared at Clarity, and in the space where our eyes met was one unspoken word: *Marian*.

CHAPTER 15

IT WAS TIME to bring an end to a long day. I was flat-out exhausted. After crossing swords with Bodhi, sheltering from violent protesters, slipping into the secret world of Clarity K, and then contemplating my mother's possibly murderous tendencies, my brain was bursting. I needed to go home, take a hot shower, eat something covered in butter, and watch a few episodes of *Shetland*. I'd started bingeing the series after dinner at the Mahars' the night before. Pretend detecting, it turned out, was a lot more relaxing than the real thing.

I walked past the Greybuck Bar on my way to the exit. Danilo was slumped on a barstool, something dark and strong in the glass next to him on the counter.

I kept walking, stopped, and reversed. *Shetland* could wait.

I slid onto the stool beside Danilo. He was wearing peacock-blue silk pyjama pants and a matching bathrobe, paired with a yellow T-shirt and high-top leather sneakers in the same canary colour—a Hugh Hefner / Japanese street fashion mashup that shouldn't have worked but somehow did. I wondered how much luggage he'd brought with him to the conference.

He nodded at me, his eyes weary and puffy. "Join me?" he asked. "I'm on my second Dark and Stormy."

I caught the bartender's eye. He shook his head, almost imperceptibly, and flashed three fingers at me. "I'll have a Diet Coke," I said. "I'm driving." More to the point, I needed to keep whatever was left of my cognitive ammunition dry. My Diet Coke arrived, along with a menu. I ordered some spring rolls, hoping the bartender would take the hint and leave us alone long enough for Danilo to unburden himself.

I patted Danilo's arm. "Tough day?" I asked.

He snorted. "You think?" He ran his hands through his hair in an attempt to smooth it but succeeded only in adding to the general air of louche dishevellment. "I'll never work in PR again when this is over. I'm finished."

"I'm sure that's not true," I told him. "You couldn't do anything to put out this garbage fire."

"Really?" He looked hopeful.

"Absolutely," I told him. "You'll be the guy who survived the worst-case scenario. Like Harry Potter."

Danilo's eyes lit up. "The boy who lived! Maybe you're right, Cat. I could spin that." Then his face fell again. "It's just so frustrating. When I got hired, I thought I'd won the lottery. Nice employers, exploding brand, a bonus structure … total dream job."

"What happened?" I asked.

His expression darkened. "Bliss happened," he said. "She started out sweet. A little dim, but not a mean bone in her body. We used to hang out on tour and watch *Queer Eye* together."

"I watch that with my mom," I told him.

"No kidding! Marian Conway likes *Queer Eye*?" He looked at me suspiciously, as if it were only now occurring to him that I might have an ulterior motive in seeking his companionship. "Who's her Fab Five favourite?" he asked, testing me.

"Tan," I told him. "She likes that he makes everyone look respectable for once." It was true. Marian put a lot of stock in personal grooming.

"It figures," he said moodily. "That's the only part I don't like. The clothes are so conservative."

His attention seemed to fade into the middle distance, settling on a television set mounted over the bar. Men with giant thighs were running down an emerald field: football. I snapped my fingers and he started. "Who's playing?" I asked.

"Playing what?" he said.

"Exactly. Stay with me, Danilo. What happened with Bliss, your slumber party buddy?"

He sighed. "Social media turned her into a monster. She was always into 'holistic living,' but she kept drifting further into la-la land as the business grew. She loved attention. That was her weakness. The more famous she got, the more people wanted her help spreading 'key information' that had been 'suppressed by the government.'" Danilo was giving his air-quoting index and middle fingers a workout.

He waved his hand to order another drink. A glass of water appeared on the bar instead. "I tried to talk to her," Danilo said sadly. "But she didn't want my advice. She had a 'personal brand advisor' who was obviously a right-wing freak and kept steering her into taking more and more outrageous positions online. She wouldn't tell me who it was, wouldn't let me coordinate with them. Once Bliss saw how her engagement shot through the roof, there wasn't anything I could do to bring her back into the fold. Bree tried talking to her as well. She was so far gone by then that she thought we were 'tools of Big Pharma.'

"That wasn't the worst part, though," he continued. "What hurt me most was how she was snuggling up to the worst people—racists, book banners, transphobes. When I was hired, the vision was all about diversity, expanding the brand to be more inclusive. Bree and

I had a whole strategy about extending our reach in the influencer community. But Bliss rejected it. She said we'd piss off our new supporters with our 'woke pronouns.'"

"Oh, geez," I said. "That sucks. I'm so sorry. You must have been angry." Not just angry, I realized suddenly. Furious. Perhaps murderously so. Had Danilo been returning to the scene of the crime the day I'd saved him from death by mondochunk? If so, he'd never have mistaken Bliss for Clarity; Bliss's hot-pink Uggs would have caught his eye as quickly as a "seventy percent off" tag at a Holt Renfrew sale. I stifled a groan. This case was making my head spin.

The spring rolls arrived, piping hot and glistening with oil. Danilo bit the end off one and cupped his hand around his mouth to muffle his crunching. "Angry? Girl, you have no idea. I'd drafted my resignation letter and given it to Bree, but she begged me to stay, at least until after the conference. She hasn't been feeling well, and it didn't sit right with me to abandon her. She told me she had a plan to make things right."

I snagged a spring roll of my own, thinking. "Do you know what it was?"

He shook his head. "There were schemes afoot on both sides, but I wasn't in on them. They were both attached to their phones twenty-four-seven, talking in whispers, closing their laptops when I walked by, that kind of drama. I figured I'd take some vacation after the conference, book a few business lunches, and put it out in my network that I was open to a move."

"You didn't think Bree could fix it?"

"Maybe?" said Danilo. "But I got the feeling that Bliss had poisoned the well. Bree threw me a bone when I tried to resign and told me to invite a few influencers of my choice to the event. But when I circulated the offer, I got a lot of resistance. Bliss's toxic bullshit was out there in the community and it wasn't landing well. I could only get one local queer influencer to sign up. Your friend, Kaydence."

KAYDENCE, A QUEER influencer? How had I missed that? During the summer she'd drooled over Declan Chen-Martin, one of the stars at the Playhouse, but that didn't preclude her loving girls too. I could feel my brain reshuffling and reorganizing information. Kaydence's estrangement from her evangelical family made more sense now, as did her brother's hissed insult at the rally: *pervert*.

God, poor Kaydence. Why were so many parents apparently incapable of executing on the one—the only—essential component of the job beyond providing the necessaries of life? Why was unconditional love so hard to give? Undoubtedly because it wasn't easy to come by in the first place. An intergenerational cycle of families enacting the same worn patterns of rejection and loss. I hoped I was doing better than that with Jake. A profound sadness settled over me.

It was dark as I drove to town, the clouds obscuring whatever moon was in the sky. I rounded a corner and my headlights illuminated the entrance to the driveway I'd pointed out to Kaydence—the one that led to the convoy's encampment. A red pickup was at the intersection, waiting to turn onto the main road, and I slowed down to give it space. It was the same truck I'd seen Debbie Halloran sitting in this morning as she'd waited to ambush me, with a little Canadian flag decal in the side window. But why was she visiting the protesters? I could feel my curiosity stirring.

Don't be an idiot, I told myself. *Stop right now. Don't do it.*

But I was already making the turn, leaving my better angel pouting on one shoulder and my shit-disturbing devil grinning from ear to ear on the other. For all their talk of conspiracies, I wanted to know if the protesters had any solid information about Bliss's death. The only way to find out was to ask them.

The road was a bumpy one-lane dirt track lined with scraggly pine trees. There was nowhere to turn around or to make way for an oncoming car, and almost immediately I began to regret my decision. A pine bough brushed the window on the passenger side and, alarmed by the unexpected sound, I clenched my hands on the wheel.

The road ended abruptly, and I drove into a meadow to the familiar chords of a stadium anthem. "Welcome to the Jungle," naturally. There were a couple of RVs (how they had managed to drive them in from the road was a mystery to me), a minivan, and a few pickup trucks parked in a semicircle; a few tents were scattered around the clearing as well. Three men stood around a burning barrel fire, drinking from beer cans and yelling along to the music, occasionally nailing one of the lyrics. Two older women sat nearby on collapsible lawn chairs. One walked over to the fire and threw in a log and a copy of the *Quill*. The flames jumped.

I shivered. This had been a mistake. I put the car in reverse, planning on a three-point turn followed by a swift exit, but I'd caught the attention of the campfire gang. One of them broke away, running in my direction, and planted himself in front of my car before I could make my escape. Kyle Johnson. I took a deep breath and rolled down my window. "Kyle," I said. "Listen to me. I don't want any trouble. I'm going to drive out of here now. Have a nice evening."

He waited a beat as if considering my proposal, then turned his head and bellowed, "It's Cat Conway from the Shill and Racket, here to make trouble. Let's show her what trouble is!"

The doors to the RVs opened and more people than I would have imagined fitting inside began flooding out—like clown cars full of rageful misanthropes. Tents unzipped and even more protesters emerged. The two men who'd been drinking with Kyle sauntered over, no hurry, their mouths curling in menacing smiles. One of them took a running hop that reminded me of elementary school track and field day, and kicked at the side of the CR-V with a steel-toed boot. I heard a crunch. I shrank in my seat.

A woman with back-combed blond hair and worried eyes placed herself beside my still-open window. Her nails, long and frosted pink, clicked against the glass. "You shouldn't be here, honey," she said. "This is no place for you."

"Deeandra?" I asked. "You're Kaydence's mom, aren't you?"

"You need to leave," she repeated.

"What do you think I'm trying to do?" I asked. I pointed at Kyle. "Your boy won't get the fuck out of my way."

"Did you swear at my mother, bitch?" Kyle yelled.

"My apologies if I offended you, Deeandra," I said. The car began rocking. There were now two large men on either side of the CR-V, pushing it back and forth like a toy. I revved the engine and they stepped away for a second before resuming their game. They clearly meant to topple the car onto its side, and if they did, I'd be trapped.

I put the window three-quarters of the way up so

that no one could easily reach inside, and then stuck my hand in my backpack and felt around for my phone. It was time to call for help. Another jolt shook the CR-V like a bumper car and sent the phone tumbling to the floor. In the rear-view mirror I could see the size of the crowd that had gathered. A dozen, maybe fifteen?

"That's enough," said a commanding voice. Peter Johnson came to stand next to his son. "Deeandra, go to the trailer, now."

Deeandra scuttled away.

"I came here to get your side of the story of Bliss's death," I called out. "The police think it's a murder, same as you do. I thought you might want to tell me what you thought happened to her. I'm not here to upset anyone."

"Upset?" said Kyle. "Hell no. This is a good night's entertainment."

Peter Johnson turned and slapped Kyle across the face. "Shut up," he said. Kyle's face turned bright red under his ginger boy-beard. His eyes, when they met mine through the windshield, were murderous. He'd never forgive me for witnessing, even causing, his shame; I'd bet on it, and I wasn't a betting gal. I was equally sure that Peter Johnson didn't need a reason to humiliate his family, beyond his own pleasure.

"No one here is going to speak to the likes of you," Peter said, moving closer to me. He was standing right next to the driver's-side window now, bending down so that his eyes met mine through the opening. "You're paid to spread manure, Miss Conway. You're the poison in the body politic. You're the problem. We're not interested in helping the problem. We're fighting against it with everything we've got. You've crossed over into enemy territory. Not smart. Not smart at all."

I rummaged on the floor for my phone, swearing under my breath.

"I'm only trying to report the facts," I said, as calmly as I could. "I care about this community and everyone who lives here. You don't like my series, and that's okay. You're entitled to your opinions." My voice was shaking. I swallowed, hard. "I did a lot of research for those articles. The newspaper's objective is to provide people with accurate information that they can use to make the best decisions for themselves and their families. That's our only agenda."

Peter Johnson chuckled. "I'm sure you believe that. Which goes to show just how deluded you are. Get your phone out, Kyle. Let's get a video of Miss Conway for the record."

Suddenly I was catapulted into the past, into the most disastrous night of my life. The night when everything changed. I saw flashes of the bros high on testosterone and entitlement. I could feel it, the wild rush of blood in my veins. The fury at the injustice of it. Would Peter Johnson be leering down at Amir as if he were a tasty snack on a plate? Would the anti-vax wrestling team be rocking Bruce's Subaru for giggles? I thought not.

I looked straight ahead and saw Kyle holding up his camera like a third eye, an evil eye. My body went cold.

"What the fuck is wrong with you?" I heard myself shriek. "Do you get off on this? Scaring the shit out of people? You're a bunch of psychopaths. And you"—I pointed at Peter Johnson—"you belong in jail. If I have anything to say about it, that's exactly where you'll go, you sick son of a bitch."

I leaned on my horn, a shrill noise that sent birds skyward from the nearby trees. Kyle, perhaps doubting my sanity at last, leapt out of my path.

I gunned it.

CHAPTER 16

HAVE YOU EVER woken up to a bird mocking you? I don't recommend it. Outside my window, a blackbird was trilling out his version of a Tinder profile, but to my ears it sounded like *You iddiiioooot. You idiooooot.*

I clamped a second pillow over my head, trying to shut out the noise. I had been an idiot to drive down that country road last night. And shouting at Peter Johnson and the protesters had been a stupid move, even if they deserved it. My instincts often took me in the right direction, and then my temper threw a banana peel right in my path.

But wasn't anger often justified? Even if it led to disastrous consequences? In my case, my unchecked rage had led me here, to Port Ellis. A year ago, I'd been a high-profile television reporter, having been lured from my newspaper job with the promise of time to do investigative reporting. And, let's be frank, the promise of a fatter paycheque as well. For a while it had gone well. I'd done some important work, in between having my hair teased and my lapels lint-brushed.

Then, in one blinding flash, it had all changed. I'd been doing a live stand-up outside Toronto city hall when a group of boys, high on their own audacity, had zoomed up behind me. One of them screamed, "Fuck her right in the pussy!" into my camera. Something in me had snapped. Instead of brushing them off, or ignoring them, I'd confronted the jerk. And by confronted I mean I grabbed him by the throat and shook him like a dirty rag.

It had felt good, in the moment. It had made me a heroine, briefly, to all the women out there who wanted to snap but couldn't. It had also gotten me fired.

I'd paid for that mistake. But, deep down, I still didn't think what I'd done was wrong. Rash and short-sighted, yes, but not wrong. And I'd been right to tell Kaydence's dad and his cult of imbeciles that they were lying about the *Quill*'s reporting. I might have been less sweary about it, though. I wondered if Amir would hear about it, and whether "I was hangry" was a valid excuse.

My feet hit the floor, and I shivered. With the

Second Act unoccupied beneath me, my apartment was now chillier than usual. I shoved my feet into fuzzy slippers and wrapped my bathrobe around me. I'd preprogrammed the coffee maker, and the rich scent drew me into the kitchen. I drank my first cup staring out the window, wondering if blackbirds were a protected species and whether I could throw a potato at this loudmouth anyway.

There was only one cure for this sourness of mood: I would write my way out of it. I checked the *Quill* website and saw that Bruce and Hannah had written a story about the protesters interrupting Bree's speech. I surfed a bit and checked my Google alert for Bliss's name. There were lots of follows about her death, interviews with her estranged parents back home in Alberta, but no one had written about the possible dissolution of the Welcome Goddess empire.

That one was mine.

WET LEAVES SQUELCHED under my feet as I huffed my way up the steep path to the lookout. It had rained overnight, and my fingers scrabbled at damp roots to haul myself higher. I really needed to ride my bike more. I sounded like a pack-a-day smoker sitting in death's waiting room.

At least the cops hadn't blocked off this route, the secret path to the top. My foot caught a beer bottle and I nearly fell. Okay, so the path wasn't secret to the intrepid teens of Port Ellis. The sky was heavy and grey above, and a few orange leaves drifted lazily to the earth. It was good at pretending to be peaceful, this town.

I didn't know what I was expecting to find at the top, but I knew I needed a look around before I wrote another story. Maybe I'd find nothing; Cheryl Bell's troops had been combing the area for days. Or maybe I'd find a footprint left behind by one of Danilo's flashy Japanese sneakers. Or Bodhi's Fitbit. A strand of Bree's glossy hair. A fibre from Clarity's Creativity Cocoon.

Or a cigarette butt left by my mother.

I shook my head to get rid of the thought and resumed my climb. To my right was a dense forest. To my left was a precipitous drop, beyond which I could see the grey glint of Lake Jane. A forest creature scuttled through the wet leaves.

After a few more steps, I heard the scritch of leaves again, louder this time. I stopped to listen. The noise stopped, almost as if it were following me. When I resumed climbing, I heard a branch snap. I stopped, quivering, like Bambi's mother with the hunters on her tail. My heart beat a snare drum in my chest.

Then there was a shuffling sound, like feet dragging through wet leaves. I darted a glance over at the cliffside, nothing but a cushion of air between me and oblivion. I started to run, my feet scrambling on the wet dirt. Either it was a coyote or the killer and I didn't want to meet either one. I flew up the path, lungs burning, until I burst into the clearing at the top.

I stood for a moment, bent double, gasping. At least there was no one up there to mock me as a chicken, and an unfit one at that. I straightened up and took a few steps into the clearing. Police tape, draped between trees growing at the cliff's edge, fluttered in the wind. The low stone wall that prevented careless plunges was hardly suitable to the task, as Doug had noted. At the centre of the clearing was a wooden bench, worn smooth by the bums of countless lovers.

I walked over and crouched down to examine the various engraved testaments to enduring love. *DD* plus *CH*. Darryl Danby, that love rat, had sanctified his love with Carly Haverman, and not me. Story of my life.

"I didn't expect to find you here," said a familiar voice behind me. I whirled around to find my mother, elegant in a Lululemon hoodie and yoga pants. She was tucking her hands into her pockets. "I mean, mornings and exercise are hardly your favourite things on their own, and together …"

I made an effort to control my puffing, and said, "I should ask what you're doing up here."

She shrugged, and flopped onto the bench. "Getting my steps in. Contemplating the destruction of my life's work."

I decided to ignore the fact that she did not consider me, her daughter, to be her life's work. I sat down beside her. "Mom, you might be overreacting the tiniest bit. I mean, your book hasn't even come out yet. I'm sure you'll get wonderful reviews and lots of great publicity. You're just dealing with a few trolls at the moment."

But her eyes were locked on the horizon. "You know, boys were always trying to get girls up here. 'There's a full moon, let's go to the lookout.' And you'd go with them, because you were intrigued. And everything else was so boring. It was like living in a coffin, this town."

A strand of her hair disobeyed orders and drifted into her eyes, but she made no move to fix it. I watched, fascinated, and said nothing. This was more than my mother had ever told me about growing up in Port Ellis. She said dreamily, "If I'd stayed, maybe things would have been simpler. If I'd followed the rules."

I'd never heard her express these kinds of doubts. "But then you wouldn't have had the life you've had. Your success. You wouldn't have met Dad. You wouldn't have had me." Her eyes met mine, and they were still lost in some reverie. This was not a Marian I recognized. How many facets of my mother had been hidden from me, all along? And was one of them capable of murder?

I took a deep breath. "Mother, I wanted to ask you about the night—that night—when Bliss was killed. She was wearing a cloak, just like Clarity's. Did you happen to …" I couldn't finish the sentence. *Did you mistakenly push Bliss off the cliff, thinking she was Clarity?*

"Clarity," my mother said. "Meaning clear or transparent. That girl's not very honest with words if she chose that as her nom du plume. She was a liar when I knew her, and she's a liar now." Marian slapped her thighs and stood up. "We'd better be heading back. You'll need more time than me to get down the path."

She started down the other trail, the one that led to the Pinerock, with the agility of a Pilates-trained mountain goat. I huffed and puffed behind her, my mind pinballing between last night's meltdown and the story I had to write when I got to the newsroom. With any luck, I wouldn't run into any protesters along the way. But I'd have to tell Kaydence about the dust-up with her father. And maybe even gently inquire about Danilo's enigmatic "queer influencer" comment. My friend probably needed a friend.

We came out of the trees onto the Pinerock's back patio. Despite the grey skies and the chill, several of the outdoor tables were occupied. And one of them was occupied by a man and a woman, heads together, deep in discussion. Bree Guthrie and Bodhi Rubin. The put-upon Mrs. Baker-Rubin and her brood were nowhere in sight.

I told my mother to go on ahead, and that I'd see her inside. I needed to get a quote from Bree. What had she known about Bliss and Clarity's plans to ditch her and form their own wellness empire? I smoothed my hair as best I could, and walked toward their table.

Bree had her back to me, a dove-grey pashmina wrapped around her shoulders. She was so intent on her conversation that she didn't hear me approach. "We need to make this decision together, Larry," she was saying. "We'll have to plan—"

"I'm sorry to interrupt," I said. "I was hoping I might ask you a question, Bree."

Bodhi's head jerked up. The look he gave me would have made Freddy Krueger blanch. Bree turned gracefully in her chair and regarded me for a moment. I could see that she was pretending to search for my name. I had to admire the power in her game.

"I'm afraid I'm not speaking to the press at the moment," she said calmly. "It's such a difficult time. I'm sure you understand."

"I do, and I am very sorry to disturb you. I certainly don't want to add to your pain." Bodhi Rubin was now clenching a fork in his paw. It seemed inconceivable to me that this lovely young woman would be making the beast with two backs with formerly-Larry, who was currently married. I turned my attention back to Bree. "I've come across information that suggests Bliss might have been intending to dissolve your partnership. Is that something you'd like to comment on?"

If the news surprised her, she didn't let on. She just held my gaze and said sweetly, "Like any partnership, we had a legal framework in place for such an eventuality. Beyond that, I have nothing to say."

And I had nothing to lose. "I was at SkyWords," I told her. "I saw you write the word *murder* with your sparkler."

Bree stiffened. "Someone I loved was murdered. I'm processing that grief in my own way. Privately."

"Murdered by whom?"

"I have no idea," she said. "I'm sure the police are doing their best to find out." She stood up. "Larry, let's go."

"My deadline is at five this afternoon," I told her. "I'll send Danilo a few questions that he can forward to you, if you change your mind."

"I won't," she said. "I've already declined an interview with the *New York Times*, so ..." *Why would I talk to your insignificant rag* hung, unspoken, in the air between us. Oh, she was good.

And well-protected. Bodhi seemed to gnaw at the air as I took my leave.

AT THE SELF-SERVICE counter of the Pinerock's café, I picked up two coffees, an almond croissant for myself, and a fruit cup for Marian. None of the members of the Conway clan functioned well on an empty stomach. My mother had texted me to say she'd meet me in the café, and I paid and went in search of her.

I caught sight of her in the corner and made my way over—and stopped dead when I realized there was someone already seated with her. Dark glossy hair, pink lipstick, pearl studs: Debbie Halloran looked ready for a magazine shoot even first thing in the morning.

"Cat!" she said, with genuine pleasure. "It's so lovely to see you."

I couldn't say the same. I sat down across from them. "You sure take your job as my mom's guide seriously," I said, hearing a childish note of hostility in my voice before I could pull it back. Why was the First Lady of Port Ellis surgically attached to my mother? Did I need to make an appointment if I wanted to see Marian alone? If so, I imagined I'd have to book it though Debbie. "You must be practically living here."

"Not at all," she said coolly. "Like you, I have other responsibilities. Spending time with Marian is something I do for fun. A choice." She tilted her head and looked me straight in the eyes, as if issuing a challenge.

On the table, her hand lay next to Marian's, and I noticed how similar they were, with their shapely fingers and manicured nails. My own nails looked like they belonged to a raccoon after an all-night dumpster binge. I tucked my hands under my thighs.

Challenge accepted, I thought. I flashed back to the night before, seeing her red pickup turn onto the highway in front of me. "What were you doing at the protesters' encampment last night?"

Both Debbie and my mother's expressions froze. Debbie spoke first. "I'm sorry, Cat, but you're mistaken," she said. "I was nowhere near the encampment. I was at a board meeting at the hospital. Chairing it, in fact. You know, tending to some of those other responsibilities I mentioned."

Debbie was ice, but my mother was fire. "What has got into you, Catherine? Your behaviour is outrageous. You are being extremely disrespectful to Debbie. She's going to think you were raised by wolves."

If the designer shoe fits, I thought.

A FEW HOURS later, I was nearly finished the draft of my story about the Welcome, Goddess empire and the schisms that had threatened it. I sent an email to Danilo with questions for Bree, knowing that she probably wouldn't respond. Then I called the OPP to see if there were any updates on the case, an even more fruitless task.

While I was waiting for Danilo's response, I typed his name into a news database. He'd graduated from the communications program at an Ontario university and was quoted in a story about the school trying to ban TikTok on campus. (He'd objected, unsurprisingly.) Danilo was younger than he looked; wellness had not saved his skin. I couldn't help but think that it hadn't saved Bliss's either.

I switched gears and typed Lewis Kinross's name into the database. During the pandemic, he'd been widely quoted in a variety of media about the dangers of not wearing masks and of using holistic remedies instead of vaccines. I could practically see the lasers shooting from his eyes. His story for *The Loft* was going to be a doozy.

I stretched, then opened my story again. After I'd added a final quote from "a source close to Clarity K," I sent the story to Amir for editing and stared at his closed door. It had been closed since I'd arrived at the newsroom. It was hard not to see it as a metaphor. *Let me in, Amir. Tell me about your failed marriage and your anxiety about your parents and your fears about the future of the paper.*

The door to his office burst open. Maybe I was a witch.

"I just filed," I said, and he nodded, distracted, and wandered in a tight circle like a dog at the vet's. He stood, fists on hips, and stared at the ground.

"Do you want to tell me about it?" I asked.

He stared at me for a minute, and then made a decision. "You might as well know. Flannery's has cancelled their contract with us."

"Oh, Jesus," I said. Flannery's, the venerable grocery chain, had four stores in the tri-lake area. It sold copies of the *Quill*, took out full-page ads every week, and paid us to publish a fat insert listing all the weekly sales. It was our lifeline. Our last one.

"All of it?" I whispered.

"Apparently, old man Flannery is in a weekly prayer group with Peter Johnson, and he asked for spiritual guidance. Or some such bullshit." He leaned over me, outstretched arms on either side of my desk. There was something wild and unfamiliar in his eyes. "You know what I think? I think that fucker Gerry Halloran is trying to sabotage us. He's always hated the *Quill*. We're the only competition for his stupid radio stations. And it drives him crazy that Bruce is always asking questions at council meetings."

"Did I hear my name?" Bruce came into the newsroom, ushering Hannah in before him. "Are you already talking about Secret Santa? It's never too early." Then he saw our faces, and he flopped down at his desk. "Damn. There's not going to be Secret Santa this year, is there?"

Hannah's eyes darted between the three of us. "What's going on?"

Amir sighed. "Cat, do you think you could call Kaydence and ask her to come in? We'll talk it through together. Meanwhile, I'll edit your story." He went into his office and shut the door behind him.

I called Kaydence and asked if she could abandon her booth for an hour or two. Bruce rose and stretched.

"Well, I don't know what's going on but we're probably going to need kombucha. Good thing I just made a fresh batch."

YOU KNOW WHAT really doesn't work when you mix them together? Kombucha and Jägermeister. But after three cocktails, my gag reflex stopped working. Everything had stopped working, including my eyes and my tongue.

We sprawled around the newsroom in various positions of drunken despair. Hannah lay on the ground, her head pillowed on a bound copy of the Ontario Municipal Act (2001). "I'm gonna have to go to law school," she muttered.

Amir had broken the news about Flannery's, and shortly after that he'd broken the seal on a bottle of Jägermeister that young Aaron Flannery, who was less godly than old man Flannery, had given him for Christmas the year before. "Fucking hypocrites," Amir said into his mug, which had "World's Best Editer" written on the side.

"They always have been," Bruce agreed. "Even way back when. Dorothy found out when she did that series about their anti-union policies."

The words cut through the booze fog in my brain. "I'm sorry—Dorothy Talbott? Our publisher, Dorothy Talbott?"

Bruce's head flopped forward, which I took for a yes. "She was just a general assignment reporter at the *Quill* when she heard that the Flannery's over in Patrick's Harbour was planning to unionize. Old man Flannery was trying to bust it up. So she got a job at the checkout and wrote about it from the inside."

"Boss bitch," Hannah murmured from the floor, then burped.

I'd had no idea. Dorothy had seemed ancient and crotchety when I'd arrived at the *Quill* less than a year ago, her vision impaired and her tone always testy. I knew she'd fought to keep the newspaper safe from her grasping children and her selfish husband. But I hadn't thought much about her role at the newspaper her family had founded more than a hundred years ago.

I choked down the rest of my drink and held my glass out to Amir for a top-up. "I don't understand how she can let her horrible kids sell the *Quill* when it means so much to her."

"I know the answer to that one." Kaydence had come into the newsroom carrying a tray of snacks she'd foraged from the depths of the kitchen: some broken cheese straws, four Oreos, and a pat of crusty hummus. "The mayor golfs with Dorothy's son."

"The one who looks like a model in a Walmart ad?" Bruce asked. "Or the one who looks like he tortures cats?"

"Both, I think." Kaydence offered me the tray, and I took an Oreo. "You know Gerry's whispering in his ear that the paper's a burden."

We sat in glum silence. Finally, Hannah's plaintive voice from the floor: "What are we gonna do?" Four pairs of eyes swivelled toward Amir, who did not meet any of them. I knew he'd been fretting over this very question since the day he'd taken over the *Quill*. He deserved one night of rest.

"Maybe," I said, "we could kidnap Dorothy's children and leave them in Nunavut."

"Not fair to the people of Nunavut," Kaydence said. "Maybe the five of us could record a charity single and it'll make a bazillion dollars and we can buy this place." She raised her glass to Bruce, and some of the foul cocktail slopped out the top. "You've got a rock star in the family, Bruce. Get him to write us a song."

"I'll do that," Bruce said. It was a running joke in the newsroom that Bruce's famous nephew, Ryan, would one day arrive and take us on a global tour with him. "I'll ask him. But first I think I need a nap."

AN HOUR LATER, Kaydence and I were in the basement archives, flipping through old copies of the *Quill*. We'd left Hannah and Bruce snoring upstairs, and Amir bent over his computer, tinkering with headlines on my story. As if he could save the *Quill* by sheer willpower alone.

I could barely focus on the page in front of me. It was an edition from the 1970s, featuring the first woman in the tri-lake area to be elected to Parliament. "Our Gal in the House," the headline said, next to a picture of the MP balanced on a desk in a tiny miniskirt.

"Nice," I said, pointing it out to Kaydence. She cackled in appreciation. After a minute she said, "Look," in the way that drunken people say *Look*, meaning, "I have something important to say, and I can only say it when I'm hammered."

"Look, I know you heard what my dipshit brother said. You know. *Pervert*."

"I was kind of surprised he even knew that word," I said. "It's not exactly in fashion."

"It is in my house," Kaydence said. "Or at least the house I grew up in. My dad caught me and my friend Fern once … well, let's just say we weren't doing our calculus homework." Her finger wiped away a smudge of dirt on the cover of the old *Quill*. "After that, they started in on me. You don't want to know what they said. Or did."

I slipped my hand around her waist, and I gave her an awkward sideways hug. "I'm so sorry you had to go through that."

"They couldn't believe that I was attracted to boys and girls. According to my dad, Satan was rolling out the welcome mat for me. He was yelling some Bible verse at me when I left for the last time. I had just turned sixteen."

I gave her another squeeze, and she patted my hand, as if I were the child who needed comforting. "It's okay, Cat. I found my real family." She bent her forehead to mine. "I think we both did."

CHAPTER 17

I WAS DOZING on the bathroom floor when the phone rang. What was it about alcohol and the midlife body? It was as though all of those years of practice drinking counted for nothing. I'd slept for approximately forty-five minutes before lurching out of bed, already heaving, and sprinting for the toilet's cool embrace. I'd spent the rest of night sweating on the ceramic tiles, a towel draped across my midsection: portrait of a non-functional adult.

"Hey, Amir," I said. "I hope for your sake that you feel sprightlier than I do."

His voice suggested that he did not. "You've seen the video?"

"The video?" I could feel thoughts attempting to push their way through my brain tissue. It hurt.

"There's a video of you at the convoy campsite. What were you doing there?"

I sat up, thought better of it, and eased into a fetal position. "It was stupid, I know," I said. "I'm sorry. I should have told you."

There was a long pause. "Cat. I need you to be completely honest with me. What did you say to them? The protesters?"

Ugh. I felt myself getting hot with embarrassment, or nausea, or both. Regrets, I had a few. "I told Peter Johnson that he was a psychopath and he belonged in jail," I said reluctantly. "In my defence, acknowledging that I shouldn't have been there in the first place, it was a freakshow out there. Peter's goons wouldn't get away from my car. They were swarming me. They scared me half to death."

"Did you discuss the mayor with them?" Amir's voice was cool, formal.

"Gerry? No. Although I think he was out there before I was. I saw his pickup leaving. I thought it might have been Debbie giving out sandwiches or doing some other saintly shit, but she says she wasn't—"

"Cat. Focus. Did the mayor come up in your discussion with Peter Johnson or anyone else at the campsite?" Amir never interrupted when someone else was speaking. Dread skated down my back like a drop of ice water.

"No. What's going on?"

"I'm sending you a video. I'll stay on the line while you watch it."

I was so tired. I closed my eyes for a few seconds, and when I opened them, there was a text from Amir with a reel attached. I clicked on it.

And there I was, viewed through the windshield of the CR-V. I was wearing an expression I'd seen before, on the faces of stray dogs trapped in cages by well-meaning rescuers, beasts who'd experienced too much in the way of human cruelty to welcome fresh captivity. I looked feral.

I screamed straight into the camera. "Gerry Halloran is a monster and you are all his puppets! You're a bunch of psychopaths, and you should be put out of your misery. Jail's too good for you. Gerry Halloran should hang from that tree"—I pointed out the car window—"and if he knows what's good for him, he'll watch his back."

"Jesus Christ," I said into the phone, suddenly and shockingly sober. "What the actual fuck. I did not say that. I swear to you, Amir—" I was interrupted by a knock at the door. "That's not what happened. Hang on, I just have to answer the door."

I pulled on a bathrobe and walked out into the living room. Amir was still talking. "Cat? Cat! Listen, this is important."

"I know it is," I told him. I opened the door to find Dick Friesen and Pamela Jones on the landing, in full uniform, complete with expressions of absolute seriousness. "Oh, shit," I said.

Dick spoke. "Catherine Conway, you are under arrest for uttering threats. You have the right to remain silent. Anything you do or say may be used in evidence. You have the right to a lawyer. If you cannot afford a lawyer, one will be provided to you." Dick paused. "Do you understand?"

Constable Jones looked profoundly uncomfortable. "We'll wait while you get dressed," she said. "Then we'll go down to the station."

"Amir," I said into the phone.

"I heard," he said. "I'm calling a lawyer. Don't say anything until he gets there."

THE CELL WAS painted in a shade that I recognized. In another life, I'd spent time puzzling over distinctions a designer insisted were crucial among the grey tones in the Farrow & Ball catalogue. This was Manor House Grey, a long fall from its namesake, knocked off by some institutional supplier. I doubted my former designer would admire the stainless-steel sink with a toilet protruding from its base, though what it lacked in privacy it made up for in efficiency. I stretched out on the concrete slab with the foam topper sheathed in vinyl and closed my eyes.

I'd been here for what felt like hours, but Dick had

taken my phone, and I had no way to know for sure. A buzzer sounded, followed by the *thunk* of a security door opening and closing. Footsteps approached. I sat up. I did not remotely recognize the man standing on the other side of the bars. He was as tall and spindly as the last Christmas tree on the lot, and his hand, when he waved, was long-fingered and bony at the wrist. His friendly brown eyes met mine.

"Hello there," he said. "I'm Gus Demetriou. Your lawyer. I'm a friend of Amir's."

Gus. I'd heard of him. He was … "You were Amir's roommate at university," I said.

"Unofficial," said Gus. "My mother wouldn't let me move out until I got married, but I crashed at Amir's so often that it seemed like I lived there. I'm sorry you've been stuck in here so long. There was a ton of traffic on the 400."

"Amir asked you to come?" If Amir had asked his best friend to come and help me, that must mean that Amir believed me. That he trusted me, even though I'd fucked up.

"That's right," said Gus.

"I didn't say those things," I told him. "I swear, I didn't."

Gus nodded. "I know," he said. "It was a deepfake. Not even a very good one. Hannah Shim had already found flaws in the lip-synching before I arrived in town. She's smart, that one."

"She's incredible," I said. "Who made the video? How?".

"I don't know the who," Gus said, "but the how is easy. You were a television journalist. There are hundreds of clips of your voice online to choose from, and one in particular where you're ... upset." He cleared his throat. "Someone fed your voice samples into the cloning software, uploaded the video of you at the campsite, recorded the message they wanted you to say, and asked AI to put it all together. Fortunately, they didn't take much time with it, and they used one of the cheaper apps. Good news for you. It didn't take much to persuade Inspector Bell to spring you."

"I'm getting out?"

"They're doing the paperwork as we speak."

"Okay," I said. "Okay." I kept repeating the word like a mantra, but I couldn't feel it. The pressure that had been building all day was too intense now. It could only be discharged in one way.

I put my head in my hands and bawled.

I could hear Gus in the background trying to calm me, but I ignored him. When the crying fit finally subsided, leaving me limp, shuddering, and gasping for breath, I looked past the bars through swimming eyes to see Gus with a sympathetic smile, and Dick Friesen with a contemptuous scowl. Swiftly, Dick punched a code into the access panel on the door, releasing the locking mechanism. The door slid open.

I stepped out and reached for Gus's hand. He shook it gingerly. "Nice to meet you," I said. "Shall we?"

Dick led us upstairs, where I reclaimed my phone. Cheryl Bell was nowhere to be seen, not that I was keen on a reunion at that moment. "You'll stay out of police business if you know what's good for you," said Dick.

"Is that a threat?" asked Gus.

Dick didn't meet his eye. "Inspector Bell said that Miss Conway should keep to her side of the street. She said, and I quote: 'Obstruction is a serious offence.' Capisce?"

"Noted," I told him. I turned to Gus. "Get me out of here, please."

In the parking lot, Gus unlocked a pretty BMW. He caught my appraising glance and shrugged, sheepish. "I don't usually work for free," he said.

"Lucky me. What favour did Amir cash in?"

He laughed. "I'll tell you in the car," he said. "Amir told me to drive you home."

We pulled out of the OPP detachment and turned toward downtown. "You were saying?" I prompted him.

"Journalists," he said. "So persistent. I could say that I'd do this for any friend."

"Would you?"

"Probably? But I doubt you'd accept that explanation."

I didn't bother to answer.

After a brief pause, he continued. "I owe him because I was Amir's best man when he married Julia." It was unexpected, and I felt myself wince before rearranging my features into an expression of casual interest. I didn't think Gus had noticed; he was still speaking. "I took him out for dinner the night before the wedding, nothing too debauched, just a few of us at a steakhouse. He drank a bottle of red on his own, and he told me he was having doubts. I cut him off, said it was the booze talking. Bad friend."

"That's what most people would have said," I told him. I felt suddenly lighter.

"Maybe," he said. "But I could have done better. He knew it, and I knew it." He looked straight at me. "He wouldn't have called me for just anyone. You get that, right?"

"I get it," I said. We rode in silence for a few minutes as I contemplated Gus's message. Amir cared. It was an idea that both warmed and terrified me. My brain wasn't capable of higher thought at the moment. It needed rest, and calm, and sugar.

Gus dropped me back at my flat, and asked if he could go get me something to eat. "It's my inner Greek." He smiled. "Nothing I can do about it." But I told him I'd be fine, and I wearily hauled myself up the steps to my apartment. Never had I been happier to see its tiny rooms; never again would I refer to it as a "prison cell." It was infinitely preferable to the real thing.

I took a couple of Tylenol for my headache and ate a quarter of a McCain Deep'n Delicious cake straight out of the freezer. It had been meant for Jake, but he'd understand. He might even think it was cool that his mom had spent the morning in jail.

I threw my clothes in the tiny washing machine in the kitchen and put on my bathrobe. When I turned my phone back on, I saw dozens of messages from Amir and my other *Quill* friends, which lifted my heart, and one calendar notification, which froze it solid: dinner with Marian, Pinerock, 7 p.m.

Flopping on the sofa, I contemplated cancelling on my mother. She'd surely understand, after the day I'd had. On the other hand, if I wanted to prove to the good people of Port Ellis that I was not incarcerated and had been the victim of a frame job, the Pinerock was a good place to do it. I'd be seen by everyone, and lips would start flapping. Lip-flapping was Port Ellis's main sport, after sailing and pickleball.

I was drifting gently toward the land of nod when I heard a knock at the door, then a second one, louder this time. I sat up groggily, clenched for a horrible second by the thought that Dick Friesen was back to re-arrest me. A familiar voice carried through the door: "Cat? Are you there?"

I tugged the bathrobe's belt tight and—I am not

ashamed to admit—smoothed my hair in the little mirror next to the front door. When I opened it, Amir was standing in the hall, looking wide-eyed and haggard. Before I could say anything, he'd taken me in a hug, his arms tight around my back. We stood that way for a minute, caught in our own little bubble.

Finally, I pulled away. I was pretty sure I'd flushed scorching red, an unflattering contrast with a dusty-pink bathrobe. "Lou Grant never hugged Billie like that," I said as I led him into the living room.

"Lou Grant was a grouchy old prick," said Amir. "Not a stylish new editor model such as myself." He did not look particularly stylish—it looked like he'd been lying on a jailhouse cot, not me.

I went into the kitchen to make us a coffee. "Instant okay?"

"Fine by me," he said.

We sat on the couch, blowing on our coffee. After a moment of silence, Amir said, "I owe you an apology. I should have known you would never say something so stupid, especially on camera."

I burst out laughing. "You know nothing of the sort. As you may recall, I have history in this particular field. I think we talked about it when you hired me."

"Yes, and at the time you told me it wouldn't happen again. And you were provoked when you lashed out at those idiots in Toronto. Now we're facing even worse idiots here. Way more dangerous, too."

"You mean Kyle and Peter."

"Not just them, Cat. They're pawns. There's something more alarming going on, something bigger." He looked over at me. "You remember that first year at Ravenhead, when the outhouse by the dock started to fall over, and nobody did anything about it until it collapsed with a camper inside?"

"Is this your way of saying Port Ellis is a shithole?"

I thought he'd laugh at that, but he didn't. "Sometimes I think this town is rotten from the inside. And everybody looks the other way because it's just easier."

"Or because they want the contract to rebuild the outhouse."

We drank our coffee and contemplated the weird twist of fate that had brought us back to the place where we'd started. At least, I contemplated it. I snuck a glance over at Amir. The setting sun came through my window at a slant and caught the flecks of amber in his eyes. He needed a haircut. Perhaps he even needed a nice girl to remind him to get a haircut, as she was running her hands through it.

He put his mug down on the coffee table, and turned to face me. "I hope you know that I trust you." He cleared his throat. "There's not many people I'd say that about."

That traitorous blush was creeping up my throat again. I wished I could say *I trust you too*, but the small matter of his semi-secret marriage had thrown rocks in that path. But I wanted to trust him, to tell him about all my fears and worries. I said, "Thank you for sending Gus my way. I give him an A-plus on the lawyer front."

"He's as solid as they come," Amir said. "I've never had a better friend. At least, not until I ended up back here."

He shut up abruptly, as if he'd said too much. There was too much silence between us, too many years. He was watching me intently, his gaze flickering between my eyes and my mouth. He was looking at me the way he had that one August night at the last dance of the season, the moon making diamonds on Lake Marjorie. We'd been out behind the bandstand. Seal was singing about a kiss from a rose when Amir leaned in and I leaned in and we met in a moment of pure longing. It was the best kiss I'd ever had, not that I'd ever admitted it to anyone. For decades, I barely admitted it to myself.

The moment had come again. I could feel it between us, the electricity that precedes lightning. I'd stopped breathing. I was suddenly stifling in my bathrobe, and there was a glisten of moisture on his upper lip. I could brush it away with my fingertips, with my lips. His head tilted toward mine—

meep meep meep meep

We sprang apart, shocked. "Stupid fucking phone,"

I hissed, which was not the kind of romantic expression recommended by Jane Austen. The phone was reminding me of my dinner date with my mother, which, frankly, was not where I wanted to be in an hour's time.

Amir dropped his head between his knees like a runner after a long race. When he popped up again, I was surprised to see that he was laughing. And that made me laugh too.

"Do you think the universe is trying to tell us something, Conway?"

"Maybe it's telling me I shouldn't sleep with my boss?"

He stood up, stretched, and tilted his head at me. The heat hadn't completely left his eyes, and I knew that if I took his hand that would be it, and my mother would have to find a different dinner partner. But he was my boss, and my friend, and my life was too tangled to accept new knots.

He went to the door and opened it. He leaned on the door frame and looked back at me. "I won't always be your boss."

CHAPTER 18

MY CHEEKS WERE still warm an hour later as I entered the Pinerock. I'd never savoured my own desire in younger days, treating it as an automatic reflex, an inexhaustible spring. Midlife, with its bouquet of stressors, aging parts, and scarce opportunities, had taught me otherwise. In spite of the complications with Amir, and there were many, I felt buoyant with possibility. Hopeful.

"Cat!"

So much for lust. Debbie Halloran had me in her sights. I squirmed inwardly. I'd owed her an apology before the video incident; now she likely thought I'd threatened her husband with a gruesome death.

"Debbie," I said. "The video is a fake. I'm so sorry. You must be upset."

"Not at all," she said. "I'm upset that someone did that to you, but otherwise, no. By the time I heard about the video, it had already been debunked. I think Gerry was disappointed. He would have liked to have a bigger fuss made about him."

I started to laugh, and Debbie joined me. Soon we were doubled over, hooting, the stress of the day finding a giddy outlet.

When we finally caught our breath, Debbie said, "I hate to spoil the mood, but I wanted to catch you for a reason. It's about your mother."

When is it not? I thought. I prepared to be told, yet again, that Debbie had identified another shortcoming in my maternal tending.

"We don't know each other that well, yet, but I care a lot about your mother. She's been a real personal inspiration to me, and I like to think that we've become friends during her stay."

"She definitely seems to like you," I agreed. "I owe you an apology, Debbie. My mom and I push each other's buttons. You're a lot better with her than I am. It got under my skin yesterday. I was rude and I regret it."

"I accept your apology," said Debbie. "And I understand. Families, well, they're complicated. I'm adopted, and I assumed for most of my life that whatever issues I had with my parents were a consequence of that. But then I had my own daughter, and god knows I love her, but she takes after her father and we drive each other nuts. Anyway. What I wanted to say is this: I've noticed some worrying signs while I've been with your mother this week. Bursts of anger, secrecy, mood swings. I'm going to come right out and say it, Cat. Is it possible that Marian is developing dementia?"

THE GLOOP ON my plate did not look much better than prison food: two oatmeal-coloured mounds of mush, a shrivelled beet, and three tiny shoots that appeared to have been pulled from the mommy plant too early.

"Designed to hyper-stimulate the biome," Lewis read off the menu. "Unprocessed and seed-oil free." His tone could shave bunions. He waved the menu in my face, as if I personally had banned seed oils from the kitchen. "These know-nothings will be the death of us!"

"I think this purée will kill us first," I muttered. Lewis had joined my mother and me for dinner at the Pinerock, and we had made the doomed decision to try the Welcome, Goddess tasting menu, which should have been called Four Weeds and a Foam. Beside me, Marian flung down her fork. "Catherine, I have no idea how you can make jokes at a time like this. With the smell of the jailhouse still on you."

I ducked my head toward my armpit—subtly, I hoped. I smelled like I always did, somewhere between fresh laundry and exhaustion. "Why did you think it was a good idea to threaten the mayor? I would have thought you had learned a lesson about the need to control your temper in public." She plucked a seedy roll from the basket and plunked it on my bread plate. "Fibre is good for an unmanageable temperament."

I resisted the temptation to hurl the bun at her. "I did not threaten the mayor, Mom. That video was manipulated to make it look like I'd said things I hadn't."

"Why would someone do such a thing?"

That was an excellent question, and one I was still puzzling over. Lewis, abandoning his struggle with the tenacious beet on his plate, came to my aid. "Marian, you know that we're in a period of great upheaval in the information ecosystem. Why, before I came to the conference, I had a group of students tell me that the Illuminati are real, and headquartered in the Denver airport. They'd seen a video about it on TikTok." He shoved his plate away. "The Information Revolution will be as disruptive as the Industrial Revolution, but instead of mechanized looms we have to contend with credulous citizens who don't have critical literacy skills."

Marian gave the beleaguered sigh of a woman who struggled with the burden of fame. "Soon there won't be very many of us who remember what life was like before the internet. For me, despite the dangers you mention, it's astonishing to be able to reach so many people with positive ideas. My ideas. We find friends and supporters in places we never would have expected. Debbie Halloran, for example. What a balm she has been these past few days." I could feel the unspoken end of that sentence: *while you've been rotting in the clink, ignoring your poor mother in her hour of need.* If my mother did indeed have dementia, her surgical ability to slice would be the last thing to go.

"The mayor's wife?" Lewis asked. "Quite lovely, with dark hair? I saw her a few times in the background of my Zoom calls with Gerry."

The exhausted haze in my brain vanished with his words. How had this professor from Alberta ended up on a first-name basis with the sleazy mayor of our little town? I asked Lewis the question, though I omitted the judgmental adjective.

"Mayor Halloran was actually quite generous with his time, once I'd outlined the parameters of my article," he said. "It's not every town that becomes besieged by a small group of crackpots."

"Is *crackpot* the academic term?" Marian asked dryly. She was fidgeting in her seat, a gesture I knew well. When Marian was ready to go, the whole family had to follow. She'd once walked out of my grade-six Christmas concert because a badly tuned trumpet had offended her ears.

"Believers in outlandish conspiracies, then," Lewis

allowed. "The mayor had a stake in trying to understand their behaviour, obviously. And, if I may be so immodest, he realized that I could help him in that regard."

Unless he was actually fuelling those conspiracy theories, I thought. Agitating from within. Controlling the crackpots for his own gain. I thought again about Kyle Johnson. What if he was "assisting" Mayor Halloran with a special project? I was about to probe Lewis further, but Marian abruptly stood up. She must really have been jonesing for a smoke. "It's been a delightful evening, Lewis. But I'm afraid Catherine and I have a long-standing date upstairs with five handsome men."

WHAT MY MOTHER had failed to mention was that the handsome men were confined to the screen, where they pampered and primped a hapless father of six who'd lost his mojo. *Queer Eye* was our Switzerland, our Christmas truce. As I'd told Danilo, it was the place my mother and I laid down arms and took up peanut M&M's.

On TV, Jonathan Van Ness was attempting to explain how the sad dad had lost interest in personal hygiene. "Struggling to function," Jonathan said. "Strugz to func is what he is." Beside me on the bed, my mother cackled. "Strugz to func," she echoed, turning to look at me. In case I'd missed her point, she dug her elbow into my ribs.

I put a peanut M&M in my mouth, which was healthier than biting my tongue. At one stage in my life, I would have struck back, wounded. But the benefit of being forty-five is that there's more ballast in your trunk. You don't tend to skid into overreaction quite the same way. And Marian was right, in a way. By certain metrics—let's say the standard of the tennis club, where Marian and Stewart engaged in competitive parenting—I was struggling to function. I barely scraped by, paycheque to paycheque. I was divorced. I spent a lot of time reporting about sewage. And we could not ignore the fact that I had just spent a day in jail.

Yet, on all the levels that mattered to me, I was doing fine. My son had rediscovered the pleasure of my company, and I no longer had to bribe him to visit. I was proud of my reporting, even if it had proved personally costly. I was surrounded by new friends. Possibly even one who was more than a friend. For once, I had a small lump sum in the bank, thanks to my consultation fee from the Hollywood executives producing the Eliot Fraser film. Granted, I was going through it rather more quickly than I wanted to, but in the big picture, I was functioning like a well-oiled machine.

I wasn't about to start that fight with Marian.

Instead, I turned to her and quite ostentatiously sniffed. Immediately she bolted upright and lifted her sweater to her nose. "Wait," she said in alarm. "Do I smell?"

I shrugged, a gesture she would understand. Despite the fact that she'd opened the window, letting the frosty October night in, she did indeed stink of tobacco. I don't know how many cigarettes she'd managed to smoke while she was outside after our dinner, but she smelled worse than Don Draper at the end of a five-martini night.

"Oh dear," she said, and leapt out of the bed. "I'm going to have a quick shower."

Once I heard the taps running, I got up and muted *Queer Eye*. I walked over to the window and grasped the old-fashioned wooden frame. Outside, it was still overcast. I could barely make out the hill rising steeply toward the lookout on my right. The hill that Bliss had walked up on the last night of her life. Why? Who had she been meeting? And who had been angry enough to send her plummeting to her death? I was loath to give Debbie any detective points, but she was right about one thing. Marian was behaving very strangely.

Shivering, I tugged the frame until it shuddered closed. I crossed my arms to keep in my body heat. A tiny wisp of steam curled up from the bottom of the bathroom door, but it wasn't enough to heat the room. The suite came with a set of matching white bathrobes, plush and warm. Marian had taken one into the bathroom with her, so the other must be in the closet.

I opened the door of the closet, and the delicate scent of Chanel No. 5 drifted out. A comfort and a pain, that scent. During my childhood, its absence meant my mother was gone; when I sensed it again, I'd rush out of my room to find her, returned to us once more.

I rifled through the clothes on the hangers—pant-suit, pantsuit, Lululemon tracksuit. But no bathrobe. I looked on the top shelf, but there was only an iron and an extra blanket. I flipped through the clothes again, yanking them to one side so I could search the dark corners of the closet. An ironing board leaned against the wall, and in the dimness, I could see something soft and pale crumpled in a ball beneath it. I bent and tugged it free.

Then I saw what it was, and hurled it away with a shriek. Behind me, I heard the bathroom door opening, and whirled around.

"Where did you get this?"

It came out sounding angrier than I'd intended. My mother paused in the doorway of the bathroom, wrapped in her Pinerock robe. The hand she'd been using to towel her hair grew still. She stared at me, and then at the object next to me on the bed. Her eyes were huge.

It was a pale cashmere cloak, identical to the one that Clarity had been wearing during the conference. Exactly like the one she had shown me in her room. Except instead of the initials *CK*, this cloak had a different monogram embroidered on the silk lining. Two elaborate *B*s, intertwined.

"Mom? You need to tell me what the hell is going on."

Marian was still staring at the cloak as if she'd never seen it before. For one wild moment, I wondered if Debbie might be right to worry about senility. The caginess might just be forgetfulness. The wandering off might not be sinister, it might just be … wandering off.

Because the alternative was too horrible to contemplate.

"Oh, Catherine," she whispered. She sat down on the bed next to me. She ran a finger over the cloak, and I wanted to yell at her not to touch it, that it was evidence. Evidence the police should already have seen. The garment was mud-streaked, and bits of grass clung to it. All of it evidence; all of it potentially pointing to a murderer.

Marian must have had the same thought because she tucked her hands in her lap. "You know how you said at dinner that the video of you threatening the mayor wasn't what it seemed? That you hadn't said those things? Well, this is the same thing."

"Mom, you can't deepfake a robe. It's right here in front of us." My voice was climbing. "Did you follow Bliss that night? Did you grab it off her?"

"Oh my god, no. Of course not!"

"Well, it's here in your room, Mom. And not in the possession of the OPP. So you'd better start talking."

Marian got up and began pacing the room. On TV, the *Queer Eye* crew were silently celebrating their latest win for fabulousness. I did not feel fabulous. I felt sick to my stomach, and panic-stricken. My mother strode over to the minibar, yanked out a half-bottle of red wine, and unscrewed the top. She sloshed most of it into a coffee mug. No time for stemware. Now I knew for sure something was wrong.

She slumped into a chair by the window and gulped down her wine. After a minute, she said, "I had nothing to do with that girl's death. But I did do something foolish."

I waited. My mother always took her own time, like cold ketchup leaving the bottle.

Finally, she sighed. "It was Clarity I was hoping to talk to. I was out having a cigarette when I saw someone in a robe heading into the woods. I assumed it was her. But she was moving so quickly that I soon lost sight of her. I swear I didn't follow her up the hill."

"Why did you want to speak to Clarity? Because you thought she was writing the shitty reviews of your book?"

Marian stood, retrieving the wine bottle. She poured the remainder into her mug. "I haven't been entirely frank with you. Or with your father. Or the world." She closed her eyes. "I-I'm something of a fraud, I'm afraid."

She seemed to be shrinking before my eyes, no longer a powerhouse but suddenly a wizened old lady. It was horrifying to witness. "You see, Clarity wasn't just my intern at the thinktank. She was a talented writer. She was able to breathe life into reports about the most mundane things. Trade infractions. International water disputes. So when I was starting my first book, and it was so difficult—so hard ..." she lapsed into silence.

"Clarity was your ghostwriter," I said.

Marian's face seemed to melt. "If anyone found out," she said. "If they knew ... I'd be ruined."

"Mom, for god's sake. All sorts of people use a ghostwriter."

Some of my mother's spirit returned, and she said, waspishly, "Not when your entire message is gutsy self-determination." She drained the mug, turning it almost upside down to get the last dregs. "I just wanted Camilla to promise me that she wouldn't say a word, ever."

My thoughts were raging. If my mother had lied about this, what else had she lied about? Was her beloved image important enough to kill for? Had she shoved Bliss off the lookout, thinking she was Clarity?

"I don't understand," I said. "If you didn't follow the person you thought was Clarity up the hill, how did you end up with this cloak?"

"I wandered around the grounds for at least an hour looking for her," Marian said. "I was in a panic. And I must have smoked half a pack, but it didn't help my nerves. I decided I'd climb up the lookout path, but I'd only gone a short distance when I found the cloak at the base of a tree."

"And you just decided to take it?"

"I still thought it was Clarity's, at that point. Maybe it was important enough to her that I could use it as a bargaining chip." Marian looked at me, and for once her expression didn't convey disappointment or irritation. It was full of fear.

"I may be an idiot," she said. "Possibly even a fraud. But I am not a murderer."

CHAPTER 19

I WAS STILL fretting about Marian the next morning. My mother was in serious trouble—potentially an improvement over dementia, but in my view too early to call. I'd spent a long day behind bars, and it wasn't the five-star experience Marian preferred. The best thing I could do to help her was find a better suspect.

And where better to start than at the top? I locked my bike to a gas meter and stood looking at the sign on the frosted glass of Gerry Halloran's radio station on the edge of town. The radio station shared a building with a mixed martial arts studio, a dentist's office, and a fish-and-chip shop called the Highest Perch.

I took off my helmet, put it in my backpack, and let the cool morning air ruffle my hair. There were places

I'd rather be, like hunting for snakes in the Australian Outback. But there was a job to do, and it wasn't going to do itself. I pushed open the door.

The reception area was empty, its walls lined with photos of Gerry Halloran and various people who had once identified as celebrities. "Is that Hulk Hogan?" I asked the young man behind the reception desk, who sat with the stiffly alert posture of an on-duty meerkat. He looked up at the photo and nodded. "Mayor Halloran had Mr. Hogan on his show during Monster Truck Days. In 2019, I believe." The young man's mouth snapped shut as if he'd already given too much away.

I stepped closer, resting my elbows on the edge of the counter, next to a guest book open to that day's date. "I wonder if it might be possible to speak with the mayor? I believe he's here today for his radio show."

The young man's mouth pursed. "Do you have an appointment? Because the mayor—"

"You can tell him it's Cat Conway." At the sound of my name, his face grew slack with surprise. I saw him try to do the mental math: how could this pleasant middle-aged lady in a sweater and cargo pants possibly be the Medusa who'd swearily threatened the life of his boss? I put on my most harmless smile, just to mess with him a bit more.

"I'll see what I can do," he said. I'd hoped he might leave the desk so that I could leaf through the visitors' book, but he just swivelled his chair away from me and had a whispered conversation on his phone. I snuck a peek at the book, trying to use my forearm to quietly slide the page back. The receptionist whirled around and said, "The mayor can see you in a few moments. Would you like to take a seat?"

He indicated a shabby couch sitting next to a fern that looked like it had needed a drink since Brian Mulroney ran things. I nodded and picked up my backpack, playing for time. The dust motes caught in the morning sun gave me an idea. I coughed, putting my hand up to my throat. The young man watched me, indifferent. I coughed again, and a third time. By the fourth cough I'd gone full Meryl Streep, clawing at the air. "Water," I managed to whisper. The receptionist leapt from his seat, panicked. He disappeared through a door behind the desk.

I had maybe a minute, tops. I dropped my backpack and flipped to the previous day's page, then the one before that. Would Kyle's name be in there? If he was in league with the mayor, maybe he'd bypass the book when he visited. No trace left behind.

I let out another hacking cough, my finger flying down the pages. Even Debbie signed in when she visited. No Kyle, though. I was about to flip back to today's page when I saw a name that stopped me cold. My finger traced the huge, looping letters. *Bliss B.*

The door opened and the receptionist came out again, holding a glass of water. He stared at me, and then at the guest book, and handed me the glass. I took a deep gulp, imagining that I was Meryl Streep recovering from a coughing fit.

"The mayor will see you now," the receptionist said, and buzzed me through a turnstile beside him. It seemed like a lot of security for a small-town radio station; it seemed like the kind of security you'd need when you'd made a lot of enemies.

I put on my best neutral face as I walked down a corridor, which ended in an open lounge space with rooms branching off to the side. Through an open door, I saw a soundproofed studio, an engineer wearing headphones bent over a control panel.

The mayor was waiting for me in the lounge. He was tall, built like a grain silo to last the years. He had a greying crewcut, which made him look a few years older than Debbie. He wore a suit but no tie, an affectation of casualness, and he smelled like the interior of a brand-new luxury sedan. Like me, he was wearing an expression that he'd just slapped on, but he had much more experience and his showed a practised congeniality.

"Mayor Halloran," I said, extending my hand. "Thank you so much for seeing me on such short notice."

"Anything for our friends at the *Quill*," he said, and I was amazed that a lightning bolt didn't strike him dead. He hated the *Quill*, and wanted it for his own.

We both knew it, and we both smiled through our lies. He indicated a sofa by the window, and we sat down.

"I just wanted to clear the air," I said. "About what happened at the protesters' camp. The video that surfaced was a hoax. Of course I would never say those things. It had been doctored to make it look as if I was threatening you."

He leaned back, spread his arms wide over the back of the sofa, an explorer taking in his conquered territory. "I gather that's what the police believe."

"Because it's the truth." I tried to keep the testiness out of my voice.

He shrugged. "I'm not much of one for modern technology. I've still got a flip phone, and everyone in town's got my number." This was true: the fact that anyone in town could reach him at any time to complain about a pothole or a broken traffic light was one of his signature policies. I liked to think of it as an opaque curtain of transparency. There was so much hidden behind.

"Or they can call in to your show," I said. "It's a great way for people to reach you."

He inclined his head, a humble acknowledgement of his popularity.

"You're obviously very busy," I continued. I stopped to take a sip from the glass I'd brought with me. "Being mayor, obviously. Your radio station, which I understand you'd like to expand beyond Port Ellis. It's even been said you might be building a media empire."

The genial expression began to unpeel from his face like sagging wallpaper. "Is this an interview? Because if it is you'll have to go through our communications office—"

"No, no, of course not. I'm just here on my apology tour." We both knew that he had not given the *Quill* an interview since our anti-vaccine series had run. "I guess I'm just curious about some things. Like, for example, what you were doing out at the protesters' encampment the night I visited. I saw your truck pulling out."

He was working valiantly to keep his tone warm. "Is there anything wrong with meeting with your constituents? Especially ones who have vocal grievances? I was trying to bring the temperature down. For the sake of peace in the town."

The practised smile again. He was daring me to contradict him, to call him out. He had a bully's confidence that the game would always be his, no matter how it was won. I wondered how Debbie had managed to tolerate him for all these years. I thought of the name in the guest book, my ace in the hole.

"I was wondering if you wanted to say anything about Bliss Bondar?"

Now he wore a mask of concern. "A terrible business. Shocking. That poor young woman. I'm glad to see the police working so diligently to find the culprit."

"What did you think of her?"

He shrugged again. "I can't really say. They seemed

like lovely young women but"—he spread his big hands—"I can't really say I know much about aromatherapy and the like."

You lying, disingenuous asshole, I thought. But of course that's not what I said. "So you didn't know her? I'm just curious because her name is out there in your guest book. She visited the station."

The mask didn't so much slip as crash to the ground. Halloran pushed to his feet, towering over me. But the inner politician saved him, and he managed to find another smile. "As you must know, this is a busy place. Regular train station. Lots of people come in to record interviews." He extended a hand to me in farewell. "If you want to talk further, feel free to call my office."

LATER THAT MORNING I was back at the *Quill*, putting the finishing touches on an essay about being the subject of a cyber-hoax. I'd cycled home first to pick up my car, trailed all the way by a creeping sensation that someone was following me. Or maybe it was just a cloud of lies that I couldn't shake off.

I looked over at Hannah, who was hunched over her computer, chipping away at an equally painful personal story about the underside of new technology. She was a self-taught expert on deepfakes, after an ex-boyfriend had pasted her face into a porn video and circulated it. It went some way to explaining why this bright light had chosen to intern with a tiny local paper instead of racking up contacts in Toronto.

She'd needed a break, she told me. Every time she caught someone looking at her—in a café, at the library, at a concert—she'd wondered if they were imagining her naked. It had messed with her head. And, she said, you could see the stars here. Kaydence had taken her to the dark sky preserve in Hawker Jetty in September. No bugs, no human noise, only the sounds of night creatures and an immensity that finally silenced the voices in her head.

I got up and stretched. In the kitchen I boiled the kettle and put a vanilla tea bag in a mug, pouring the water over. Hannah's favourite. She looked up when I set it down beside her and gave me a wobbly smile of thanks. It was horrible writing these stories about yourself; horrible to swim through the muck of the past again.

Back at my desk, I tried to make my thoughts stand in a straight line. What had Bliss been doing at Gerry Halloran's radio station? If they were having an affair, I'd eat my keypad. I couldn't imagine her tastes ran to small-town politicians with delusions of grandeur. I didn't believe that she'd been there for an interview, either: there was nothing on the station's website to indicate that she'd ever spoken to anyone there.

None of it made sense. Which meant I had to start back at the beginning. I opened the Welcome, Goddess website, hoping the goddesses might shed some light for once. Some of their pandemic podcasts had generated a surprising number of views and comments. I put on a set of headphones and selected one on Parenting through Uncertainty. I wasn't sure what either Bliss or Bree purported to know about child-rearing, but the guest, Dr. Melissa Wainfleet, had a PhD and a *New York Times* bestseller, so I figured it wouldn't be a complete waste of a half-hour.

BREE: Thanks so much for joining us today, Dr. Melissa. I was fascinated by your book, *Even Unicorns Do Fractions*, about how parents are struggling to adapt to a scary and rapidly changing world. In your words, "we've created a false dichotomy in which parents feel that they have to become either entertainers, softening the impact of the pandemic by making each day a series of magical and memorable childhood experiences; or parodies of nineteenth-century one-room schoolhouse teachers, hitching their sanity to a rigid adherence to formal lesson plans." Now, I don't have children, but I definitely see what you're talking about when I look at my friends with kids. Would you like to—

BLISS: What do you think about the government closing the schools and demanding that kids get vaccinated? Don't you think that's trampling on our human rights?

DR. MELISSA: Um, well, I think it's a question of checks and balances. We have to use the available information to make the best choices for parents and kids.

BLISS: So you support the government forcing our kids to be poisoned?

DR. MELISSA: That is not at all what my book is about. Did you read it?

BLISS: No.

DR. MELISSA: It's possible that you didn't fully understand my point, then.

BLISS: Why should I? You don't understand mine.

BREE: Dr. Melissa, let's talk about how parents find a style that works for them and their values in the midst of so much contradictory information.

DR. MELISSA: I'd love to do that, but I feel I should address the point about vaccination. I don't want to participate in letting misinformation stand. We know the science of vaccination. We know that kids are safer when they are vaccinated.

BLISS: Don't they have a right to go to school?

BREE: Let's let Dr. Melissa talk about her book, Bliss.

BLISS: Her book is about parents and choice, right?

DR. MELISSA: Yes.

BLISS: That's what I'm talking about too. Parents being allowed to make choices and not being tools of the government.

DR. MELISSA: If I could just say, I think that parents need to make choices within the parameters of evidence-based research on child development and public health. It's not a free-for-all.

BLISS: Are you calling me stupid?

BREE: I think we'll wrap there. Thank you so much for tuning in, everyone. Again, Dr. Melissa's book is *Even Unicorns Do Fractions* and it's really good. You should read it.

I took off my headphones and stretched my neck to one side and then the other, trying to release the tension that had infected me simply by listening. What must it have been like to try to work alongside Bliss?

I scrolled through the comments. The vast majority echoed Bliss's position: *Our kids are not your science. Fear is the real virus. No more mandates.* Occasionally a brave voice would dissent and raise the concept of herd immunity, only to be taunted by other commenters writing *baaaa* or *poison your kid then, not mine.*

An exchange between Bliss and one of her fans caught my eye.

ALLISONP: Bliss, you are so right and I'm sorry that Bree doesn't get it! Stay strong.

BLISS: thank u angel. dont u worry, im fighting for u and yr rights.

ALLISONP: It's so hard. My parents don't understand and I have to keep them away from my daughter because they are so judgy. I won't put that poison into my precious girl.

BLISS: you are doing the right thing. love u.

ALLISONP: Your support gets me through the day. Please don't quit even if Bree is a bitch to you. Your voice matters!

BLISS: id never quit no matter what. over my dead body.

Had it come to that? I thought back to my earlier encounter with Bree and Bodhi. Exactly what legal arrangements had the women made, anticipating a future end to their partnership? Whatever they were, I guessed that Bree was better off in a scenario where her partner died than in one where Bliss forced a division of company assets during her life.

"Hey, Bruce," I said, beckoning him over. I showed him AllisonP's conversation with Bliss. "I don't think we've pushed Bree hard enough. She has a better motive than anyone. I'm going to take another run at her. Care to take a ride out to the Pinerock?"

"Sorry, Cat," he said. "Hannah's struggling with this story—it's so personal. I told her I'd give it a read-through." He smiled at me. "Don't tell me you're afraid? You can take them. They live on micronutrients alone."

"I'm a big girl," I agreed.

He gave me a thumbs-up and returned to Hannah's desk. In his own understated way, he was telling me to suck it up. He knew I didn't need a babysitter, and he wasn't going to coddle me now that I was out of danger. He was right. I grabbed my jacket and my trusty backpack and hit the road.

I was miserable anyway, so I turned on the radio and tuned in to Gerry Halloran's station. He was talking—surprise, surprise—about me. "I don't know about all this deepfake nonsense," he said. "The police

explained it to me, but it sounds like some clever lawyer took them for a ride, if you ask me. Now, you all
know that I respect our friends in law enforcement—
they do a great job for us. I'm just saying that there
should be consequences for people who threaten duly
elected officials such as myself. But the corporate
media doesn't think the law should apply to them.
And they wonder why we don't trust them! What do
you all think? Let's go to caller number one."

I punched at my radio and made Gerry's voice
disappear.

CHAPTER 20

BREE WAS ONSTAGE, giving one of the final seminars of the ill-fated convention. I slipped into the room and stood by the door. Bodhi had folded his muscular body into a chair in the front row. He glanced at me but didn't try to throw me out. Small wins.

Bree looked even paler than usual. She was seated on a high stool, on a riser, in front of her audience. I worried that she might topple over. She was reading off a set of PowerPoint slides on the topic of medical misogyny and women's role in managing their own fertility. The content should have been thrilling both in its outrage for past and present practices, and in its optimism for the future, but Bree was flat and tired and her audience drooped. As she wrapped up to luke-warm applause, Bodhi bounded to her side.

"This is a fantastic new direction for Welcome, Goddess! We all know that women's bodies are sacred and full of wonder, yes?"

The audience mumbled.

"I can't hear you!" Bodhi cupped a hand to his ear.

"Yes!" called the audience, stirring in their seats.

"Bree's expertise in chemistry is going to change the fertility game and put the power in women's hands where it belongs!"

"Yes!"

"Welcome, Goddess supplements are only the first step in the revolution! Are you with us?" Bodhi cried.

"YES!" The audience roared and clapped.

"Thank you for being here today," Bree said, into her microphone. "Your support means so much to me."

The energy dropped again and the crowd dispersed, but now at least they seemed to be awake and smiling. Bodhi had saved the day. But why?

I approached Bree as Bodhi helped her down from the stool. "Could I have a quick word?" I asked.

"No," said Bodhi. "Bree is tired. You can make an appointment."

"It's fine, Larry," she said. "Let's sit for a minute." She took a chair from the front row, moved it so that it faced another one, and then sank into it. I wasn't sure why she'd agreed to speak to me now, when she'd been refusing all along. Had my badgering worked? Was she just exhausted? Or had she decided that the best way to throw me off the scent was to lay a false trail?

She gestured for me to join her. "What would you like to know?"

"Were you aware that Bliss was in discussions with Clarity K about breaking up the company?"

Bree glanced at Bodhi. "No comment."

"On the night Bliss died, she was wearing a cloak identical to Clarity's Creativity Cocoon. At least one person mistook Bliss for Clarity that night. Is it possible that you followed her as well, thinking she was Clarity? Did you want to confront Clarity about her efforts to destroy your business?"

Bodhi's face was red and furious. "That's enough," he said, stepping between us. "You've got a fucking nerve."

"Larry, stop. Don't sink to her level." Bree raised a hand to his waist and gently pushed him to the side so that we were face to face again. "I have three things to say to you, and all of them are off the record," she said. She held up a finger. "One: Welcome, Goddess has been extremely good to me personally. I'm not living paycheque to paycheque. I don't have to work ever again if I don't want to. And candidly, I was never interested in being in the public eye. That was all Bliss." She held up a second finger. "Two: The company employs a lot of people who are not in my fortunate financial position. So if you really believe Bliss died because of her plans to fold the business, you should be looking at our employees, not at me." She extended a third finger.

"Three: I wasn't climbing up to the lookout, not that night or any other. I've been on bedrest most of the week. I'm allowed up for a couple of hours a day to do events and that's it. Doctor's orders."

Maybe she and Bodhi were better matched than I'd thought. They both knew how to throw other people under the bus. Was she talking about Danilo? That seemed like the obvious conclusion. I liked Danilo, but maybe it was a case of traumatic bonding—I'd saved the guy's life, after all.

As for her final point, I was pretty sure I understood what Bree was signalling. There were only so many reasons a doctor would put a young, healthy woman on bedrest. I glanced down, and sure enough Bree's hand rested lightly on her abdomen. I pictured a world with even more tiny Larrys on the loose, wreaking havoc.

At least Bree could afford a nanny.

A HALF-HOUR LATER I had a call from Amir. He told me that he wanted to see me, but there were a few convoy trucks circling the *Quill* building, so I should meet him at Glenda's. The subject of this meeting was unclear. Did my monkey brain rush to fill the void? It ran shrieking in circles.

Maybe he wanted to tell me that I was fired (unlikely) or that the paper was closing for good (more likely) or that he wanted to give me a raise (about the same possibility as an asteroid obliterating Port Ellis). Or maybe he was going to tell me that his divorce from Julia was final, and that he regretted keeping the secret from me in the first place.

Death by asteroid seemed a safer bet.

As soon as I entered Glenda's, I was wrapped in a blanket of delicious aromas. I had started to think of it as the smell of home—much more than Chanel No. 5. I felt a twinge as a particularly pungent note of cinnamon hit my nose. Was this home? If so, for how long? No *Quill*, no job. I'd be forced back to the big city with my tail between my legs. My poor tail needed to spend a bit more time in the air first.

Amir had found a table in the corner, and I weaved my way through the crowded space to reach him. A cappuccino sat on the table in front of my chair, beside an almond biscotti.

"Someone else is joining us," Amir said.

"Who?"

"You'll see in a second. But it'll be a good meeting, I think. And it's thanks to you." He gave me an unusually smug smile. The secrecy irritated me. Bletchley Park Amir was a new development, and I wasn't sure I liked it.

"Sorry I'm late." A man dropped into the empty chair beside us. He looked familiar, but then he also looked like half the men in town: a baseball cap, a beard, a dark polo shirt. I peered more closely and saw the logo of Flannery's grocery store—a singing tomato—on his chest.

"Aaron Flannery," he said, and held out his hand to me. "I read your story online this morning. The one about the deepfakes. It was wild." He shook his head. "What a crazy goddamn world we live in."

I nodded my thanks but didn't say anything. So this was Aaron Flannery of the Flannerys who had shafted the *Quill*. Who had cancelled their lucrative ad contract with the paper. Cutting us adrift. Although this Flannery didn't look old enough, or insane enough, to be in a prayer group with Peter Johnson.

"Can I get you a coffee?" Amir asked, but Aaron said he was fine, and that he couldn't stay very long. Aaron leaned over toward me. "Your story today really hit home. Last year our computer system got hacked pretty bad. All the customers' data was compromised."

"We'd heard that," Amir said. "Bruce chased that story for weeks but he couldn't pin it down."

"My dad pulled every string to keep it quiet," Aaron said. "But in the end that just meant shoppers got mad. They thought we were keeping secrets from them, which we were. And we lost lots of customers to SaveFest, of all places." His face twisted. "I mean, have you seen their produce?"

I still had no idea where this was going. I dunked my biscotti and waited. Aaron slid the salt shaker from hand to hand. Finally he said, "Between us, I'm not sure all of my dad's decisions are good for the company." He shot a glance up at me from under his ball cap. "Like cancelling our ad campaign because some lamebrain said we should." A blush ran up his neck. "The lamebrain is not my dad, in case anyone asks."

I tapped the side of my nose, and Flannery chuckled. "I've told Amir that Flannery's will reinstate its ad buy. And we're thinking of producing a special flyer at Christmas, and hoping the *Quill* will distribute it."

Amir now looked like a cat who had bypassed the canary and eaten an ostrich instead. The grin brought an adorable, rarely sighted dimple to his cheek. "Thank you, Aaron. It means a great deal to us."

"And you really do have the best tomatoes," I said. "But your stores need more bike racks." Aaron laughed again, said he'd bring it up at the next operations meeting, and waved farewell. Once he'd gone, Amir pumped his fist, a boyish moment of triumph.

"Good job, boss," I said, returning to my biscotti.

"It's all you, Cat. Your deepfake story triggered some remorse tripwire in him." He reached over and clasped my forearm. I felt the warmth of his hand on my skin. Suddenly it was stiflingly hot in Glenda's. My eyes rose to meet his.

"Is this chair being used?"

The voice, tight with stress, burst my little happiness bubble. I looked up to see Jenny Baker-Rubin,

surrounded by whirling children. "It's free," I said.
"And we're just about to go, so you can have this
table." Jenny looked as if she were about to burst into
tears with gratitude, and she went to the counter to
order. It occurred to me that if I sat with Jenny for a
little chinwag, she might open up about Bodhi and
his wandering pleasure gong. "I'll see you back at the
newsroom later," I said to Amir.

"Great. I presume you're working on a follow to
the Bondar story? But don't forget the feature on the
seventy-fifth anniversary of Pepley's Pumpkin Patch.
It's also Great-Granny Pepley's one hundredth birthday. They're making a carrot cake the size of an suv."

"The glamorous life of a local news reporter," I
said. "I've already been in touch with the Pepleys, and
I'm heading to the patch next week." Amir turned to
go, the smile still lighting his face. I liked smiley Amir
better than secretive Amir, but if you shone a bright
light in my eyes I'd cave and admit that I liked both
of them quite a lot.

I walked over to the bathroom, waving to Glenda,
who was frantically buttering a bagel behind the
counter. She grimaced in return, hands flying. If I
ended up short on dough, I could always pick up a
few shifts at the bakery. Where I would spend my days
making bad puns.

When I came back out, I saw that Jenny's children
were busy at their table making a fort out of sugar

packets and salt shakers. Their mother stood by the front window, clutching a coffee mug, her gaze lost in space. I recognized the look: a woman experiencing the nirvana of child-free time.

Back at the counter, I asked Megan for a plate of rocky road triple-fudge brownies and brought them over to the table. Two of the tiny Baker-Rubins lunged for the treats. A third was under the table, manically shaking its legs. I broke off a piece and handed it to her. She snatched it from my hand and stuffed it into her brownie hole.

I left them to their games and walked over to Jenny. She said, "That was very kind of you, thanks."

"You might be paying for it later. I think I just filled their tanks with super unleaded."

She gave me the ghost of a smile. "I'll bring them to Larry's room tonight. He can experience the joys of the midnight stuffy hunt for a change."

Up close, I could see that she was wearing two different earrings. Probably not a fashion trend; more likely the result of dog-tired hands fumbling around in the pre-dawn gloom. She jerked her chin toward the table and said, "You really seem to enjoy the kids. Not a lot of people do."

Her honesty deserved the same from me. "Look, Jenny, I'm trying to put the pieces of this story together. I don't need to quote you directly, but I am trying to figure out what was happening between the

Goddesses. And your husband—well, he seems to be playing a role."

She snorted. "Goddesses. You mean like in Ancient Greece? The ones who were always messing with mortals' lives? No matter what the cost?"

"Is that what you think Bliss and Bree were doing?"

"I felt sorry for Bliss," she said. "She thought she was in charge but really she was just a puppet. And then somebody cut her strings."

I kept my mouth shut. I noticed that the hand clutching her mug was white with tension. "It's the other one who's a monster. Playing at being so superior and serene. Let's see how serene she is at three a.m. when she's all alone at feeding time."

Then she stopped, abruptly. She shot me a sideways look: Had I received her message?

I had. She was telling me that the behaviour of goddesses had not improved very much since ancient times. They were still playing with mortals for sport.

CHAPTER 21

THERE WAS ONLY one person—aside from Bliss and Bree themselves—who knew the truth about their relationship, and I was determined to get him to talk. I'd brought my version of truth serum, too. I knocked on his hotel room door.

I was shocked to see Danilo's decline. His eyes were bloodshot, but more disturbingly, he was wearing a plain grey tracksuit, the type issued in minimum-security prisons. He'd accessorized it with bejewelled loafers, but still. I handed him the box of crullers before asking a single question.

He waved me inside. "You win," he said. "I don't have the energy to resist you. I'll tell you what you want to know, but everything's off the record."

I took a seat by the window. Danilo placed the doughnuts on the bedside table and then stretched out on the bed, his head resting on two pillows and his arms folded across his chest like a medieval tomb effigy. "This has been the worst week of my life, and that's saying something," he told me. "My therapist says I can't set boundaries." He gave me a dark look, and then rolled onto his side and reached for the bakery box. "This is a perfect example."

"Since I'm here, though …"

He extracted a doughnut, chewed contemplatively for a few seconds, and then swallowed. "You want real talk? Here it is: the company was imploding. On the one side, you had Bliss conspiring with Clarity K to build a spiritual empire—although if you ask me, Clarity was planning on strip-mining Bliss for followers and then dumping her within a year. Clarity's an evil genius; you can't trust a word that comes out of her mouth. On the other side, Bree was sneaking around with Bodhi. She wanted to get away from the woo-woo stuff and break into the market for nutritional supplements and generally be more science-y. But then Bodhi knocked her up and the pregnancy turned out to be high-risk, and she ended up on bedrest. She insisted on coming to this conference against her doctor's orders because she didn't want to give Bliss an advantage in their little war."

Danilo finished his first doughnut and licked his fingers clean. He hesitated momentarily before plucking a second one from the box. "Has anyone told me any of this directly? No. I know it because I'm a professional-level eavesdropper. The best around. Also because all four of them took me aside and told me— hush, hush—that even if there were changes in the Welcome, Goddess empire, I'd still have a job. A job! I can get one of those on my own, thank you very much. Don't do me any favours." He sniffed, then said plaintively, "I was invested, you know?"

I did. I'd seen countless others fall for this late-capitalist shell game. I knew without asking that Danilo had thrown himself into Bliss and Bree's world, staying up late, sacrificing his personal time, skipping vacations—giving his all to execute their precious vision. His brilliance had earned reputational and financial gains for the company. He was an invisible hand, a consummate insider, a backroom star. But ultimately, he was an employee. An asset, not an actor. He didn't own any part of the creation he'd brought to vivid life. It belonged to Bree now, and she could do whatever she liked with it, including selling it off for parts.

I also thought about what Bree had said about employees having a motive. Danilo's tale of exclusion and resentment had just put him into the frame. I wondered if he was telling me the truth about Bliss. It sounded like she'd been listening a lot more to her personal brand advisor, whoever they were, than to Danilo. Would she really have promised him a job?

"Do you think Bree killed her?" I asked.

"Not on her own," he said. "She's really fragile with the pregnancy and everything. But when you factor Bodhi in, it's possible. He's a mega-dick. The way he treats his wife and kids is disgusting. I bet he thinks Jenny will give him an alibi but that is so not happening. She hates his guts."

I had to agree. "Has he been staying in Bree's room for the entire conference?"

Danilo nodded. "I can't believe Bree hasn't figured out that he's in it for the money. Sure, Bodhi could have shoved Bliss off a cliff, no doubt about it. Have you seen his arms? He did not get those the natural way. If I had to bet, I'd say he had a fit of 'roid rage, killed Bliss, and then told Bree he did it for her and the baby. He's that kind of guy. Total gaslighter." Danilo finished his final cruller and lay back down, exhausted. "That's my story. Now, if you'll excuse me, I need a nap."

I told him I respected his boundaries. In truth, I knew I'd be back once I'd done some further digging into his story.

As I stepped outside his room, my backpack started ringing. I dug inside for my phone. "Dad?" I said, seeing his name on the screen. "Can I call you back in a few minutes?" It would be a good tonic to put my feet up for a half-hour and play word games with my father, I thought. I headed in the direction of the stairs.

"No," he said. His voice was tight and strained.

"Are you okay?" I asked. As a rule, my father was endlessly accommodating. Married to my mother, it was the difference between survival and a slow death of the soul.

"I'm fine," he said. "But I'm worried about your mother. I haven't been able to reach her in hours. It's not like her, Cat. And she hasn't been herself the last few days. I need you to find her and make sure she's safe."

"Why wouldn't she be? Is this about the reviews of her book online? She's really bugging out, which doesn't make any sense. It's not like she cares about other people's opinions."

My father hesitated for a moment. Finally, he said, "She just has a bunch of things on her mind. She's fretting. And your mom's not a fretter."

Now my ears were fully pricked. "Fretting about what? What's going on, Dad?"

"It's not my story to tell. Once you've found her … well, maybe we can have a talk."

I promised my father I'd hunt Marian down and that I'd call him with an update as soon as I had one. Marian's room was on the same floor as Danilo's, only a short jog from my current location, and I knocked, half expecting to find her with a tumbler of the minibar's finest, wreathed in contraband cigarette fumes. But instead there was only silence.

I dug around for the key card she'd given me on the day she arrived, "just in case." Was this the circumstance she'd had in mind? What kind of trouble was my mother in, exactly?

The room was empty and tidy. The cleaning staff had been through, and the linens hadn't been disturbed since. Marian's clothes were hanging in the closet, her shoes organized in a neat row at the bottom, but the cloak I'd found hidden last time I'd been here was gone. I pressed my fingers to my temples and massaged gently. Surely, I thought, my mother would have had the sense not to dispose of it. But lately, her usual prudence had been as hard to locate as shoreline designated for public use on the Three Sisters lakes.

I scanned the room, then dropped my bag on a chair and did a thorough search. No laptop, no purse. Whatever clothes Marian hadn't hung up were folded in her suitcase. The bedside tables were empty, aside from a hotel-issued Bible, but in the desk drawer, I found an advance reader's copy of Grit and Gumption. So she did have an extra one. I felt a prick of annoyance. Was my mother's embrace of Debbie Halloran strategic, or did she genuinely prefer her to me?

I sat down at the desk and flipped through the pages, looking for the acknowledgements. They were lengthy, and included her entire publishing team, her former consulting colleagues, everyone she'd interviewed for the book, her tennis instructor, and her Mastermind group. My father was mentioned as her "strength and stay," a deliberate (I assumed) casting of herself as Queen Elizabeth to his Prince Philip. And there at the end: "My daughter, Catherine, reminds me that women still have a long way to go, and that the message of this book continues to be urgent and important." My mother, queen of the Hallmark sentiment.

I held the book by the spine and shook. A piece of loose paper fell out and landed on the desktop. It was a bit of Pinerock stationery with three words written on it in bold black marker: *YOU WILL PAY.*

My gut dropped. I should have taken my mother's fears more seriously. Was that why she hadn't shown me this note? If the author was the same person as the one who'd been leaving toxic reviews of her book online, Marian might be dealing with a delusional fan who'd decided that negative attention was better than none. Maybe that person had gone to extreme lengths when all other efforts had failed.

I was trying to rid myself of a mental image of Kathy Bates wielding a sledgehammer in *Misery* when the phone rang. It was my dad again. "Dad," I said. "She's not in her room."

"Yes, I know," he said. "That's because she's in jail."

I MUST HAVE set a personal land speed record sprinting from my mother's room to the parking lot. My father was in a car driving north with my mother's lawyer, a venerable Bay Street litigator, but I didn't want her to be alone for any longer than necessary. Call me crazy, but I wasn't confident in her ability to make great decisions just now.

My mind raced with all of the actions I'd failed to take—any one of which might have prevented my mother's incarceration. I should have pressed her to confide in me earlier. I should have insisted that she turn the cloak over to the police. I should have gone with her to the detachment, rehearsing her statement on the way. I should have been the type of daughter who practised non-judgmental listening—someone like Debbie Halloran, for example, who had inexplicable patience for Marian's drama. I should have done more to protect her when I saw her crumbling.

Preoccupied with my own shortcomings, I was startled when a black pickup braked hard in front of me and then swerved so that it was angled across both lanes. I pumped my own brakes and came to a stop on the gravel shoulder. I assumed an animal had darted out onto the road; deer were common on this stretch of highway, especially as mating season got underway. But then the driver and passenger doors of the pickup opened, and two men hopped out and strode toward me with intention.

No dead deer, then, but the realization provided little comfort. Before I could formulate an escape plan, Peter was banging on the window next to my head, while Kyle placed his hands on the hood of my car, his glare piercing and furious through the windshield. Déjà vu, but this time, he had a tire iron in his hand.

"Open the window," Kyle yelled.

"Not a chance," I shouted. Kyle reared back and booted my front fender. I felt the car rock.

"I saw your latest piece of garbage online," Peter said.

I tapped my ear apologetically and shrugged. *I can't hear you.*

"You can hear me fine," said Peter. "How does it feel to be on the receiving end of fake news? Turn around is fair play, eh?"

"Payback time!" shouted Kyle. He came to the passenger side, swung the tire iron in a wide arc, and smashed the side mirror.

The terror was immediate and visceral. They wouldn't take me without a fight, I thought, as I groped around for possible weapons—keys? a ballpoint pen?

Deliverance, in the form of a battered green Volkswagen hatchback, appeared in my rear-view mirror. It slowed to a stop right behind me. A woman in her early seventies emerged, an avenging angel clad in pink fleece.

I rolled down my window and yelled for help.

"Has there been an accident?" the woman asked. "Do I need to call the OPP?"

"Yes!" I called.

"No," said Peter. "There's no problem. Just a friendly chat."

"Doesn't look that way to me," said the woman. "Doesn't look like this lady wants to chat with you at all. Move along. You're blocking the road, and the bingo starts in a half-hour at the Legion."

"Keep your hair on," said Kyle.

"Kyle!" said Peter. "Get in the car." To the woman, he said, "Our apologies for the inconvenience. We're done here."

If he expected the woman to return to her car at that point, he was disappointed. She crossed her arms and tapped her foot ostentatiously. "Tick tock," she said.

Turning away from her, he leaned into the open space between us and said, with quiet intensity, "Our movement has friends in very high places, and they don't want you here. If you know what's good for you, you'll hightail it back to Toronto."

He stalked to his vehicle and climbed in. Kyle revved the engine before driving away with a squeal. The green hatchback was hot on their heels.

I gave myself a minute to stop shaking. Then I got out of the car, walked around to the passenger side, and inspected the damage. The side-mirror housing was crunched against the door. I pulled at it to see if it might miraculously pop into place and sliced the palm of my hand in the process. I closed my fist around the wound, opened the trunk, and pushed the contents around with my uninjured hand until I caught sight of a package of microfibre towels that my mother had given me for Christmas. ("So handy for cleaning spills in your car when they happen!") I extracted one and created a field bandage by wrapping it around my palm and then sliding a hair elastic overtop of it, securing it in place.

I thought about calling for help—Amir, Bruce, even Debbie—but I knew I'd lose it if I tried to explain what had happened. There would be time for that later. Right now, my mother needed my help. This time, I promised myself, I wouldn't fail her.

CHAPTER 22

WHEN I BURST through the doors of the cop shop, Inspector Cheryl Bell was at the front desk, consulting with Dick Friesen. She took a second to assess my current state of distress—lunatic hair, sweaty face, hand encased in a neon-green towel—and said, "Ah. It's you again."

"I think at this point you should give me a loyalty card," I said. "One more stamp and I get one of your delicious prison lattes."

"Ha," she responded. If sounds had cutting edges, my head would have rolled free of my neck.

Friesen had obviously had enough of this witty banter. "Can we help you, Ms. Conway?"

I refrained from expressing my true thoughts

(*yes, Dick Friesen, you turd bonnet, you can give me my mother*) and instead said, "I understand you may be detaining my mother, Marian Conway. May I ask why?"

"Are you here in some official capacity, Ms. Conway?" Bell asked, crossing her arms over her chest. "I believe your mother has already been in touch with her lawyer." Her eyes shifted down to my hand, noting the blood leaching out from the edges of the towel. "Did you have an accident?"

In my frenzied drive over, I'd forgotten the pain in my hand. "Would you call it an accident if you're attacked?"

Her eyes narrowed. "Elaborate, please."

Did I really want to get into it? Was it a wise idea to escalate my feud with the Johnsons? Kaydence might despair over her brother and father, but that didn't necessarily mean she wanted them arrested. On the other hand, they couldn't rule the town with threats and violence. I loathed bullies, especially ones who said they had powerful friends in their corner. And it seemed like their violence, at least toward me, was escalating. *Sorry, Kaydence*, I whispered to myself.

"I was driving here from the Pinerock when a pickup swerved in front of me and blocked the road. It was Peter Johnson and his son, Kyle. I'm not sure which of them was driving. They approached my car and threatened me. Kyle smashed my side mirror with a tire iron. I cut myself clearing the glass off the road so that no one else would be hurt."

Friesen let out a noise that sounded like a snort of disbelief, and Bell shot him a withering look. "This happened when?"

"Maybe fifteen minutes ago." Suddenly my legs felt like they were about to give way. If that woman hadn't intervened ... "Wait. There's a witness. I don't know what her name is, but she was on her way to the Legion for bingo."

"It is Tournament of Champions week," Friesen acknowledged grudgingly.

Bell reached behind the front desk, pulled a pack-aged alcohol wipe from the drawer, and handed it to me. "You should get that looked at," she said. "Meanwhile, would you like us to pursue this with the Johnsons?"

I appreciated that she had given me agency in this decision. She would understand the choice I faced: speak up, or capitulate to the small-town mafia in hopes of buying peace. I could use a minute's peace at this point. Or a year's peace. Maybe the Johnsons would respond to efforts to de-escalate. They were Christian, after all. Hadn't Jesus said that peacemakers were the children of God?

Kyle's face, twisted with wrath, swam into my vision: he was definitely working from the Old Testament playbook.

"Bring them in," I said.

Bell gave Friesen a brisk set of instructions, and he set off to find someone to occupy the front desk while he went in search of the Johnsons. Bell nodded at me curtly and turned to leave. I grabbed her sleeve with my non-bloodied hand. "One favour," I said.

"Five minutes," she said. "And don't make me regret it."

FOR THE FIRST time I could remember, I saw myself in my mother. That is: her hair was not impressively groomed, at least two of her nails were broken, and she was starving.

"Do you have any of those peanut M&M's left?" Marian asked when I walked into the tiny room. I was pretty sure this was the officers' break room, judging by the empty Nespresso pods in the garbage and the sign-up sheet for the 2018 softball team on the wall. Pamela Jones had let me in, and now presumably stood guard outside.

"Mom, have you ever known me to hold onto chocolate overnight? If you're hungry, I'll ask Pamela to bring you something to eat."

"No, it's fine." She attempted to pat her hair smooth, and this one gesture twisted my heart. "Your father and Stanley will be here shortly, and this whole ridiculous charade will come to an end." Stanley had been my parents' friend for ages, a senior lawyer with a lake view from a corner office in a law firm known for its impeccable reputation and blue-chip clients.

"Do you have any idea why you're here?"

My mother slumped in her plastic chair. "The police showed up this morning with a warrant to search my room and they found ... they found ..."

"Bliss's cloak."

Marian shot upright and snapped, "Well, I'm sorry I'm not an expert at disposing of evidence. Not that it is evidence, seeing as I witnessed no crime."

"I'm not sure the rules of evidence work that way, Mom."

She wasn't listening, though. "Who could have told them what was in the closet?" She gave me a wild look. "It wasn't you, was it?"

"Yes, Mom, it was me. I turned you in to the cops. I'm planning to write a tell-all memoir that will land me on *Good Morning America*."

My sarcasm was lost on her. She was too busy frantically running through her list of enemies. "It could have been Clarity. She despises me. And she saw me outside that night. Or perhaps it's that absurd Bodhi Rubin. He's angry that I ruined his sausage party."

I burst out laughing, and after a second she joined me, and soon the two of us were chortling like fools. My mother wiped her eyes. "Jake taught me that expression," she said. "I never thought I'd have an opportunity to use it."

The laughter didn't last long, and an anxious silence took its place. I reached across the table to take her hands, not something I would normally do. But Marian was being detained at a police station, and for all I knew she'd be charged with murder. Normal had left the building long ago.

She gasped when she saw my bloodied hand. "Oh, sweetheart—what happened?"

Sweetheart. That wasn't normal either, but I'd take it. I felt tears pool, and didn't make any effort to fight them back. I was exhausted, scared, at the end of my rope. I needed my mother. "I'm fine," I said. "I'll tell you about it when we get out of here."

There was a knock at the door, and Pamela Jones stuck her head in. "Time's up," she said.

Marian clutched my wrist, pulling me closer. "Call Debbie," she said.

"Debbie?" I couldn't keep the disbelief out of my voice. "Why?"

"She's the mayor's wife. We could use all the help we can get right now." My mother's eyes were wild. I didn't like what I saw there. She was frightened, but it was more than that. There was pleading in her expression, as if she desperately needed me to know something but was afraid of what I'd do when I found out. A terrible tension.

Officer Jones rattled the doorknob. I stood, and Marian stood with me. She leaned forward and hissed, "Just call her."

I SAT IN the small lobby, watching a tall man complaining to Pamela Jones about a ticket his son had received for a DUI on the water. She wasn't having any of it, and he left in a huff. She went back to clacking on her keyboard and ignoring my pleading eyes.

The most recent text from my dad said they were nearly in Port Ellis. I imagined him at the wheel ignoring speed limits, Stanley riding shotgun and urging caution. But was Stanley the right man for the job? He was revered as a mergers and acquisitions expert, a rainmaker, and an all-around gentleman, but he'd spent his career in boardrooms, not courtrooms.

I had to do something. Marian needed me, and I wasn't about to let her down. I'd called Debbie Halloran, who'd let out a yip of distress and said she'd be right over, but surely there was more I could do?

The door slammed open, making me jump. Dick Friesen thrust his way in, tugging Peter Johnson by the arm. Peter's wrists were fastened behind his back, and his face was as washed of colour as a November sky. He looked to me, for the first time, like an old man. I guessed he wasn't much used to having his power taken away, and he was finding it a sobering experience. Kyle, on the other hand, was spitting mad. Steam practically rose from his magenta ears, and he shouted his opinion that Dick Friesen was almost certainly destined for hell.

"Wait until the mayor finds out about this," Kyle yelled. "You'll be sorry!"

Dick responded that it was his opinion some people should learn to keep their traps shut.

Suddenly, there was more commotion at the door, and Kaydence burst in, with her mother huddled against her. Unlike her father, Kaydence just looked furious. She stomped over to me. "Cat, what the hell are you doing? Siccing the cops on my family?"

I was so tired of people asking me what I was doing. My job, maybe? Trying to help other people? "You need to talk to the men in your family about their anger issues," I said. I held up my hand, the hideous green towel dark with dried blood.

Kaydence's face stilled. "They did that to you?"

"We didn't touch her!" Peter bellowed from across the room.

Deeandra, huddled in her daughter's armpit, suddenly began to sob. Her voice rose in a terrible howl, an animal in pain. Her husband hardly merited these histrionics, but who was I to judge? Peter's thundering curses rose over the wailing, and Kaydence began shouting, even louder, that he should pipe down.

Cheryl Bell, striding in from a side hallway, halted

in the middle of the melee. She raised her hand in one decisive motion, and silence fell miraculously over the room.

"All right," she said. "Would someone like to tell me what's going on?"

The voices rose again, a cacophony of Johnsons and cops. Bell's eyes met mine, and I thought I saw a little flicker there. "Okay. We're going to start with—"

The door flung open again. We turned as one, and all I could think was: *Great*. Now we had a full Marx Brothers movie. For there was Debbie Halloran, looking fetchingly flushed, her hair wind-tousled.

"Finally!" Kyle Johnson shouted. "Someone here to explain our side of things."

Debbie looked startled. She shook her head briskly and trotted over to my side. "I'm here for Cat," she said. "Well, specifically for Marian, but I'm here to support Cat, too." She looped her hand through my elbow, as if they were all about to rush at us and we needed to make a wall.

Peter's head spun around so quickly that he reminded me of the kid from *The Exorcist*. "Debbie Halloran," he said. "You've forgotten who you're beholden to. You're a traitor to your family."

"Gerry's going to hear about this," said Kyle. "You can count on it."

I felt Debbie rise and expand beside me, an eagle defending her chicks. Her eyes shone with a righteous fury. "This is my family," she said. "Cat is my family. And I don't answer to Gerry."

Peter scoffed. "None of your garbage. You are a wife. You need to honour your family the way our Lord intended. With loyalty."

Debbie was quivering with rage. She clutched my arm tighter. "She is literally my family," she shouted. "Literally my sister. My blood."

Some small part of my brain was irritated that Debbie did not know what *literally* meant, though it was the wrong time to educate her. Then my breath stopped, frozen in my chest. What if she did know what *literally* meant?

Literally her sister.

Her sister.

CHAPTER 23

DEBBIE SLAPPED HER free hand across her mouth. "Oh my god," she said. "Cat, I'm so sorry. We didn't mean for you to find out like this."

"We?" I asked. "You mean, you and Marian?"

"Let's sit down," she said, and led me over to the station's waiting area: a row of moulded orange plastic chairs locked together on a rail and secured to the floor.

I sat, feeling dazed. My hand throbbed. At least the Johnsons had stopped shouting. I shifted onto one hip so that I could face Debbie. I examined her closely. Could I see a glimpse of my mother in any of her features? Maybe her eyebrows, although Debbie seemed like the sort of woman to have them professionally

275

shaped. Maybe her chin, pert and determined like Marian's.

"Cat! Hey. Are you in there?" Debbie waved her hand across my path of vision.

She'd been speaking, I realized. "I'm sorry," I told her. "It's a lot to take in. Start again."

She nodded. "I understand." Her forehead was furrowed with worry. "I was saying that your mother—my mother—gave me up for adoption before you were born. I knew I was adopted, but my parents didn't ever discuss it with me. It was only after they died a couple of years ago that I found my birth records in their safe deposit box. I hired a private investigator to help me put the pieces together. It didn't take that long—we found a genetic match on 23andMe."

Jake's anniversary present to my parents. I fought the impulse to put my hands over my ears. It was too much. I stood up. "I need a second," I said. I walked outside and propped myself against the squat brick wall next to the entrance. I bent over with my hands on my knees, letting my head hang and feeling the stretch in my spine and shoulders. The air was cool and crisp, and it was quiet enough to hear birdsong from the woods behind the station.

I heard tires crunching to a stop near me, followed by footsteps.

"Kitty Cat?" said a voice brimming with love and concern. "Are you okay, honey?"

I straightened up, saw my father's gentle face and threw myself into his arms.

"Oh, sweetie," said my dad. "It's going to be okay. Stanley, you go ahead. I'm right behind you." He rubbed my back. "What's happened? Is it your mother?"

"Why didn't she tell me I have a sister?" I blubbered. "She's been lying to me my whole life."

"Ah." My father put his hands on my shoulders and nudged me upright so that he could see me. He fished a packet of tissues out of the pocket of his navy canvas jacket and handed it to me. I blew my nose. "She wanted to tell you. She didn't know how. I think being reminded of that time in her life was overwhelming for her."

"For her? What about me? I feel like a complete idiot. Mom and Debbie have been talking behind my back for days. Weeks, even!" As the words emerged, I could hear how much I sounded like my son, when he'd been even younger than he was now, railing against some schoolyard injustice.

My father's voice was calm and reasonable. "It happened a very long time ago, Cat. Several years before Marian even met me. She was young, in her second year at university. She'd come home for the harvest festival and had a fling with her ex-boyfriend from high school. She didn't want to be with him and she didn't want a baby. It took her a few months to figure out that she was pregnant, and by the time she got her head around it … well, it wasn't easy to have an abortion in those days."

He kept his arm on my shoulder as he steered me around the corner of the building so we could sit on the edge of a planter filled with the summer's dried stalks. He paused for a minute, gathering his thoughts. "She didn't want her parents to know. She didn't want her friends to know. She finished her term, told her parents she was working abroad for the summer, and found an agency for unwed mothers that gave her free room and board and set her up with prenatal care. She gave birth in the summer and was back at school in September. I honestly believe that she stuffed it down and never thought about it again until Debbie Halloran got in touch."

I could well imagine my mother burying a traumatic experience. She was adept at repression. "It must have changed her," I said. "An experience like that."

My father nodded. "I'm sure it did," he said. "She was determined never to let her guard down after that. Never to let anything stand in her way."

"When did she tell you?" I asked him.

"Two weeks ago," he said. "That's when she finally agreed to meet Debbie. Debbie had been pursuing her for at least a year before that." He smiled wryly. "Seems like persistence runs in the family." He tucked his arm through mine. "Let's go in. Your mother needs us."

A METAL DOOR leading to the office area opened, and Stanley emerged, along with Kaydence and Deeandra. Kaydence had an arm around her mother's shoulders, and she fixed me with a dark look. In my backpack, my phone vibrated, and I reached inside, breaking Kaydence's gaze. It was Bruce, that pillar of competence and good sense. I answered.

"Cat?" he said, sounding uncharacteristically rattled. "Some serious shit is going down over here. Dorothy's little monsters left a few minutes ago. It's official. They're selling the *Quill*. Do you know where Kaydence is? I can't reach her."

"She's here," I said. He didn't need to know where "here" was, at least not yet. "I'll let her know. I've got another situation I'm dealing with, but I'll be there as soon as I can."

"I'm worried about Amir," he said. "He's not doing well. It's like someone turned the lights off inside him, you know?"

"Yeah," I said. "I know the feeling."

I sank into one of the moulded orange chairs and dug in my pocket for the tissues I'd taken from my dad. The day felt like an escalating joke with no punch line in sight. I wanted to jump in the nearest lake and float away from all the drama and pain and struggle and uncertainty.

"Cat?" Debbie was sitting next to me. "What is it? What happened?"

279

"Dorothy is selling the *Quill*," I said. I raised my voice so that Kaydence could hear. "That was Bruce. It's over."

"No!" Kaydence said. She flopped down beside me. Our little skirmish was over; we had a bigger war to fight, together. She pounded her fist on my knee. "We're not going to let them shut us down."

I didn't want to ask her how that would happen. It was too late to start buying lottery tickets.

"Oh, no," said Debbie. "I can't believe it. Port Ellis needs the *Quill & Packet*, whatever Gerry says. Is there anything I can do to help?"

"It's too late, Debbie," I told her. "The paper's fucked."

"Cat?" My father broke away from the hushed conversation he'd been having with Stanley and came over to where I was sitting with Debbie. "I'm sorry about your newspaper, honey. But Stanley needs our help. The police seem to think that your mother is a serious suspect in a murder, for heaven's sake. It's ridiculous. Apparently, two other speakers at the conference, Clarity K and Bodhi ..."

"Rubin," supplied Stanley. "They're witnesses to some odd behaviour by your mother. I'm sure there is a perfectly innocent explanation, but in the meantime, it would be helpful to know more about these people. Do they have any reason to cast suspicion on Marian?"

"If they do, Cat will find out," said my father, with

absolute confidence. "No one can keep a secret from her."

It didn't seem like the right time to mention that my mother and Debbie had done exactly that, the former for my entire life. "I'll do my best," I said.

"I'll help," said Debbie. "Put me to work. I may not know much about criminal investigations, but I'm better connected than the Wi-Fi up here."

"I'm coming too," said Kaydence. "Cat, I owe you an apology. What my father and my brother did—it wasn't right. I can't expect you to protect them the way I do. It's not like it's healthy for me, either. I just hate seeing my mom like this."

"I'll meet you at the *Quill*," I told them both. "There's someone I need to see."

I HADN'T BEEN to Dorothy's home on Millionaires' Hill in a few months, and I was surprised to see signs of change. The dented Cherokee had vanished from the parking pad, signalling, I assumed, the termination of Dorothy's driving privileges—either by the province or, more likely, by her children. The pine-needle-soft driveway had been paved. The flower beds, choked with weeds on my last visit, were tastefully planted with young perennials and blanketed with fresh mulch.

I knocked on the door and was greeted with a familiar chorus of barks, howls, and whines. Last time

I'd been here, the *Quill*'s owner had opened the door herself, her dogs falling over themselves to defend her from invaders. Today, I was admitted by a woman in uniform, who held the dogs on leashes. They'd been groomed recently; the little mop with legs was now recognizable as a poodle. "Dorothy is on the screened porch," she said. "I'll take you to her." She lowered her voice as we walked. "She tires easily. Please keep your visit as short as possible."

"There's nothing wrong with my hearing," a familiar voice called. "I'll decide for myself when my guest has overstayed her welcome."

We stepped into an outdoor living room. It was a warm day for October, but the breeze from the lake was chilly through the open screens. "Of course, Mrs. Talbott," said the woman. "I'll take the dogs and come back with your medication. Are you sure you're warm enough?"

Dorothy glowered at her from underneath a mound of throw blankets. "I'm fine."

I took a seat, and she turned her hazy eyes toward me. "Cat Conway," she said. "To what do I owe the honour? Oh, let me guess. You don't want me to sell the paper."

I felt queasy with shame. I should have come to visit Dorothy long before now. As soon as her husband had died. I'd done the basics, of course—I'd gone to the visitation with the newsroom crew to pay my respects, and I'd made an appearance at Calvin's funeral, but those were displays of duty, not friendship. Dorothy had offered me employment at a time when my prospects were limited, to say the least. I owed her, and she was a person who kept score.

What can't be cured must be endured: one of my grandmother's favourite expressions. I took a breath and forged ahead. "I wish you wouldn't sell," I said. "Amir is trying so hard to make a go of it. We're doing work that matters."

A crepey hand emerged from the nest of blankets. I don't know what I'd expected, but it wasn't a gentle pat on the knee. "I shouldn't give you a hard time," she said kindly. "I'm truly proud of the paper the *Quill* has become. You and Amir were excellent hires."

"So why sell?"

Dorothy looked out at the lake. I wondered how much of it she could see. "I'm selling everything," she said. "The house, the paper, a couple of rental properties in town. I'm moving. More accurately, my children are moving me. They want me to be closer to them so they can keep an eye on me. My son's wife has constructed an in-law suite for me in her basement." She grimaced. "It could be worse. I can take the dogs. And I won't be living out my days in Martha Mercer's retirement village." A sly grin played around her mouth. "I hear she's had some difficulties with the planning permissions."

I laughed. "I hear the same." I wondered if Dorothy still had enough pull in town to tangle Martha's application in red tape. I imagined she did.

"The *Quill* was my father's paper, you know," said Dorothy. "He inherited it from his father, when it was already an institution. Boring as hell, I should add, but it influenced opinion. He was an ambitious man, my father. Had his eye on a political run. He was way ahead of his time in the advertorial game." Her expression was wistful. "We weren't doing hard news then."

I laughed again. "Maybe you had the right idea. Hard news has cost us."

She shook her head. "I believe in independent journalism, even if my father didn't. But, you know, he could have given the *Quill* to one of my brothers, who would have continued in the same vein. Instead, he gave it to me because he knew I loved it. I worked there every summer during high school and university, and even after I married Calvin and had the children, I still wrote a weekly column. It was my escape, my way of existing as a real human person in the world beyond my family roles."

"If you sell it, it'll get scooped up by some vampire conglomerate and slowly drained of life," I told her. "Is that what you want?"

She rose haltingly from her chair, like someone who'd lost faith in their legs. "You must know that Gerry Halloran has been trying to buy the *Quill* for years. He'll outbid everyone." She shooed away the aide, who had rushed to her side.

"You can't sell it to Gerry!" I said. The thought was devastating. The mayor wouldn't be buying the *Quill* as an income property; he'd be buying it for revenge. He'd relish tearing our paper to shreds and making us watch the massacre.

Dorothy interrupted my doom spiral. "I said I was selling," she said, her tone mild. "I didn't say I was selling to the highest bidder. My children might scream, but there's not much they can do beyond that. I have all my marbles and they know it."

Her milky gaze settled on me. "If you love the *Quill & Packet*, make me an offer."

CHAPTER 24

THE NEXT MORNING, I sat in Centennial Park, waiting for the arrival of a person who might give me some answers. Touch grass—wasn't that the modern panacea for anxiety and stress? I was willing to try anything at this point. I lay on my back on the lawn, eyes closed, feeling the sun warm my face. And then I felt something snuffle my crotch.

My eyes popped open to the sight of a Shiba Inu enthusiastically sniffing my jeans. Its owner was hauling back on the leash as hard as she could. "Oh my god, I'm so sorry. Walter, you are a terrible canine ambassador." She grabbed the dog's collar and yanked him away, apologizing as she went.

My head sank back into the grass. I tried to

concentrate on the sun, the sound of the waves hitting the pier, the shrieking of gulls fighting over a crust of hamburger bun. Normal sounds. Inside my brain, though, it was a death-metal symphony. My mother was possibly a murderer, and definitely a liar. That was bad. I was about to lose my livelihood, also bad.

And I had a sister. Was this bad, or good? I couldn't tell. Debbie seemed stable, and resourceful. She had terrible taste in men, true, but I could hardly cast stones in that direction. Perhaps it was a genetic failing.

A shadow fell across my face, and I squinted upward. Three shadows, to be precise. One of them was Clarity K, arms folded across her chest. Behind her, two minions stood at attention, like hockey enforcers protecting their prize goal scorer, if hockey enforcers wore matching Alo outfits. I sat up.

"Thanks for coming, Clarity. Do you want to pull up a piece of grass?" Silently, the one called Zed unfolded a square of cloth, and Clarity lowered herself onto it. Her posture was extraordinary. Then she opened her mouth.

"I've got like five minutes, so hurry up. We've found a property we need to go see."

I couldn't keep the astonishment to myself. "You're moving to Port Ellis?"

She sighed at my obtuseness. "CK Centres for Belonging and Creativity. We opened the first one in Prince Edward County last year. We're always on the

287

lookout for new community hubs. So what did you want to talk to me about?"

"Marian didn't try to kill you that night. She found Bliss's cloak on the path, and she stupidly took it to her room. My mother can be …" I searched for the words. "Kind of self-sabotaging sometimes."

"Really," Clarity said dryly. "Like having me fired after I wrote her book? And lying to the world about it?"

A seagull landed near Clarity's knee and the acolyte not named Zed chased it away. "I understand how angry that must have made you," I said. "Angry enough to report my mother to the police. Angry enough to try to sabotage her new book."

Clarity let out a shriek of laughter that was not un-gull like. "You thought I was tearing her up online? Oh, sis, I do not have time for that bullshit. And number two, I don't consort with cops."

"Are you telling me that you didn't report my mom? You didn't find the cloak?"

Behind her, the two minions exchanged uneasy glances. Clarity spread her hands, a regal butterfly. "I unfortunately cannot be responsible for the diligence my team demonstrates on my behalf." She shrugged. "But I've told these two geniuses that they're making things worse."

The tumblers in my brain clicked into place. "Oh," I said softly. "I get it. Your protectors. They review-bombed my mother's book and thought they were doing you a favour. But that still doesn't explain how the police found out about the Creativity Cocoon."

Clarity crooked a finger, and her assistants came forward. "Zed and Sharon were perhaps overzealous in their efforts to trash your mother's reputation." For a moment I stared at them, sparing a moment's pity for the acolyte saddled with the earthbound name Sharon. I pictured them in the clearing at the SkyWords workshop, lording it over the mere mortals.

And then it made sense.

"The hotel cleaner," I said. "The one who was at SkyWords. She was only there because you were paying her off. Did she give you the key to my mother's room?" The threatening note had said *you will pay*, in the same black Sharpie used to write my invitation to Clarity's suite.

"We didn't think your mother would take it seriously," said Zed.

"It was meant to be ironic," added Sharon.

"And did you report her to the cops ironically after you'd found the cloak?"

"All right, enough," Clarity said. "I've already revoked their spa privileges. They've learned their lesson. They're going to remove the negative reviews. And tell their friends to stop it, too. And restore your mother's website to its original state. Am I right?" Zed and Sharon nodded in unison, refusing to meet my eyes.

Clarity made some tiny movement, and her minions crouched and helped her to her feet. She glared at them. "These two should be focused on engagement, not revenge. Actually protecting me, as you say." She shivered. "I can't say I feel very safe here. And not because of your whack-job mother, either."

I thought of Bree and Bodhi, new parents. Bringing a baby into the world, and trying to hatch a lucrative fledgling empire at the same time. "Do you think it was Bree and Bodhi out in the woods that night? Did they mistake Bliss for you? But why would they target you?"

"Do you think that Bliss could have made something epic on her own? That girl had tofu for brains." Clarity brought her hands together at her heart. "Sorry. I promised myself not to diss the dead. But really, Bliss was not a threat to them."

"But you were?"

She shook out the wrinkles from her skirt. Zed snatched up the cloth she'd been sitting on and folded it. "Let's just say that I wish Bree and Bodhi well. And if I ever see them again, I'll keep my back to the wall. And my eyes open. You should too."

AFTER THEY'D LEFT, I checked my messages. My dad had sent a text saying that everything was under control with Marian. I texted him back the news about Clarity's assistants—that they'd been the ones to find the cloak and report Marian, and they'd been behind the review-bombing. It would stop now, which should bring my mother some peace of mind.

A small victory, but I still hadn't won the war.

I walked back across the street to the newsroom, the wind brisk at my back. How many more days before the first snow? Would the *Quill* even exist long enough for us to print Flannery's fat Christmas flyer?

At least there were no trucks outside the newsroom when I arrived. The Johnsons' slap on the wrist must have filtered down to their cultists. Good. Maybe they were rethinking their path in life. Or, more likely, they were out chaining themselves to the door of the local medical clinic, or storming Parliament Hill.

But I had other things to worry about. Like finding a murderer, and thus saving my mother's neck. And finding a new job. And a fresh bandage for my hand.

Bruce and Hannah looked up when I opened the door. "Fight with a bear on the way here?" Bruce said, pointing at my hand.

"Nope," I said. "Just Dorothy."

"Ah," Bruce said, leaning back. "Well, that can be dangerous too. When she was younger, before her eyes went all wonky, she was quite the wildcat." He curled his fingers into a claw, and Hannah screwed up her face in distaste.

"No, I'm serious," Bruce said. "One year it was Wienie Bite Day—"

"Stop," Hannah said. "Back up. Sometimes I think you just make this all up."

"Not at all," Bruce said, offended. "I've got the pictures here somewhere. Once a year, the local bikers would descend on town. They'd have all these games, with the proceeds going to charity. During the wienie bite, they'd have to race underneath a hot dog hanging from a string and try to bite it without falling off. Dorothy took a fancy to the winner. She said she admired a man who was good with his tongue at high speeds. She almost hopped on the back of his hog and ran off with him."

"Was this before Calvin?" I asked.

Bruce reached for a slice of dried mango. "Possibly during," he said.

"It's astonishing that she had such boring children." I flung my backpack on my desk and took a seat, my chair skittering underneath me. Now I'd never get a chance to fix it. Kaydence walked in from the kitchen and perched on the edge of my desk. She gave my uninjured hand a squeeze, and I knew we were good.

The door to Amir's office was closed, and I left him to his important work—possibly signing divorce papers—while I told my colleagues what had happened at Dorothy's house the previous evening. Yes, she was going to sell, and yes, Gerry Halloran wanted to pay top dollar, but it was entirely possible that she might sell to us.

"I have four hundred and twelve dollars in my savings account," Kaydence said. "No, wait." She checked her phone. "It's actually four hundred and fifty-two. I got an e-transfer for the Ogopogo-print skirt I sold yesterday."

Bruce was gazing off into the distance, his hands steepled in front of his face. "Bruce?" I said. "Do you have any concert T-shirts from the seventies we could sell?"

"Oh, sure," he said, but his voice was far away. "Give me a minute. I'm thinking."

My phone buzzed. It was Dad. "Your mom is out on bail, honey. I've rented an Airbnb and I'm taking her there. I'll text you the address. She doesn't want to darken the door of that hotel, and I can't say I blame her. Not after what you found out about those poetry crooks."

"I need to talk to her, Dad," I said. "She needs to think about strategy here."

"Not today, Kitty Cat," he said, firmly. "She's exhausted. She spent the whole day explaining herself to Stanley and the police. What she needs is a hot bath, a glass of wine, and some time to herself. You can see her tomorrow." I could hear a muffled voice in the background, and my father said, "Your mother wants to thank you for uncovering that bad business about the reviews. What is it, Marian?" He sounded as if he was covering the phone. When he came back, his voice was a little choked. "She says she's proud of you. I am too."

"Dad," I said, "I've got to go. I'll call you soon. I love you both."

Hannah sat slump-shouldered at her desk. I wanted to go over to her and hug her. I wanted to scream at the unfairness of it all. She was exactly the kind of journalist we needed—smart, resourceful, quick on her feet. And we were going to lose her.

I wandered over and sat next to her as she scrolled through her phone. She was flicking through a long WhatsApp chain, pausing occasionally to read a message. "UMWOO," she said to me, as if I lived in a universe where the word made any sense. My face must have displayed my confusion, because she laughed. "Unemployed Media Workers of Ontario. We have a group chat. People sometimes post job listings, but mainly we just share coupons and talk about whether we should go to law school."

"You should ask if anyone knows about jobs at *The Loft*. Seems like they're hiring everybody these days. No, I take that back. You're not allowed to go work in Toronto. It's a sea of sin and pestilence."

"Really good bulk stores, though," Bruce said. "Really, really good." He stood up and stretched. "Anyway, you're needed here, Hannah. Unless I'm mistaken we're supposed to be at the meeting of the emergency infrastructure committee at city hall in twenty minutes. And you know what they say: drains don't cover themselves."

"Wah-wah," said Hannah, pulling a face as she began to pack up her stuff.

"I'll head out with you," Kaydence said. "I'm going back to the Pinerock. My mom's going to help me pack up my booth." They left together; the glass door rattled shut behind them. The peeling letters still said *Quill & acket*. Dorothy had promised to have the sign fixed and never got around to it. Now she never would.

Suddenly the door to Amir's office burst open and he radiated out. And I mean radiated: like the sun on a June day. His smile would have blinded a lesser woman.

"Wow," I said. "Did somebody buy you an ice cream?"

"I'm a free man in Paris. I'm unfettered and alive."

I melted a little, I'm not going to lie. We stared at each other, not saying anything. Finally, I said, "So that means you're—"

"That was Gus on the phone. It's over. I'm not a married man any longer. Not that I had been for a long time, of course. Although I know that was unclear ..." He stumbled to a halt, shook his head. In the awkward pause he flung his hand up for me to high-five. I met it with my own grungily bandaged palm.

Amir flinched when he saw my hand. I started to say *It's nothing, don't worry*, but he gripped it, gently, and bent his head to look. "Is this an occupational injury?"

"Aren't they all?"

He turned my hand this way and that. I didn't pull away. He said, "Do you ever wonder …"

All the time, I thought. But what came out was "Do I wonder about what?"

He lowered my hand, but didn't let go. "Whether it's worth it. All of this." His chin pointed to the corners of our shabby newsroom: the mousetrap against the wall, the pile of ancient *Maclean's* magazines sunfaded on the window ledge. "I mean, we could have proper jobs somewhere else. In an office at the top of a skyscraper. With pensions and benefits and company cars."

"Oh, Amir," I said, squeezing his hand. "We'd be bored. We'd be so bored."

CHAPTER 25

TWO HOURS LATER I was, it must be said, quite bored. Also frustrated. I'd chased every lead I could think of, following the online lives of every suspect on our list until I found myself staring at a picture of Larry Rubin, aged eleven, posed in the middle of his Little League team. My brain was doing doughnuts, and I could feel my synapses frying like overheated tires.

I returned to Bliss and Bree's YouTube channel and began scrolling through episodes of their podcast again. Surely there was something I'd missed. I was halfway through an episode about ancestral eating, which somehow did not involve cannibalism, when my phone rang.

"You need to come to city hall," whispered the voice on the other end.

"Who is this?" I asked.

"It's Debbie." She raised her voice slightly. "Hurry. I need you to see something. I'm in the ladies' room across from Gerry's office."

I'd been summoned to meet sources in some odd locations in my career, but this was a first. I waved to Amir through the open door of his office and jogged down Main Street toward Port Ellis's iconic clock tower. I bounded up the stairs, past the sculpture of "Industry"—a man carrying a pickaxe and a jackhammer—and up to the second-floor hallway. I knew the building well; I'd been here many times since moving back to town, covering council meetings, or trying to doorstop the reluctant Mayor Halloran for a quote.

The ladies' room was empty but for a locked stall at the end of the row. I leaned against the 1920s sink with its original brass taps and hoped it wouldn't come crashing off the wall. "Debbie," I hissed. "Are you there?"

The door to the stall popped open. "Oh thank goodness," Debbie said.

"Where's the fire?" I asked.

"It's Kyle Johnson," she said. She was flushed with excitement. "He arrived just before I called you. He insisted on seeing Gerry without an appointment and he got quite agitated. Mitch—that's Gerry's PA—offered to call security, but Gerry said no, he'd handle it himself."

"Then what happened?"

"They went into Gerry's office."

"That's it?" I asked. "Why couldn't you tell me this over the phone?"

"Because then you wouldn't have been able to eavesdrop on them," she said, with irritation. "I'm giving you a lead, Cat. I told Gerry's events coordinator that I was throwing a cocktail party for Marian, and you were coming by to help me with the guest list. Come on, let's go!"

In the mayor's office, Debbie announced airily that she'd be using Gerry's conference room for a few minutes to go over details for a party with me. From the expressions on several staffers' faces, they weren't sure how to tell the First Lady that I was persona non grata in the mayor's office.

"Ma'am?" A man in his thirties, wearing a suit and tie, stood up from his desk and came toward her. "The mayor is in a meeting and doesn't wish to be disturbed."

"I have no intention of disturbing him," said Debbie. "The conference room is next door to his office. He won't even notice we're there."

She swanned past the man, ignoring his protests, and I followed. Someone was most definitely having an argument behind the brass-plated door that read Mayor G. Halloran. Debbie slid into the adjacent room, closing the door behind us and drawing down the Venetian blinds. She put a finger to her lips and pointed to the air vent on the wall adjoining Gerry's sanctum.

"... you got me into this, and you better get me

out." I recognized Kyle's voice, gritty with rage.

Gerry's voice was lower, more controlled, and harder to hear. "… threaten regret …"

"Are you fucking firing me?" yelled Kyle.

"… relax … time … calm down."

"I'll calm down when you fix this!" The door slammed hard enough to rattle the blinds.

There was a moment's pause, and then: "Mitch!" Gerry shouted. "In here, now!"

Another scuffle, another round of doors opening and closing, and then Debbie stuck her head into the hallway and declared that the coast was clear. "So?" she said, brightly. "What do we do now?"

THERE WERE ONLY a couple of places in town where I could be sure we wouldn't be overheard by someone in Gerry's pocket—my apartment and the *Quill* office. The *Quill* was closer.

As we entered the newsroom, Amir straightened from his position behind Hannah, where he was reading her story about Port Ellis's dilapidated sewer system. "Mrs. Halloran? Can I help you?"

"It would be easier for all concerned if you told them, Cat," Debbie said.

"Let's not and say we did," I returned.

She tilted her head to one side. "Has anyone ever told you that you're avoidant?" she asked. "I can lend you a book about attachment styles if you like. Enlightening stuff."

I sighed. Debbie could be relentless in her polite way. "Okay, everyone, it turns out that Debbie is my sister. Moving along, it appears that her husband may be in league with the protesters. Kyle Johnson is working for him."

"Not so fast," said Bruce. He closed his eyes as if the world was spinning too fast for him. "What was that first part again?"

"Marian is my biological mother," said Debbie. "She gave me up at birth and we're reconnecting now. Cat is my sister."

"Half-sister," I said, hoping it didn't sound cutting.

An itchy silence fell over the newsroom.

"I know it's a lot," I said. "I'll explain it all over a beer when things calm down."

"Well," Hannah said slowly. "Plot twist, I guess. Which I did not see coming."

"You think?" I asked. I sent a pointed look in their collective direction and then turned to my new family member.

"I might be overstepping here, Debbie," I said, "but are you and Gerry having problems? I can't help but notice that you seem to be throwing him under the bus."

"Hardly," she said. "I'm saving him from himself. But this is the last time. I'm done."

"Why does he need saving?" I asked. Gerry seemed

to be doing pretty well for himself from where I was sitting. Sure, his wife wanted to ditch him, but he had money, influence, and friends in high places.

"Because he's up to his neck in this whole mess with Bliss Bondar," she said. "He was acting as her 'personal brand advisor,' trying to persuade her to launch a syndicated talk-show that would air all over North America." Debbie shifted uncomfortably in her seat and then continued. "I'm not proud of this, but I snooped on his phone while he was in the shower. I thought he might be having an affair with her. It wouldn't have been his first time."

"Was he?" I asked.

"No," she said. "But he was supposed to meet her that night to talk about his offer. Gerry sent a message to Kyle the night Bliss died, telling him to come to the Pinerock. He said he was meeting Bliss and he wanted Kyle to be there. Kyle's his 'intern,' whatever that means."

The newsroom absorbed this information. Bruce nudged me. *Ask the tough question*, he seemed to say. I took a second before I said, "Are you saying you think he killed her?"

Debbie shook her head. "Gerry has more than a few flaws," she said. "He craves attention and he blows with the political wind and he's a poor judge of character and"—Debbie was really warming up now—"he's vain and honestly he only graduated university because I wrote all his papers. But he's not a killer, for heaven's sake."

CHAPTER 26

"ALL RIGHT, TEAM, we've got work to do," said Amir. "Hannah, roll the whiteboard over here, if you don't mind."

Hannah put her shoulder into it, and the whiteboard rattled across the vinyl floor. On its well-worn surface you could just make out ghostly words from story meetings past: *parking, rooster, drownings, dunk tank.* Overtop, Amir scrawled the word *SUSPECTS.*

"Right," said Bruce, looking over the top of his reading glasses. "We've got Gerry Halloran and Kyle Johnson at the top of the list." Amir wrote the names as if taking dictation.

"Bree Guthrie and Bodhi Rubin," said Hannah. "And maybe Clarity K as well. That's some toxic wellness."

"They certainly spend a lot of time stabbing each other in the back," I said. "Very cozy. And then there are the people who have reasons to be angry at the whole Welcome, Goddess business. Lewis Kinross, for example. He despises influencers who peddle lies. And our friend Danilo—Bree was about to drop the big glitter guillotine on his neck."

Bruce nodded. "I know you won't like this, Cat, but we have to include your mother." Amir's hand wavered, then wrote *Marian Conway*.

"I think you should take my mother's name off the list," I said.

"Got to disagree with you there." Bruce gave me the face Jim Rockford used to give his most deluded clients. "Just my two cents."

"She's been freed from custody," I said.

"Technically," Hannah said with an apologetic smile, "freed on bail. But still a suspect."

Amir divided up tasks while I wheeled my chair back to my desk in a huff. They were not wrong. Okay, they were right. They were keeping me in line, asking the right questions. Doing their jobs. Which I also should have been doing, except that my thoughts were jumping like the Rockettes on steroids. I needed to learn to calm my brain. Maybe Debbie had a book I could borrow.

Borrowing a book from my sister. The thought popped into my mind and floated there, sparkling.

I had a sister. Too late to pull her hair or borrow her curling iron, but in plenty of time to bond over a glass of wine, or complain about our kids. I pictured us travelling to Fogo Island together, going to see a show at the Playhouse, fighting over who would cook the turkey this Christmas. Arranging to see our mother on the penitentiary's visiting day.

I shook my head. My priority was to save Marian, which meant trying to narrow the focus on the other suspects. I was starting with Bree and Bodhi, although they weren't my top picks; they seemed more interested in their own reflections than bloodshed. Nevertheless, I scrolled through recent stories about Bliss's death, noting the speculation about who might fill the vacuum in the wellness empire. A bunch of gossip sites were dissecting my scoop about Clarity's planned liaison with Bliss, and how this would have pissed off Bree. But none of them actually came out and made any accusations.

I was about to ask Hannah to do a search for me when I noticed her glum expression.

"What is it?" I asked.

She shrugged. "I'm just worried that every story is going to be my last one for the *Quill*."

I did my best imitation of Michael Keaton in *The Paper*, gruff but kind. "Listen, kiddo, this paper is tougher than it seems. It's the Betty White of newspapers. There's lots of life in the old girl yet." Bruce and I exchanged glances. We were the panicked parents in the front seat, telling our kids in the back that everything was going to be fine—even as we drove toward a wall of flame.

I asked her to do a corporations search and see if Bree or Bodhi had registered any new titles or companies lately, or if Clarity K, a.k.a Camilla Khe, had. Then I slid over to Reddit to see if there was any chat about Welcome, Goddess in the forums. There was an entire thread about whether the special menu had given everyone diarrhea, and another about where to buy the yoga pants Bree had been wearing when the convoy protesters interrupted her speech. Another thread hinted at a possible romance between two of the key players, which led to dozens of guesses. *As long as it's not Bree and that gross Bodhi*, someone had written.

My phone buzzed. It was a text from Debbie: *Come to the mayor's office now. I've got Kyle here stuffing envelopes.*

I burst out laughing. "Come on, Bruce," I told him. "We have an interview with Kyle Johnson."

BRUCE AND I could have won a speed-walking contest on our way to city hall. We burst through the doors to the mayor's office, panting. Mitch gave me a sour look and pointed down the hall. "Conference room," he said. "You know the way.

In the conference room, which I now thought of as Debbie's secret spy headquarters, Kyle sat at the table, dwarfed by a mound of invitation cards and envelopes. Debbie was flipping through a binder full of spreadsheet pages and seemed to be instructing Kyle in the fine art of highlighting with yellow, green, and purple fluorescent inks, each deployed for a certain coded purpose (dietary intolerances, hostility toward other prospective guests, campaign donors). Kyle appeared perplexed.

"Oh, good, you're here," said Debbie. "I've been trying to round out Kyle's internship experience with some event skills, but I think we're both ready for a break. I'm going to grab a coffee. Would anyone else like some?"

"We're good." Bruce and I sat down across from Kyle. Call me oversensitive, but I preferred to have a solid object between us. Kyle clenched his jaw.

"I don't have to talk to you," he said, pushing his chair back and beginning to stand.

"You don't," Bruce agreed, pleasantly. "Before you go, though, we know you were hanging out with Gerry Halloran at the Pinerock the night Bliss died."

"Were you up at the lookout?" I asked. "You and Gerry planned to meet Bliss." My voice rose. "Did you lose your temper?"

"I didn't!" Kyle seemed to be torn between vomiting and beating us up. "That's not true!"

"Are you saying the mayor pushed her?" Bruce

asked. "Did she tell him she wasn't going to work for him?"

"If you think Gerry Halloran is going to take the blame for this when he could pin it on you, you're dreaming," I told Kyle. "Maybe that's why he invited you in the first place."

He covered his ears. "Stop it." There were tears in his eyes. "He cares about me. He would never do that."

"So what happened then?"

For a moment, it seemed like Kyle might make a run for it. "We're the only people who know about the meeting," Bruce said. "If you tell us what you know, maybe it can stay that way."

Kyle's shoulders sagged. "Gerry asked me to be there when he talked to Bliss. There was a big dinner at the Pinerock, and they were going to meet up afterwards. But Bliss changed her mind. First she said she needed an hour to meet with her fans, and then she needed to go up to her room and"—he curled his lip—"'decompress.' Gerry was getting really mad. Like, he's the mayor! She wasn't giving him proper respect."

The conversation was taking a turn. I felt Bruce's eyes on me. What if Debbie's assessment of Gerry was wrong? We were going to have to deal with a mess even larger than the Great Manure Explosion of '75 if our killer was the mayor of Port Ellis, my sort of brother-in-law.

Very calmly, I asked Kyle to tell me what Gerry had done after Bliss put him off.

"He went up to her room to talk to her. I went with him. He knocked on her door and she opened it. She was wearing this long bathrobe thing with a hood on it. She said she'd been meditating on Gerry's offer, and she'd decided to take another path. Those were her words: 'another path.' Then she said she hoped he would keep shining a light on injustice, and shut the door in his face."

"And?" I asked.

"And then he went down to the Greybuck Bar and had a couple of glasses of super-expensive Scotch, and I drove him home. He was pissed. At Bliss, I mean, though he was also pissed." He mimed downing a drink. "He said she was a flighty little bitch. But he didn't hurt her and neither did I."

CHAPTER 27

"I BELIEVE HIM," said Bruce, as we trudged back to the *Quill*. "I don't think he did it."

"I don't think so either," I said. "Where does that leave us on suspects? Don't say my mother."

"Hey, Cat?" Hannah flagged me down as I walked into the newsroom. "Remember I told you about UMWOO?"

"Yes?" I had no idea where she was going with this, but if it wasn't about one of my family members, I was willing to listen.

"It's weird. There's a guy on here who got a job at *The Loft* recently. Senior editor. Pretty big deal." She held up her phone.

"And …"

"And I asked him about Lewis Kinross's story about the conference." She sat, quite smugly, and did not say another word. I didn't know if I should hug her or throttle her.

"You don't want to make me work for this, Hannah," I told her. "I might be your boss one day."

"Or I might be yours." She relented, and burst out: "Lewis Kinross isn't writing a story for *The Loft*. This editor had never even heard of him. There's no story on their sked about the Welcome, Goddess conference. He seemed totally surprised when I asked him."

Amir came over to join us. "What do we know about Lewis Kinross?"

"I've been doing a bit of digging," Hannah said. "Lewis has one child, a daughter named Allison. I found an account on Facebook for a woman named Allison Kinross Persson, who has been posting a lot about Bliss's death. Apparently, she and Bliss were old friends and roommates from university." Hannah opened a tab on her laptop and showed me a photograph of two twenty-something women with their arms wrapped around each other. Both were wearing University of Southern Alberta sweatshirts. One was unmistakably Bliss Bondar. The other was a past-life version of the profile photo on the account. The caption beneath the photo read: *I still can't believe this angel has left Earth. She taught me so much. She gave so much* to the world. *She was brave and beautiful and I'll always remember her. It's up to us to continue the fight!*

Hannah scrolled down in Allison's feed. "This is her husband, Lars, and her daughter, Olivia, who seems to be eight, based on her last birthday photos." Hannah paused on a photo of an adorable child wearing a cardboard tiara bedazzled in plastic gemstones, her face covered in chocolate icing and sprinkles. (*Eight years with this gorgeous girl! Blessed to share the occasion with our family! Happy birthday, Olivia!!!*)

"Are we sure it's Lewis's daughter?" I asked. There was no sign of him in the extensive family photos that accompanied Olivia's birthday post.

"Yep," said Hannah. "We need to go back a few years, but … here." She scrolled for a long while, then pointed to a photo of Lewis Kinross holding a toddler in his lap. (*Happy Father's Day to Olivia's grandpa!*) I felt my breath catch. I leaned closer, to confirm that my eyes weren't failing me. They weren't. I recognized the little girl's smile, the dandelion puff of pale hair. It was the same child in the photo that Lewis had showed me at the opening-night banquet. His granddaughter, Olivia.

Hannah was still scrolling. "Allison's posts were fairly normal at that point, but it looks like she had a bad pandemic. She got really freaked out about vaccinations—there's a lot of reposting of convoy propaganda. And then, last year, she said that she was taking Olivia out of school and that education should be for everyone, not only for sheep. Ah, here it is: 'I pay my taxes like everyone else but my daughter can't get an education without getting a government chip implanted? No fucking way. I'm going to protect her from the forces of evil no matter what it costs me personally. If you are reading this and you can't support my choices, you aren't my friend and I don't want you in my life.'"

"Whoa," said Bruce. "That's a dark place to be."

"Sure is," I said. Allison Kinross Persson. Something about the name seemed to pull at me. What was it?

I shot upright and began typing, my fingers flying. Finally, I found it: the podcast episode where Bliss had melted down over the educator's approach to keeping children safe during the pandemic. The episode was posted on the Welcome, Goddess YouTube channel, and I raced to the comments, scrolling as fast as I could. There it was, the comment from AllisonP: *My parents don't understand and I have to keep them away from my daughter because they are so judgy. I won't put that poison into my precious girl.* Were AllisonP and Allison Kinross Persson one and the same?

I googled Allison's name and found her website, which highlighted her works of crochet—shawls, blankets, sweaters. She took custom orders, too. Bland, ordinary stuff. I took a screenshot of her contact details and went back to the angry comments she'd left on Bliss and Bree's channel.

I put her name into the YouTube search engine, hoping she'd have a channel. Bingo. The oldest content she'd uploaded was cooking videos, filmed in a pretty pastel kitchen. Allison was a natural, funny presence as she made oatmeal—"toddler gruel"—and budget-friendly pasta dishes. The videos from the past couple of years were coloured with a darker, paranoid tint. She began to parrot Bliss's language about personal liberty, toxins, and "the body's natural path to healing."

Near the end of 2021, she'd posted a tearful video about how hard it was to deal with family estrangement at Christmas. "Sometimes," she said, "the family you're given will let you down. And you have to be strong enough to walk away, knowing that you're walking in your truth." A little girl wandered into the shot and smiled at the camera, her face lit with an adorable gap-toothed grin.

I tapped my pen against my teeth. Lewis Kinross had never struck me as particularly violent, but then I'd never gotten in between him and one of his children. Or grandchildren. I'd gone into beast mode when my mother was in danger. How might he react if someone he loved was in danger? What if his daughter had taken away his beloved Olivia because she'd been listening to some crazy influencer?

What wouldn't I do if someone threatened Jake?

"Guys," I said, "come take a look at this." My colleagues clustered around my desk. "Allison Persson is Kinross's daughter, and this is his granddaughter, Olivia. His only grandchild." I pointed to Allison's comment about being strong enough to walk away from your family. "She refused to get her daughter vaccinated, probably because she was tuned in to Bliss's woo channel."

Amir peered over my shoulder. "And you think Kinross was angry enough to confront her about it?"

"Possibly," I said. "I'm trying to imagine how furious I'd be if someone broke up my family." I opened the tab that showed Allison's pre-pandemic Facebook post. Lewis Kinross beaming, with Olivia on his knee. "This is the picture Kinross showed me at the banquet. I thought it was weird at the time. He said his granddaughter was eight, but in the picture she was a toddler. Now we know why he didn't have anything more recent. Because he hadn't seen her. Allison had cut him out of their lives."

My phone buzzed. Another text, this time from Danilo: *So long, Cat. We've been given the all-clear to go home. Last workshop is in an hour and then I'm going to click my heels three times and swoosh out of this hellhole.*

Shit.

I stood up and grabbed my keys. "Looks like the circus is leaving town," I said. "Last chance to catch the bad monkeys."

BRUCE PUSHED HIS Subaru to the limit—I imagined the Phish bumper stickers being stripped off in the wind—and we reached the Pinerock in ten minutes. I leapt out of the car and raced to the door, with Bruce on my heels.

We ran past Kaydence and her mother dismantling her booth. "What the—" Kaydence cried, and I held up my hand in the universal sign for *can't stop now, on my way to confront a criminal*. I skidded to a halt in front of the security office. Doug was inside, chomping on a bagel, his eyes on a bank of security cameras.

"Doug," I panted. "What room is Lewis Kinross in?"

His mouth downturned in disapproval. "Cat, you know I can't—"

There was no time for this. "You need a reference to get into PI school, don't you? Well, I'm your reference. And it will be glowing."

Bruce piped up from behind me. "And free ads in the *Quill* when you finally set up your business."

Doug sighed and wiped some poppy seeds from his chest. He tapped on his keyboard with one index finger. My whole body vibrated with impatience. "Doug!"

"Okay, fine. Room 213. One floor up." I turned to dash down the hall, and I heard, from behind me, "It had better be glowing!"

We sprinted toward the stairs and tore up two flights. I slammed into the fire door and it crashed open. "To the right," Bruce called, sounding like an aerobics instructor from the late eighties. I was panting like a dog after a hard run; Bruce exhaled the steady deep breaths of a man with a regular yoga practice.

Outside 213, I paused for a second to catch my breath. Bruce waited politely until I gave him a nod, and then knocked on the door.

Lewis was either genuinely shocked to see us, or he deserved an Oscar. The skin on his jaw was still damp from shaving, and I could see, on the arm that held the door open, that his wristwatch had already been set back to Alberta time.

"I'm sorry?" he said. "Did we have an appointment?"

"No," I said. "But Bruce and I have discovered something that might be pertinent to your research."

"Can you give me a call when I'm home?" Lewis looked irritated. "I'm just heading out. I've got to drive back to the city to catch my flight tonight."

"It's about Mayor Gerry Halloran." I hoped the name would draw him like chum drew a shark. "And his relationship to the convoy protesters. Even more important, his relationship to Bliss Bondar."

Lewis looked torn, and he darted a glance down the hallway. His desperation to know more about Halloran and Bliss won out. He swung the door open wide. "Fine, come in. But it really will have to be quick."

His roller bag sat upright by the bed, with his suit

jacket draped over it. I went and sat at the desk, and Bruce leaned against the wall by the door. Lewis stood with his arms folded, practically tapping his toe. "Well?" he said.

I told him what we'd learned about Gerry Halloran: That he'd wanted to make Bliss a star of the whacko news ecosystem. That he was going to ride her gossamer skirt all the way to even greater power and influence. That he wanted to be the most poisonous toad in a much bigger pond. That he might have used Kyle Johnson as his own private enforcer.

Kinross squinted at me. "I don't understand. Are you saying that Halloran killed Bliss? Or that Kyle did it for him? Why aren't you telling the police? Why are you talking to me?"

I picked up the pen from the desk and started clicking it slowly. Kinross let out a huff of exasperation. I said, "Here's the thing, Lewis. You know my mother, Marian."

He waggled his head as if to say *yeah, so?*

"Marian and I have had a tricky relationship over the years. We're like two magnets lined up at the same pole, constantly pushing each other away. And she takes up a lot of space in my head. A lot." I drew a giant sphere in the air with my hands.

"Look, I don't understand—"

"I'm just saying that I understand families can be difficult." Suddenly I heard a muffled ring, and Bruce reached into his pocket. He dug out his phone, looked at the screen, and mouthed "Amir" at me. He opened the door, and mimed that he'd be right back.

"Anyway," I resumed. "There's tension within families around all kinds of things. When my son was a toddler, my mother used to tell me that I was too protective. That I should let him eat peanuts and honey. She'd fed me all those things, and I was fine. Do you know what I'm talking about, Lewis?"

He shook his head, but slowly this time, like he was an ancient computer trying to process too many tasks.

"I think you do know." I took out my phone and opened it to the screenshot of Allison P's comment about how she wouldn't let her parents see their granddaughter. Lewis didn't come closer to see it, though. Instead, he took a step back.

"I have to use the washroom," he said. "When I'm finished, I want you out of this room. And out of my life. I don't know what you're playing at, but I have no interest in your insane conspiracies. You're as bad as them."

With that, he ducked into the bathroom, slamming the door behind him. I sank into the chair, closing my eyes. It was not my finest moment. I was supposed to be in the business of pumping information from people, not causing them to clam up.

I was beginning to wonder why Lewis was taking so long in the bathroom when I heard a banging at the door. Bruce was in the hallway, already jogging away.

"Lewis is on the run," he called over his shoulder. "Quick, let's go."

"He's in the bathroom," I called after him.

"Not anymore. I just saw him running across the parking lot like he was on fire."

I spun back to the bathroom door in disbelief and twisted the knob. It wasn't locked. I flung it open to find gauzy curtains fluttering in the lake breeze, an old fire escape winding down to the ground, and Lewis Kinross disappearing into the trees—and headed for the lookout.

CHAPTER 28

"GODDAMN IT," I yelled. My fist slammed the window. My brain churned. I ran out into the hall.

Bruce was opening the door to the stairway at the far end. "Let's go, Cat," he called. "I'm pretty sure I know where he's headed."

I'll say that it was easier sprinting down the stairs than it had been coming up. Adrenaline is a powerful force. As we spilled into the lobby, I spotted Danilo. Grabbing him by his smooth satin sleeves, I said, urgently: "You need to call the cops. Do you still have Cheryl Bell's contact info? Tell them that Lewis Kinross is the suspect they're looking for. And he's probably heading up to the lookout right now."

We left Danilo gape-mouthed and ran toward the

hotel's front door. I waved to Kaydence again as we raced past her, and she raised a bewildered hand. Her mother was folding a skirt with loving care, and the sight stopped me cold.

Her mother.

"I'll catch you," I said to Bruce.

"I doubt it," he called back, but kept running.

I jogged over to Kaydence and explained what I needed. It took more time than I had. I handed Kaydence my phone and then followed in Bruce's footsteps, dodging through the crowded lobby.

I couldn't see Bruce or Lewis, but I knew the shortcut.

I fought my way through the dried bullrushes in the drainage ditch. A dagger-sharp stalk snagged my sleeve, and I struggled free. Within a few minutes I was in the glade where I'd saved Danilo from the deadly muffin. Was that a week ago? A month?

I stopped and listened. Someone was coming. I braced myself to intercept Lewis, but it was Bruce who appeared. "How the heck did you get up here ahead of me?" he asked.

"Later," I said. "Where's Lewis?"

"I never caught a glimpse of him," said Bruce. "If he came this way, he's farther up."

We glanced at each other, not wanting to say out loud what we were both thinking: if Lewis had gone straight for the lookout, it probably wasn't for the view.

"Come on," I said. "It's not much farther. We can catch him." Weathered leaves caught in my hair as we re-entered the forest. Almost immediately, I tripped on an exposed root, falling onto my injured hand. I grunted in pain, and Bruce lifted me by my other elbow.

"What are we going to do if we find him?" he said. "Ask for an interview?"

It was a good question. We weren't the authorities. But all I knew was that I had to hear him say it: that he was guilty. Which meant that Marian was not. I needed her name to be cleared by the time I came back down the hill.

I shoved off against a tree, ignoring the pain. "We'll figure it out when we get there."

A patch of sunlight grew brighter in front of us. Nearly there. I tried to calm my breath, which to my ears sounded louder than the last chopper out of Saigon. The wind moved through the trees, and a sudden movement made me jump, a skittering in the leaves. Bruce jutted his jaw toward a squirrel, busy on its autumn shopping trip. Otherwise, it was silent.

I should have been sweaty from the mad climb, but I just felt icy cold and sick. What if Lewis had headed to the highway instead? Maybe he'd circled back around to the lake, where he'd steal a boat and disappear forever into the world of international fugitives. He'd transformed in my mind from geriatric professor to criminal mastermind.

KATE HILTON & ELIZABETH RENZETTI

And if he got away, we would never be able to prove what he'd done. Suspicion would fall on Marian again. I couldn't let that happen.

As we stepped out of the forest, Bruce grabbed my arm and pointed directly ahead of us. There, straddling the low stone wall that marked the edge of the cliff, was Kinross. Silhouetted against the bright blue of the sky, he stared out at the famous view. I motioned for Bruce to follow me, and we crept toward him.

My foot snapped a twig, and the crack echoed out over the void. Lewis's head jerked our way. He braced, as if ready to launch himself off the wall. I came toward him, hands open and outstretched.

"Professor Kinross," I said. "Lewis. Please come away from the wall. We were hoping we could talk to you."

He leaned in the wrong direction, his head and shoulders canting out dangerously over the abyss. "Talk about what? You want to try to get my side of things? That's not going to help anybody."

Keep him talking. How long had it been since I'd whispered my instruction to Kaydence and handed her my phone? Not long enough.

Kinross let out what he must have thought was a laugh. It was the saddest sound, half-sob and gut-wrenching. "I've buggered everything," he said. "My job. My relationships. Nothing makes sense anymore." He shook his head. "One minute, it was all fine, and the next it was like everyone had lost their minds. Like people were going around saying the moon was made of cheese and everyone was nodding and saying *so it is, it's made of cheese*."

He gave me a pleading look. "You understand, don't you? You spend your life devoted to one idea. That there is a precious thing called truth, and if you can just find it and share it, everything will be all right. You shine a light where you can and hope it helps."

I felt a catch in my chest. He'd seen me. It was how I felt, a great deal of the time—that I'd gone tumbling into an alternative world where nothing I'd ever done mattered one bit. Where no one thought the way I did.

"But I didn't kill anyone over it," I said. Beside me, Bruce slowly reached into his pocket. I knew he was hitting the record button on his phone. "You did. You shoved Bliss off that cliff because you hated what she stood for. Because she came between you and Allison. She was the reason Allison took your granddaughter away from you."

Kinross swayed toward me. His voice shook. "How do you know about Olivia?"

I took a step closer. "She's a beautiful little girl. I can imagine how much you love her. And how much it must hurt to be separated from her."

"How could anyone want to hurt a child like that? Send her out into the world with no defences?" Lewis's voice rose until he was shouting into the wind. "That's

325

what Bliss Bondar was doing. To children all over the country. And all for her own gain!"

"And you wanted that to end," I said, in what I hoped was a soothing voice.

"What?" Lewis cocked his head at me. "Do you think I did this deliberately? To silence her?" He shook his head furiously, *no, no.* "I only wanted to talk to her. She'd rebuffed all my other attempts." His head swung side to side, the momentum jerking his body toward the catastrophic drop. "I'd shown you that picture of Olivia at dinner, and it made me realize how much I missed her. I went up to my room and started scrolling through the latest pictures Allison had posted. Olivia on her first day of grade three. In her soccer uniform. And I thought: *I'll never be able to pick her up from school. Never take her to a game.* It felt like someone had cut my heart out." His voice faded, and I strained forward to hear.

"I couldn't sleep, thinking about her. Thinking about what would happen if she got sick, and I wouldn't even know. I went outside for a walk, to try to calm down. But then I saw her." He looked over at me, his eyes glittering. Rage, or despair, or both. "Bliss. She was walking to the trailhead. She was wearing that ridiculous huge cape with a hood, but she pulled it down for a moment and I saw her face."

I held my breath, willing him to go on. Willing him not to choose a violent ending a second time. "I caught up with her here. She was pacing around near the wall. I would say fate brought us together …" He let out a low strangled noise that might have been a laugh. "But I don't believe in fate." He wiped his eyes, lurching, and I nearly ran forward to grab him. He took a deep breath. "I lurked in the trees for a moment, and then I came out here to talk to her. She was startled to see me. I tried to tell her … I tried to tell her that I just wanted to talk to her, but she didn't want to hear reason. She kept saying, 'You swallowed the poison. You swallowed the poison.' It was nonsense, and I told her so. Then she told me that I was the liar. I was the baby killer." His finger shook as he pointed to himself. "Me—as if I'd done anything to harm anyone, ever. I was angry, I admit, but I just wanted to talk to her." His voice fell to a whisper. "I didn't want to hurt her. I reached for her and …"

"And what, Lewis? What happened?"

His eyes drifted to a distant moment. He reached up to grasp a phantom. "She backed away from me. She pulled away"—his face contorted with pain— "and she went too far. The momentum … it took her. It took her over the edge. I tried to grab her, but all I got was a handful of her cloak. And then she was gone. She screamed—oh my god—" He clapped his hands over his face.

I stood silently, watching him writhe in pain. I looked over at Bruce, who held his phone in his hand.

His expression was unreadable. As quietly as I could, I began to walk over to Lewis. I didn't want to startle him and send him over the cliff.

"Lewis," I said. "Let's go back down the hill. We'll talk to some people and see what your options are?"

He stared at me with bloodshot eyes, his face wet with tears. He looked like a man who'd seen his whole family murdered in front of him. "Options?" he said. "I've lost everything that means anything to me. I don't have options." He laughed hollowly. "Well, I have one."

With those words, he swung a second leg over the wall. It would only take a slight push from his shaking hands to send him tumbling to his death.

Where the hell was Kaydence? I'd given her one simple task. I spun around to scan the clearing, but I couldn't see anything but the treeline, couldn't hear anything but the birds. Lewis moaned again.

Suddenly Bruce stepped forward. "Lewis," he said, "do you think you could listen to me for just one moment?"

Never had I been so glad for Bruce's mellow FM voice. Lewis turned his head slightly to hear, which Bruce took as a yes. "You and I are of an age," he said. "And I understand what you're going through, believe it or not. I've been at very, very low points myself. When I thought I'd lost people I loved."

Lewis's body trembled, but he seemed to be listening. "Your kids?" he asked. He shifted so that he could talk directly to Bruce, bringing one leg back to our side of the wall.

"No, I never did have children. But my family, just the same."

"It's not the same!" Lewis started rocking back and forth in a frenzy, the momentum destabilizing his precarious balance. "You don't know what it's like to lose your children. Your grandchildren. Your whole line!"

I was about to leap and grab for his shirt when I heard crashing behind me. I whirled around to see Kaydence burst from the trees. Inspector Cheryl Bell and Dick Friesen were close behind, and Dick looked as if he were about to vomit from exertion.

Kaydence was holding my phone up in the air toward me. "I found her!" she shouted.

"Put her on speaker!" I yelled back. I turned back to Kinross. "Lewis! Your daughter is on the phone."

He froze in place, and when he spoke, he sounded like a man waking from a coma. "Allison?"

"Yes, Allison is on the phone, and she wants to talk to you." I grabbed the phone from Kaydence. I leaned toward the inspector and whispered in her ear, "Let me have one minute." She held one finger up at me and nodded curtly.

I set the volume as high as it would go and began to tiptoe toward Kinross. From my phone's crappy speaker, I heard a woman's voice. "Dad? Dad, are you there?"

Lewis seemed to fold in on himself. "Allison? Is that you?"

"It's me, Dad." There was a long pause, and everyone in that clearing seemed to be holding their breath. "I'm worried about you. Are you okay? Please don't do anything stupid."

There was genuine fear in Allison's voice, and I felt a pain in my throat like I was trying to swallow a jawbreaker whole. This woman had lost her father for a time, and now she was on the verge of losing him for good.

He sagged in defeat. "I did something very stupid, honey. But I did it for you and Olivia. I'm so sorry."

"I get it, Dad. I know you love us." It sounded as if Allison was crying too. "Maybe you can tell Olivia that in person. But you have to be smart right now. Don't do anything final. You want to see Olivia again, don't you? You won't believe how much she's grown."

Now Lewis was sobbing helplessly, his arms wrapped around his head. Silently, Cheryl Bell and Dick Friesen crept closer. He didn't say a word as the cuffs were slid over his wrists. Allison's plaintive voice carried on the crisp air: "Dad? Dad, are you still there?"

CHAPTER 29

IT MIGHT HAVE been one of our last editions, but it was a banger: a multi-page feature on our investigation into Bliss Bondar's death. It wouldn't stop Bliss's fans from generating their conspiracies, but we were proud of our reporting.

Yesterday, I'd been at the courthouse for Lewis's first appearance. It seemed that even hard-hearted Inspector Bell had felt sorry for that broken husk of a man, charging him not with murder but manslaughter. With Lewis's wife and daughter sitting behind him and sobbing throughout the proceedings, his lawyer requested that he be permitted to return home to Alberta until his trial date, so that he could receive the appropriate support and treatment for his mental health. The Crown attorney didn't put up a fight.

According to Stanley, who'd called Lewis's lawyer, a movement was afoot to have Lewis declared not criminally responsible for his actions that night. His lawyer believed there was a good chance Lewis would avoid a long stretch in jail. I wasn't sure that was the right result, as much as I sympathized with Lewis, but I could let it go. My mother was free, and that was all that mattered.

Free, that is, to make incomprehensible decisions like partnering with Clarity K on a female leadership summit. Having both survived Cheryl Bell's interrogations—and evened out the score of wrongs perpetrated against one another—my mother and Clarity had finally found themselves on equal footing and able to see each other as strategic allies.

"Joining forces with Clarity is an incredibly bad idea," I'd told my mother. "She literally hates you."

Marian had, infuriatingly, rolled her eyes. "It's business, Catherine," she'd said. "You can't get emotional. It wouldn't hurt you to learn that."

I'd told her not to call me when it all went south, and to hire Danilo. On the latter point, she took my advice.

Peter and Kyle Johnson's assault charges were proceeding. I didn't need them to be convicted, but I didn't want them anywhere near me ever again. I'd said as much to the Crown attorney, who agreed to offer a peace bond instead of continuing to trial. Deeandra obviously felt somewhat the same way since she remained at Kaydence's house even after her son and husband were out on bail.

Kaydence wished her mother would follow Debbie's example and ditch her marriage, but she wasn't optimistic. She told me Deeandra wasn't talking much, but they were making enough tea towel dresses to stock both the harvest festival and the Christmas fair. Sewing was the only therapy Deeandra was prepared to embrace.

Healing may be a matter of time, but it's also a choice, one that too many people won't make.

Case in point: Peter and Kyle rejected the Crown attorney's offer of a peace bond outright. They were outraged and wanted their day in court to talk about how the corrupt press was destroying society. I doubted the *Quill & Packet* would be around by the time the case made it onto the court docket in a few months' time. I'd have to be there to testify. Would I be living in Port Ellis by then? Or crashing on Kaydence's sofa after fighting traffic and using up vacation days from some crappy job in the city? Ugh. It was horrifying to be forty-five and unable to see more than a couple of months into the future. Where were my predictable plans and sensible investments? Wasn't middle age supposed to be comfortable?

THE BELLS ON the door of Glenda's bakery jangled, but the regulars barely looked up from their copies of the *Quill & Packet*. Bruce, another fine representative of the forces of evil, was sitting at a table, drinking a hot chocolate and eating an apple fritter. Beside him, Amir sat with an untouched black coffee, his gaze lost in the middle distance. He looked like a captain whose ship had just had an unplanned meeting with an iceberg.

I took the seat opposite and ordered a coffee. When it arrived, I raised my mug and clunked it against each of theirs. "Here's to an edition for the books," I said. "At least we can say we went out in style. And took Gerry Halloran with us."

"Not just yet," Bruce said. "I hear he's gunning for the Conservative nomination."

"Federal?" I asked.

He nodded. "Oh come on," I said. "That guy is toast. He'll never win."

"We'll see," said Bruce. "Is he a slimy dickweasel? Yes. But I'm not sure that's an impediment to entering the House of Commons. I'd like to see the *Quill* do an in-depth investigation into his financial dealings, though. That might do it." Bruce took a bite of his fritter and chewed it contemplatively.

We both knew it was wishful thinking. The *Quill* was out of money and on the market. I'd been putting some thought into my next move, which Marian was insisting should be to Toronto. She was making noises about buying a rental property and installing me in it as a tenant. I'd stopped short of saying what I thought of her plan—*when hell freezes over*—because there weren't a lot of options out there for a journalist without a newspaper, and certainly not in Port Ellis. Even in Toronto, the freelance market was saturated with people working for "experience"—that is, free—and every few months the major outlets released another wave of layoffs into the labour pool. It was monumentally depressing.

"I have some news," said Bruce. "I wanted you to be the second to know." He tipped his fritter at Amir. "Boss here was the first." He pulled himself upright, bony shoulders filling out his barn jacket. "You're looking at the new owner and publisher of the *Quill & Packet*."

I choked on my coffee. "What?" I sputtered.

Bruce appeared delighted by my reaction. "A couple of days ago, I made Dorothy an offer and she accepted. I signed the paperwork this morning."

"Oh my god," I said. "This is the best news ever. Are you kidding me right now?"

Bruce pulled a sheaf of papers out of his satchel. "It's all here in black and white."

"Wait," I said. "Stop. How did you buy the newspaper?"

Bruce grinned. "You have a hard time accepting

good news, don't you?" he said. "The how is a who. I have a silent investor."

I thought for a moment, and then said, "Your nephew? Ryan?"

"Uh-huh. And he's an actual rock star, so you can be sure he has better ways to spend his time than to interfere with the *Quill*. It's a carte blanche, a new day for independent journalism in Port Ellis."

I looked over at Amir, expecting joy, or surprise. Or anything, really, except the lukewarm expression of acceptance. Maybe it was shell shock? I nudged his arm. "Hey, who ran over your dog? This is good news. The *Quill* is safe. We're safe."

"And I'm glad about that." He reached over, gripped my hand. "I'm over the moon, really. It's just that ..."

"Amir's abandoning ship," Bruce said. "Swimming for the mainland. Eyes fixed on the coconut palms on the horizon."

I felt something break inside me. "You're leaving us?"

Amir was glaring at Bruce. "I am not, in fact, leaving you. But I do have to think of the future, and what I want to do with it." His eyes met mine, and it was as if Bruce and the bakery vanished, and it was just the two of us. "I've been at this too long, Cat. I've given it everything. I feel like I have to shake the bars a bit before I'm wandering around town in a walker." He reached over and squeezed my hand. "You're my inspiration, in a way. You chose a new path, and it worked out."

I was almost too afraid to speak. "What new path are you thinking about?"

He withdrew his hand from mine, and ruffled his hair. Embarrassed, but in an adorable way. "Would you think I was nuts if I wanted to run for mayor?"

I burst out laughing. "Is this because you want a henchman of your own? I think Kyle is looking for work."

He didn't seem to think it was funny. "This town's been so screwed by Halloran for so long," he said. "Maybe it's a giant ego trip to think I could fix things ..."

I thought of how he'd saved the *Quill*, how he'd taken such good care of his parents for years, how he'd rescued me when the quicksand was closing over my head. "Or maybe," I said, "you're just the man for the job."

He smiled then, one of those rare, blinding smiles. My heart clenched. And then I thought, with a little prick of shock, that he wouldn't be my boss anymore. Had that played into his decision?

"You won't be my boss anymore," I blurted.

Bruce spread his hands wide. "In fact, you would be the boss. The job's open, and I don't want it. I hate giving performance reviews. Are you in?"

Did I want to be the editor of the *Quill*? Did I want

to keep killing myself for little recognition and less pay? Did I want to commit the next phase of my working life to a dying industry, which would surely pooch my retirement and leave me regretting my folly in my twilight years? Did my love for journalism and for the people in this weirdly murderous town outweigh my sense of self-preservation?

"Hell, yes," I said.

ACKNOWLEDGEMENTS

Welcome back to Port Ellis, dear readers. We very much hope you enjoyed your second visit. We are so grateful to you for embracing Cat Conway and the rest of the *Quill & Packet* crew.

Thank you to all the booksellers, librarians, book clubbers, bloggers, literary festivals, and reviewers who championed *Bury the Lead* last year. We had a great run with it. We loved meeting so many of you at events across Canada, from Victoria, British Columbia, to Eastport, Newfoundland. We can't stop singing the praises of Nicole Magas from ZG Stories and Emma Rhodes from House of Anansi, who managed our book tour publicity.

And now here we are with *Widows and Orphans*,

backed by the same brilliant team from House of Anansi. They aren't kidding when they say they publish Very Good Books. We appreciate the talents of Shivaun Hearne, Jenny McWha, Linda Pruessen, Melissa Shirley, Lucia Kim, and Gemma Wain. We also thank publisher Karen Brochu for her personal support of this series (and for acquiring two further titles).

Our agent, Samantha Haywood of Transatlantic Agency, is a woman of exceptional skill and tenacity. We owe a particular debt to Eva Oakes, whose notes helped us complete this fictional puzzle. Thanks also to Laura Cameron, who sold the film and TV rights.

Meg Scott, a friend and a Crown attorney, made sure we hadn't bungled the criminal law process (we had). Any errors that remain are entirely our own.

Many writers we respect and admire said kind words about our series, which appear in the front pages of this book. Others provided moral support during those moments when a writer really needs cheering up. Thank you, friends.

While writing *Widows and Orphans*, Kate was beset by several family emergencies. She sends love and gratitude to the women in her life who know exactly when to show up with a hot meal and a hug. These friends include the wonderful Liz Renzetti; having Liz as a co-author is a bonus, as well as an ongoing joy and privilege.

Kate takes daily pleasure in her decision to marry Sasha Akhavi. She also very much appreciates her parents, sisters, brothers-in-law, nephews, stepdaughter, and sons. She reminds her sons that you must read your mother's books if you wish to have one dedicated to you. She remembers Shelby, the Canine Assistant, who sat in her office and radiated support throughout the writing and production of this book.

On the topic of wellness, Kate admires and appreciates her colleagues in psychotherapy who make the world better, healthier, kinder, and more responsible, one client at a time. And yes, if you are reading this, Kate thinks you need therapy.

Liz also wants to thank all the journalists, both friends and strangers, who reached out to share their enjoyment of the *Quill & Packet*'s ramshackle newsroom. Thanks also to every reporter who interviewed us—we found Cat Conway in every city and town we visited! A huge thank you to my friends and family, and to mystery lovers who borrowed or bought *Bury the Lead*. In particular, Doug, Griff, and Maud—you are my north stars, always.

© Betsy Hilton

KATE HILTON is the co-author of *Bury the Lead*, the bestselling first novel in the Quill & Packet mystery series. She is also the author of the novels *The Hole in the Middle*, *Just Like Family*, and *Better Luck Next Time*. When not writing, Kate maintains an active psychotherapy practice, working with individuals and couples. She has a particular interest in personal reinvention and life transitions. Kate has had prior careers in law, university administration, publishing, and major-gift fundraising. She lives with her family in Toronto.

Jessica Blaine Smith

ELIZABETH RENZETTI is a bestselling Canadian author and journalist, and the co-author of the Quill & Packet mysteries. Her book *What She Said: Conversations About Equality* was a national bestseller in 2024. She was a columnist, feature writer, and reporter at the *Globe and Mail* for many years. In 2020 she won the Landsberg Award for her reporting on gender equality. She is also the author of the essay collection *Shrewed: A Wry and Closely Observed Look at the Lives of Women and Girls* and the novel *Based on a True Story*. She lives in Toronto with her family.